finders KEEPERS

A NOVEL

NICOLE WILLIAMS

FINDERS KEEPERS
Copyright © 2013
Nicole Williams

ISBN-13: 978-1492353553

Cover Design by Sarah Hansen of Okay Creations
Editing by Cassie Cox

This one's for the book bloggers.
For making this series what it is, and for reading and spreading the word in ways I never could have imagined.
For helping me title this one (thank you, Natasha!), and for pushing a square sort of series through the round hole of the present book market. I love you all.
Keep on, keepin' on . . . because the world needs more lovers of books.

chapter ONE

TRYING TO IGNORE her was like trying to ignore a bull charging me. Especially when that was her fifth fake laugh in fifteen minutes. How did I know that laugh, along with the smile and the whole damn act she's trying so hard to put on, is fake?

Simple.

I've known Josie Gibson since before I figured out girls like her were disastrous to guys like me. Girls who could give a boy one look and make him feel it all the way into his boots were ones for me to avoid at all costs. Girls who could give a boy a look and make him feel equal parts irritation and infatuation were ones I didn't only need to avoid but have permanently erased from my mind.

Girls like Josie Gibson spelled one thing for me: doom. The only thing I was more sure of was that I spelled even more doom for her. Doom was too soft a word, actually.

I would infect Josie like a virus, spreading until I'd done so much damage it went way past the point of repair. That was more like it. I was a virus to Josie Gibson. A toxic one.

I tried to ignore that for too many years. After the past couple years, I couldn't ignore it anymore. Josie and I should stay on opposite corners of the planet. Unfortunately for her, we lived in the same state. In the same region. So we'd just have to figure out how to live in opposite corners of Missoula County.

Sitting across the bar from one another wasn't exactly staying in opposite corners.

I'd had too many drinks, and she'd thrown too many glances my way, for me to stay quiet any longer. "You might want to step it up a few hundred notches, Mason, because you're exciting Josie about as much as cow shit on the bottom of my boots."

When Josie's eyes flickered to mine, they narrowed into a glare. "Control yourself, Black."

"I might if I could, but since I can't, it's kind of a moot point." Lifting my once-again full shot glass, I downed it in one easy drink. I could hold my liquor—kind of a side effect of drinking like a fish since age thirteen—but when whiskey tasted like water, I knew I probably had enough alcohol sloshing through my bloodstream to kill me.

The Jack had started tasting like water three shots ago.

When Colt Mason finally noticed who was propped into the bar stool across from them, he bristled. "Come on. Let's just go, Josie."

Hell, I would have bristled too if I'd seen me sitting across from myself. I had something of a reputation for getting into bar fights, and the only reason Brandy still let me in her joint was because I was her best customer. Plus I gave her a little after-hours action when she was feeling lonely and I was feeling drunk.

"No." Josie shook her head emphatically. When it came to me, she did everything emphatically. It was my curse. "If I left every time Garth Black started running his mouth, I'd never have a chance to get comfortable. He can leave."

If I'd had a dozen shots less, the look on her face would have made me squirm. "No can do, sweetheart. You see those bottles?" I waved my finger in the general bar area. "They're still full, and I'm not leaving until a good bunch are empty."

"Your liver must be jumping for joy right now," she snapped before grabbing Colt's shot. She downed it in one drink, but to Josie's light-weight credit, her whole face puckered up.

"Come on. We're leaving." Colt nudged Josie and slid out of his stool.

She shook her head and lifted her finger at Brandy. Like the bar-tending elite she was, Brandy had another shot in front of Josie in under ten seconds. Josie downed it, her face grimacing less that time. I didn't miss the lingering look Colt gave her chest while she was mid-whiskey wince.

"Let's get out of here," he said.

I might have felt my anger flaring when he'd run his eyes all over her, but when his hands moved to her, that anger exploded. I was out of my seat and moving toward them before Colt noticed me coming. Josie knew enough to expect my next move. The rule was simple: whatever normal, sane people did, I went with the opposite.

Anyone else would ignore the couple across from them and let them get on with their Friday night. Me, on the other hand? I was less than a foot away and ready to break the guy's jaw if he didn't stop tugging on her arm. Anger management candidates had nothing on me. "I don't normally give warnings, Mason, but you're with my friend whose judgment in people, up until recently, I've never doubted. So I'm going to give you the benefit and issue one." I tried to ignore the look of horror on Josie's face. "Take your hands off of Josie, or you're going to be slurping your steak through a straw from tonight on."

That horrified look on Josie's face? Just went up a few notches instead of down.

"Get lost, Black. Josie isn't your daughter, your sister, or your girlfriend, so you have no place to order me about what I can and can't do."

He was right. And he was wrong. I wasn't a blood relation, and I sure as shit wasn't her boyfriend. The man applying for that position was the one who couldn't look me in the eyes. Since her dad wasn't there to see Colt Mason all but manhandling her out of her stool and her only brother was on the opposite side of the country, I was temporarily filling both positions.

Moving in front of him, I butted my chest into his. "Josie's been my friend since before you and your Hollywood family moved out to Montana and insulted us all with your flashy trucks and poser-itis. That gives me the right to put you in your place when I see you put a *finger* on Josie."

Josie whipped in front of me, butting her chest into mine. If I hadn't been so shocked, I would have been turned on. "Leave me alone and go ruin someone else's life."

"Spoken like a woman who doesn't want a man like you putting anyone in their place for her." Lifting his eyebrows, Colt steered Josie and himself away from me.

They made it a few steps before I slid in front of them again. I wasn't letting them leave with Colt's hand still wrapped around Josie's forearm and with her a few drinks in and wearing that dress Colt had been eyeballing all

4

night. I knew what had happened the last time Josie got drunk when a snake was around, and I wouldn't let it happen again when I could stop it.

"Fuck off, Black." Colt's ever-cool facade was finally crumbling. I was getting under his skin, and when a normal person would have backed off, I kept going.

"You want to hit me?" I said, lifting my arms. I almost wavered in place—probably because I was swimming in whiskey. When Colt shook his head, I cut him off. "Of course you do. You've wanted to hit me since the first day of high school when all the girls were more interested in me than you and all your money."

"I don't want to hit you." Colt had managed to collect his cool again, although Josie was picking up where he'd left off. If she could level me with one punch, I didn't have any doubt that I'd already be horizontal and blacked out.

"You might not *want* to—which I don't believe for one goddamned second—but before we part ways tonight, you're *going* to hit me."

From over Colt's shoulder, I noticed Brandy mouth *Take it outside.* We weren't going to make it another step if he didn't take his hands off of Josie, let alone outside.

For the second time that night, Josie got in my face. Instead of a punch, she almost leveled me with her expression. "Why don't you stop pretending to be the hero and own what you really are? The villain. Go villainize someone else's life. You couldn't possibly do anymore to mine."

Josie Gibson had just gotten under my skin. I should back up, raise my hands, and surrender, but I couldn't. Something about having her under my skin, even though it wasn't the way I might have liked, was a drug for me. One

I couldn't say no to. "How about this? I'll stop pretending to be the hero when you stop pretending you're actually interested in this eunuch in a cowboy hat."

"Ever heard the phrase 'it takes one to know one,' Black?" Josie crossed her arms and managed to narrow her eyes farther.

"I have, but I don't see how it applies. You ought to know, with our history and all, how much of a eunuch I'm not. I might be wrong, but I'm pretty sure a eunuch couldn't make a girl come the way I made you a while back." That was when the slap came. I was braced for it—it didn't surprise me—but it stung just the same.

"Go to hell."

"I've been standing in it for twenty-one years, Josie."

Colt moved to her side, and when he grabbed her forearm, he gave it a good tug. "Come on. We're out."

"Ouch," she snapped, trying to pull her arm from his grip. "Ease up a bit, Hulk."

What I did next I didn't think about. It was all instinct. When Colt Mason tugged on Josie's arm, my fist driving into his jaw was my reflex. It wasn't enough to land him on his ass, but that had less to do with Colt's ability to take a hit like a man and more to do with the amount of whiskey in my bloodstream. Josie's hands covered her mouth as she gaped at me like I was a monster. That was exactly what I was, but at least Colt's hands were off of her.

"What the hell, Black?" Colt spat, rubbing his jaw.

I lifted my finger in his face and fought the urge to deck him again. "That was because you put your hands on Josie."

"I've put my hands on her plenty of times before and never got clocked across the face."

That was the wrong thing to say. Before I knew it, my other fist was driving into the other side of his jaw. That was my reflex to Colt Mason insinuating his hands had been on Josie in *that* way. The way that made me almost as furious as imagining them on her in a harsh way. "There! That's for all the times you put your hands on her before."

Colt gave his head a swift shake and moved Josie aside as he moved closer to me. "I'm going to—"

That time, my punch was planned. I knew what I was doing before my knuckles crushed into Colt's jaw. "And that was because you irritate the shit out of me." Spitting on Colt's pristine boots, I shoved his chest. "Go back to California and leave Montana to the real men. Pansy-ass poser."

Judging from the look on Colt's face, I couldn't have paid him a greater insult. I moved Josie aside—who was in front of him fretting over him like he was dying—right before Colt charged me. It was about time I got a reaction out of him.

Colt's first punch landed square on my nose—a true cheap shot—and gauging from the crack, my nose had broken for the third time. Colt's next punch sank into my stomach, and when I curled, he drove his knee into my jaw. I went down. I didn't try to move or lift my hands to shield my face when Colt's fists came at me one right after the other. I didn't fight back. I didn't protect myself. Not because I incapable of doing it, but because taking a good beating every now and again did me good. Some people prayed, some did a cleansing, some took a vacation. I did a

7

solid beating. It reminded me I wasn't invincible and somehow that reminder made me stronger.

Josie tried to pull Colt off of me when I felt my left eye swell shut, and by the time my right was following suit, Colt's punches had slowed. I could tell they were still a long way from being done though. The unexpected bonus of getting the shit beat out of me was that somewhere along the way, my whole face had gone numb. The hits didn't sting anymore.

"What the hell are you doing, Colt?" Josie grabbed one of his arms and tugged on it. "What the hell are you doing, Garth?"

Josie had seen me in plenty of fights, but that was the first one she'd seen where I hadn't come out the winner. She hadn't seen when my dad used to lay me out with one strong backhand to the cheek starting when I was four. She hadn't seen his backhands turn into fists as I'd gotten older. She hadn't seen the guy I'd picked a fight with the night after she and I slept together. That was the first fight she'd seen where I just laid there and took it. I liked keeping those fights private, and Josie having a front seat to my twisted form of therapy was something I couldn't decide how I felt about.

"Stop it, Colt! You're going to kill him!" Josie kept trying to drag Colt off of me, but he had her by a good seventy pounds and seven times that in the rage factor.

I was close to blacking out when I heard the unmistakable sound of a shotgun being racked. Colt's fists stopped instantly.

"You better get off that boy now unless you want to see how we Montana folk use a shotgun," Brandy ordered, inching the barrel toward Colt's face. "And it isn't to decorate our walls like some kind of fancy trophy. Around here, we shoot coyotes, wolves, and assholes. And it's been a while since I've got to shoot an asshole. I'm going through withdrawals."

Colt lifted his hands and slowly lifted himself off of me. It was a smart move; I wasn't afraid of most anything, but Brandy Hansen holding a loaded shotgun in my face was one of them. And yes, it had happened to me once before.

"Now get out of my joint." Brandy waved the shotgun at the door. "I'd recommend you not come back unless you want me to ask questions second."

Colt huffed but continued toward the door. "Maybe you'll wake up tomorrow learning your lesson finally, Black. Don't mess with me."

I had to spit out a mouthful of blood before I could respond. "I learned my lesson all right. That you fight like a little girl." Leaning up just enough to make eye contact with him, I raised my middle finger and blew him a kiss.

Flames rolled through his eyes, and I could practically taste how badly he wanted to come take another swing—or ten—at me, but Brandy took a few steps in his direction and Colt kept moving for the door.

"Josie? You coming or staying?" he called.

I spit out another mouthful of blood. Good thing Brandy liked me because from the looks of it, more of my blood was splattered across her floor than I had left in my veins. "There's no chance of Joze 'coming' if she goes anywhere with you, Mason."

Colt shot me a lethal glare. "*Joes*? What the hell kind of nickname is that? " He shook his head before glancing away from me. "*Josie*, are you coming?"

"I can't just leave him, Colt. Not like this." Josie had on a brave face, but her bottom lip looked close to quivering. She'd never been a fan of blood, especially when it came to me spilling mine or someone else's.

"That's exactly the kind of guy you leave behind."

I might have been beat to a pulp, but I didn't like what Colt was implying.

Crossing her arms, her eyes narrowed at him the way I was used to seeing directed my way. "Not to me."

"You're actually going to stay behind with this loser?"

Most days, I tried to convince myself I didn't like Josie Gibson, and some days I failed. That was one of those failure days. I propped up onto my elbows. I didn't want to admit it, but that small movement hurt like hell. Colt had done a number on me. "If I'm a loser, what does that make you? Oh, wait. Never mind. There hasn't been a word created for that yet. Colt Mason is all we've got to sum up what a good-for-nothing prick your kind is."

Colt's fists balled, but Brandy and her shotgun kept him from coming at me again. "Just what kind am I? The kind who doesn't go home to a dad who's the town drunk? The kind who doesn't live in a ramshackle trailer that should have been condemned two decades ago? The kind who only has friends like Josie and Jesse Walker because they pity you? If that's the kind I'm not, then I'm good with that."

I kept my face blank. I went to that place within myself that was always angry at the world because when I was good and burrowed down in that place, I didn't feel anything. Least of all the words coming from the mouth of the jackass in front of me.

Colt shook his head at me—sprawled out, broken, swollen, and bleeding—and the look he gave me almost brought me to my feet with both arms swinging. That look, a mixture of pity and disgust, far outdid his words. I didn't take well to people pitying me. Despite Colt saying Jesse and Josie only hung around because they pitied me, that was bullshit. Jesse and Josie and I had history. We'd bled through life together. When people shared the kind of ups and downs the three of us had, the common denominator wasn't pity—it was loyalty. But Colt Mason was looking at me with true pity. If I didn't feel like I'd just been stampeded by a herd of cattle, I would have beaten his ass until he'd never even consider looking at me that way again.

"I'll call you later, Josie. Once you're done doing your good deed of the day." Colt stalled for a second in the doorway, probably waiting for Josie to hustle up beside him. Unlike me, he didn't have fifteen years of experience with Josie Gibson's unparalleled stubbornness. That girl wasn't going anywhere until she was good and ready.

"Night, Princess. Same time next week?" I called after him as he charged out of the bar. Good fucking riddance.

"Next time you do that in my place of business, I'm aiming this here barrel between your eyes. I don't care how dark and brooding and sexy they are, you hear me?" Brandy's face hovered above mine and she lifted an eyebrow.

I answered her with a weak salute. Brandy was back to the customers and the customers were back to their drinks when Josie kneeled beside me.

"What am I going to do with you, Garth Black?" She sighed, her forehead lining as she inspected my face.

11

"I've got plenty of answers for that question, Joze."

"Mind wowing me with that plethora of answers?"

A girl who knew the word "plethora" should not be allowed to date a guy who'd only graduated high school because his daddy offered to foot the bill for a new football field.

"I would, but I'm afraid I'll get slapped if I give you any of those answers, and I'm not sure how much more my face can take tonight."

Josie sighed again, not quite as long as the first. "Sure, now you decide to keep your mouth closed. That would have come in real handy five minutes ago when Colt Mason came at you with his fists."

I let Josie help me up. Even with her help, by the time I stood, I was feeling enough pain to know I was close to blacking out. It had happened before, but it had been a while. And damn it all to hell, Colt Mason hadn't only broken my nose. I was pretty sure he'd cracked a couple of ribs, too. "You and I both know if I was interested in fighting back, Colt would have left here on a stretcher."

Josie slung my arm over her shoulders and helped me to one of the tables in the corner. Having my arm around her, even though it was only to steady myself, made me feel something I wasn't ready to feel. Especially not when it came to feeling it for Josie Gibson. I wasn't made to give and accept that kind of thing. Ever.

"I do know that. I've seen you in enough fights since the testosterone switch flipped on when you were barely out of first grade to know you could have dropped Colt like you dropped first period trig." I shot her a tight smile. "So why did you let him beat on you like a flesh-and-bone punching bag?"

My smile went up a notch on the tightness scale. "Because."

Instead of sighing, she rolled her eyes. When I was close by, Josie was either glaring, groaning, sighing, or rolling her eyes. I could measure my life by her expressions. "I see you've made a lot of progress in the whole opening-up department. Bravo. Go, you."

"Opening up's never been my thing. It really gets in the way of that whole mysterious vibe I like to let off. It drives the women wild."

"It drives them something." She leaned in to inspect the left side of my face. She came so close, I smelled that coconut shampoo she'd been using since our freshman year of high school. Josie's coconut shampoo had marked many milestones in my life. The first time I'd noticed it was in ninth grade at the homecoming dance. That was the only dance I'd ever gone to, that dance with Josie the only one I'd danced, and coconut shampoo was the thing I remembered. Then that night a couple winters back, I'd buried my face into her hair right as I was about to—

Shit.

Scratch that.

Fuck.

What the hell was I thinking? My face probably looked like a science experiment gone wrong, and I was teetering on a chair dreaming about coconut shampoo and Josie Gibson. I wasn't sure what I was more disturbed by: that I was fantasizing about shampoo or that my dick was hard from remembering that night with Josie. My dick, along with everything attached to it, needed to stay far away from Josie Gibson. She and her coconut shampoo were messing with my head. Messing with my brain.

"That's going to need stitches. And probably that one, too." Josie studied my face with a furrowed brow. "I'll drive you to the hospital if you promise not to get blood all over my truck."

"I don't need doctors and stitches. I need a bottle of whiskey, a woman, and some sleep. I'll wake up tomorrow good as new." Gauging my pain level, I probably needed a couple of pain relievers too, but I wasn't about to admit that. I had a reputation as a badass to uphold and asking for a couple of Tylenol had a way of ruining that.

"Garth, you need medical attention."

I lifted my hand, catching Brandy's attention. She had a double shot of whiskey in front of me in thirty seconds flat. I swallowed the whiskey before slamming the empty glass on the table. "There. Medical attention. Check."

"You really are a stubborn pain in my ass." She sighed and started for the door. "Wait there, and try not to get in another bar fight before I get back. If you're still thirsty, try some water. You know, that stuff that comes out a faucet. It's easier on the liver."

"And I'm a pain in *your* ass?" I called after her, but her only response was a shake of her head as she disappeared out the door.

"You want another, sugar? From the looks of you, I'd say you need another after another. After another." Brandy grabbed the empty glass and waited.

Actually, I needed a line of "anothers," but I couldn't get Josie's voice out of my head. "I'll have a water."

"A what?" Brandy's mouth dropped open a bit.

"A. Water," I repeated slowly.

Brandy looked at me like I'd grown two heads. "Anything else with your . . . *water*?"

Even rolling my eyes was painful. "Ice."

Brandy gaped at me for a while longer before heading back to the bar. In all fairness, looking at me like the world as she knew it had just changed because Garth Black had ordered a glass of ice water in a bar was probably to be expected. Despite being underage, I'd been venturing into Brandy's bar since I turned fifteen, and that was the first time I'd ordered water. Waiting for my H2O, I grabbed a couple of napkins, twisted them, and stuffed them up both nostrils to stop the bleeding. As far as medical attention went, that was about all I needed.

"You sure you don't want anything else? It's on the house." Brandy set a tall glass of ice water in front of me and waited.

"No, I'm good. Me and my water. What else could a man wish for?"

Brandy shifted, dropping her hand on her hip. "I could think of a few things. You decide you need something else, *anything* else, you know where to find me." Glancing at the back room, where Brandy and I'd had plenty of after-hours "get-togethers," she winked before walking away.

Sex was, like alcohol, my go-to when I wanted to block out something like a shitty day, getting thrown from the bull before the eight-second buzzer, or taking a serious beating. I'd already drowned myself in alcohol. Sex was the next thing on my journey toward "healing," but sex with Brandy wouldn't cut it. I don't know how I knew that, or why; I just did. Sex with just anyone wouldn't work like it normally did for me. When the face of who I did want flashed through my mind, I wished I'd asked for a bottle of whiskey with my water.

I wasn't going there again. Not with her. Not ever. Once was enough to fuck a man up good for the rest of his life. I didn't want to be fucked in the hereafter as well. Not that I wasn't already fucked when it came to any kind of hereafter reserved for the likes of me, but that wasn't the point.

"Since when did you start drinking vodka on the rocks?" Josie slid into the chair beside me and dropped a first aid kit on the table.

"Since never."

She scooted her chair closer until her legs brushed mine. "What are you drinking then? Gin? Tequila? Hemlock?"

I gave her another tight smile. "What you basically ordered me to drink."

And I thought Brandy's face had been shocked.

"Water?" I nodded. "No way." She grabbed the glass and actually took a sip. "Well, crap. Just when I think I've got you all figured out." She set the glass down and shook her head.

"I go and order a glass of water? Mind blowing, I know."

She fumbled through the first aid kit before pulling out some bandages and ointment tubes. "Consider my mind sufficiently blown." She pulled out a few small squares and tore one open. Even though I felt like a panty-waist sitting in a seedy bar having a chick patch up my war wounds, I wasn't about to get up and leave. I probably should. Being alone and in close proximity to Josie Gibson did strange things to me . . .

Like making my heart feel like there was something more to it than just pumping blood.

16

Speaking of panty-waists . . . I was so far gone in the land of make-believe and shit that I barely registered when Josie lifted a damp towelette to my face. That changed real quick when she pressed it into the gash above my eyebrow.

I didn't flinch. I didn't wince. I all but leapt out of my skin. I was doing fabulous things to my notorious rough-and-tough reputation. "Shit, Joze, warn a person before you douse alcohol on a serious wound. Give them a second to brace themselves first."

She gave me an exaggerated eye roll, holding the bloody alcohol swab off to the side. "First of all, I hardly consider an alcohol swab to be 'dousing.' Second, you gave up the right to call any of your wounds serious when you refused to seek medical attention and left me strapped with the burden of patching you up in the corner of some hygienically-deficient bar. And third"—she had to work to disguise her smile—"I thought you were immune to pain."

Josie might as well have just slit me open and gutted me for as vulnerable as I felt. She was looking at me like she could see everything, *everything,* and was waiting for an explanation. I gave myself a proverbial shake before replying. "I *am* immune to pain, but no man, not even the toughest son of a bitch in the universe, is immune to alcohol applied to a gaping wound."

"Gaping? Really? You on some sort of exaggeration kick or something?"

I couldn't catch a break with Josie to save my life. "You said I needed medical attention. If something isn't gaping on my face, you're the one exaggerating, not me."

"Oh, sweet Jesus. You are the most exasperating person I've ever known," she said around a sigh, reaching for another alcohol swab. "For a man who doesn't seem too picky about his alcohol, you wouldn't think he'd turn his nose up at the rubbing kind."

"Let's get something straight. You, princess"—I lifted a brow until the pain registered. No raised brows for me for at least twenty-four hours—"are the most exasperating person *I've* ever known. And if it has the audacity to call itself alcohol and put a warning on itself saying not for personal consumption, then hell yes, I'll turn my nose up at it. Calling something alcohol when you can't drink it is kind of like Colt Mason calling himself a cowboy. It's heresy."

Josie knew from enough experience with me that I would never forfeit an argument. It just wasn't in my nature. To start an argument with me was to lose an argument with me. So instead of going a few more rounds, she gave close to her dozenth head shake before lifting the swab to my other eyebrow. "Brace yourself, you big baby. I'm about to *douse* your *gaping* wound with the red-headed-stepchild of alcohols."

I still flinched when she pressed the pad into my skin, but at least I didn't act like a cat on a hot tin roof. I bit the inside of my cheek and blew out a slow breath.

"Big baby," she muttered before moving closer and blowing on the spot she was dabbing.

Shit, that felt good. If I had a tail, it would have been wagging. No one had to tell me twice that Josie leaning in, that damn coconut-scented hair brushing my face, and softly blowing on my battle wounds was probably the worst thing that could happen to me. One step above the apocalypse. No one had to remind me that I needed to keep as much distance between her and me as space would allow. Hell, I was reminding myself of that. But when Josie broke through my walls and got close, physically and every other way she could, I was incapable of pushing her back out. No, nobody needed to tell me how fucked up that was. I reminded myself of it every day.

"This is one deja vu moment getting doctored up by you," I said to distract myself from my thoughts.

She tore into another alcohol pad and blew on the next patch of face even before pressing it against it. "After these past couple years, I actually regret that day on the bus." Her eyes looked everywhere but into mine.

I pulled out the knife she'd just lodged my chest before replying. "I guarantee you not as much as I regret it."

Josie was a tough girl, one who I'd seen cry about as much as I did, but when her face broke, I was reminded for the billionth time what a dickhead I was. My default when someone hurt me was to hurt them back. It was a reflex, but it was one I wished I could turn off with people like Josie. She tore the next alcohol swab package open like it was to blame instead of me. Even though my words had cut her, she still dabbed my face gently, blowing the entire time.

I sighed. "Shit, Joze, I'm sorry. I don't mean to be such a dick but—"

"Something about me brings out the dick in you?" She tilted her head and waited.

"What? No. Not even close." I shook my head. "Being around *me* brings out the dick in me."

It was Josie's turn to shake her head. "Sucks to be you."

19

"Especially right now." I held back the wince when she dabbed some ointment on my left eyebrow. Colt must have split that sucker right open.

"This one needs stitches, Garth. Some gauze and a Band-Aid just aren't going to cut it." Josie bit her lower lip, studying my eyebrow.

I snorted. "Yeah, right. There's no way I'm going to let Colt Mason brag about giving me a good enough beating to require stitches. No. Way."

"You don't think he's already bragging to his brothers about how he kicked your ass?"

"He might be bragging about it now. But once word gets around that I let him take his best shots with my hands all but tied behind my back and he *still* couldn't manage to land a solid enough punch to require some stitches, *I'm* going to be the one with bragging rights." Another eye roll from Josie. We had to be nearing the half a dozen count. "I'm made out of fucking steel. There isn't a man alive who could hurt me."

Josie pressed the alcohol swab back into my eyebrow but stopped blowing.

"Ow." I snapped my head away from the swab. "That hurt."

The corners of her mouth twitched before she blew on my eyebrow again. "There might not be a man alive who can hurt you"—she arched an eyebrow at me—"but I'm no man."

I chuckled. "You're a bruiser, Joze. A regular killer. Remind me to never pick a fight with you if I don't want to get my ass beat."

"Well, it wouldn't be the first time you got your ass beat by me, would it?" The corners of her mouth twitched up again.

"No need to bring up bad memories. I'm not drunk enough for that."

"I thought the first week of kindergarten when I socked you in the jaw for pulling on my pigtails was a repressed memory, not a bad one."

"A repressed memory and a bad memory are one and the same. If you had enough of them, you'd know that by now."

"Spoken like someone who has a few . . ."

I closed my eyes as she continued to work on my eyebrow. One eye was about to swell shut anyway. "Spoken like someone who only has those kinds of memories."

"Exaggerate much?" Josie muttered.

"Only about the things that are important."

That made Josie laugh. Her laugh started off small and got bigger until it almost rocked her entire body. That laugh had been one of the few constants of my past. I loved that laugh.

I shouldn't love that laugh.

"Okay, last call for stitches. Anyone? Any takers?" she said once she'd stopped laughing.

I sealed my lips and shook my head, but Josie was already grabbing a thick Band-Aid from the kit. She knew me about as well as I knew myself.

"You're impossible." Sliding my hair back from my forehead, she tore open the bandage.

"Are you just figuring this out now? That I'm impossible? Because I would have thought by now, you especially would realize what an impossible, stubborn ass I am."

My fists curled around the chair-arms as Josie settled the bandage into position.

"I know who you are, but what happened to the guy who made me believe he'd walk through fire rather than hurt one of his only friends? What happened to the guy who punched Roy Watkins at recess for calling me a prissy little bitch?" Josie leaned back, looking about as exhausted as I felt.

She was waiting for an answer, so I gave her one. "Someone he cared about fucked him up good."

Josie's hands balled in her lap. "I know your dad's hard on you. Why don't you move out already? Get away from that toxic environment." She grabbed the ointment again and dotted it on a few other areas on my face.

"My dad wasn't the person I was talking about." Why in the hell did I say that? I couldn't even blame the alcohol for my momentary lapse into opening up like a goddamned pansy. When Josie's eyebrows came together as she worked out who I was referring to, I gave myself an imaginary beating. I was already bleeding; no need to spill my guts all over the damn place too. I needed to change the topic. And the mood. I didn't do vulnerable for a mountain of reasons.

So I slid that lazy smile of mine into place. The care-free, I-could-give-a-shit one that drove girls wild. Well, every girl but the one sitting a foot in front of me. It drove her wild, I guess, although in a totally different way. "So? You and Mason, eh? How's that working out?"

"Better when some asshole in a bar doesn't pick a fight with him." She shot me an accusatory glare as she capped the ointment.

"Whatever. Getting in a bar fight will be the single most exciting thing that ever happens to Colt Mason."

"Yeah, because being with me or potentially marrying me one day wouldn't even register." She tossed the stuff back in the first aid kit, still taking out her irritation on something else instead of me.

"I guarantee if that son of a bitch even thought he had a chance at marrying you one day, that would be the highlight of his life." I leaned forward, waiting for her to look at me. "But that douche has as much a chance with you as I do."

She grabbed my hat and settled it back on my head, adjusting it until it was right how I wore it, just a hair off the brow. "He's an awful lot like Jesse. What makes you think I'd never marry him?"

I wasn't sure if she was intentionally baiting me, but it was working. "First off, that little dick is nothing like Jesse. Nothing. Other than wearing the same kind of hat, although Colt's has never so much as seen a speck of mud, Jesse and Colt are about as alike as Jesse and me. Secondly, you're not going to marry that boy because, well, you're not going to marry that boy." I lifted an eyebrow and waited for her to argue. Josie might try to deny it, but she couldn't lie to herself. She was as likely to marry one of the Mason boys as I was.

"How descriptive." She leaned back and crossed her legs. Damn Josie Gibson's legs and that dress that barely covered them. It barely *barely* covered them when she went and crossed them like that. I tried not to stare for too long, but when I did manage to shift my eyes back to hers, she was giving me a look.

I cleared my throat and tried to forget about Josie's bare legs a few inches to the side of mine. "Fine. Here's just one of the million 'descriptive' reasons I've got for you." I leaned toward her until I could smell her shampoo again, and I knew she could smell the whiskey on my breath. And then, I leaned in closer. I waited until her eyes met mine. It took a while, but when they did, my point was proven. "You look at me with more fire in your eyes than you do him."

Her eyes narrowed, but they stayed with me. Continuing to prove my point. "That's enraged fire, Black."

Damn. At that proximity, forget the shampoo; I think I could smell her strawberry lip gloss. Which, of course, made me remember the way it'd tasted that night . . .

Get your shit together, Black. This is Josie. Josie Gibson. The girl I needed to stay away from for both of our sakes. When I leaned back that time, I was sure to give my chair a good slide to put some more distance between us. "It's still fire. And if it isn't there in the beginning, it sure as shit isn't going to magically crop up out of nowhere."

"Says the love non-expert."

"I'm the expert because I'm the only person on the face of the planet smart enough to know better than to fall in love. That right there is the reason I've earned my expert badge in love." I glanced toward the bar, hoping to catch Brandy's attention, because a few shots right about then would really dull the pain. Both kinds.

"You've got one warped view of love."

"Why, thank you. That's the best compliment I've heard all week."

Shaking her head, Josie stood, grabbing her purse and first aid kit. "You want a ride home? Now that I'm dateless and covered in your blood, this girl's Friday night is a wrap." Josie smiled at me, that same gentle ghost-of-a-smile she'd given me the second day of kindergarten when I realized I was either going to marry her or no one. It took me until the end of the school year to realize I'd never marry Josie Gibson. For all of the reasons I was being reminded of.

Just like that, I dropped the curtain on those memories and the small part of me that didn't feel permanently hardened. It had become like second nature over the years. I gave Josie a slow, crooked smile. I don't know why I even gave her that smile anymore. She'd seen through it the first time I'd tried it on her. She was immune, unlike the rest of the girls. "What kind of a ride are you asking about?"

"When you find that guy who had my back instead of plotting for ways to get into my panties, let me know okay?" I was still in my seat, but she gave my chest a solid shove. "I'm sick of being treated like the other girls you've banged. I might have made a mistake, but I still deserve your respect. Until you figure that out, I don't want to be around this new Garth. I'm not so hot on him." Sweeping her eyes over me, she shot me one last glare before marching toward the door.

"You call the sex we had a mistake? Because the first word that comes to my mind is mind-blowing," I called after her. I was partly hoping she'd come back and give me one more shove and partly hoping she'd keep on marching. "The kind of sex that makes a man keep his fingers crossed for an encore production."

That stopped her in her tracks. She spun around, cross-ed her arms, and lord . . . If I thought I'd seen fire in her eyes before, I'd been wrong. "It wasn't just a mistake. It was the biggest one of my life. I lost two of my best friends in exchange for the asshole with his nostrils packed with tissue in front of me now." She didn't give me the chance to reply before shoving through the door and out of the bar. Which was good, because I didn't have a fucking clue how to respond.

Garth Black. Brought to his legendary, come-back knees by a few words from Josie's mouth.

"It looks like you need another shot." Brandy stopped beside me and slid a glass in front of me.

"No, I don't need a shot. I need the whole fucking bottle."

chapter**TWO**

HALF A BOTTLE of whiskey later, I'd closed down the bar. After telling her three times that I didn't want to pay for my night of drinking with her in the back room, Brandy finally took my money. She called me a name even I wouldn't dare repeating that close to Sunday and told me to get out and never come back.

I wasn't planning on it. At least not until next Friday night.

Brandy's bar was a fifteen-minute drive from my place, but it took a little longer since I probably had about as much alcohol in my bloodstream as I did white blood cells. The general consensus was that a person shouldn't get behind a steering wheel after drinking a bottle—or was it closer to two?—of whiskey, but I had a tolerance that would put the Irish to shame. I wasn't seeing double, my vision wasn't blurred, and my reflexes weren't sluggish. I was good.

Of course, if I got pulled over and tested, I'd be up shit creek without a paddle. The one and only positive thing about having Clay Black as a father was that the cops and the law gave us both a wide berth. The cops had had enough experience with my dad to know they didn't want a repeat, so they turned a blind eye on our minor law breaking and basically forgot the two Black men were part of their jurisdiction.

I'd lost count of how many times that unsaid agreement had kept me out of jail.

About the time I turned down the overgrown drive leading back to the trailer, the alcohol had worn off just enough that thoughts of Josie were returning. Well, they were flooding back. Whatever curtain I'd dropped, whatever dam I'd built, whatever I'd constructed to keep her out of the forefront of my mind crumbled. I was swimming in thoughts of her. The way she'd chewed her lip as she doctored my face. The way she looked at me with disappointment on her whole face before walking out. The way she'd felt that night a couple years back.

After pounding the steering wheel with my palm, I slapped both of my cheeks. Josie Gibson was off limits, and if I kept thinking about her, I would have to find someone who could remove the part of my brain that kept long-term memory in good working order. So what did my mind go and skip to after issuing that ultimatum?

The last day of kindergarten. The bus had just picked me up, and I was furiously wiping my nose with my sleeve, hoping my nose would stop bleeding before my sleeve got soaked through. I'd accidentally woken Clay when I'd been checking the cupboards for something that could constitute breakfast. I'd finally settled on a dry package of ramen noodles. My punishment for rousing the sleeping bear had been the backside of his hand across my face. It had caused a bloody nose that wouldn't stop.

The bus driver barely noticed. He'd grown accustomed to my bloody noses and swollen lips, along with the rest of the kids on the bus. For some reason, that morning, someone noticed and scooted into the seat next to me.

"Here. Use this." Josie, complete with her pigtails, had pulled a napkin out of her lunchbox and held it out for me. A note was written on the napkin, along with a few hearts. At the end, it said, *Love, Mom.*

"I'm not using your special note to wipe my blood off," I'd said, trying to will my nose to stop bleeding.

"It's okay. She leaves me one every day in my lunch." Josie'd shrugged, holding the napkin out for me again.

I remember being shocked, floored by the fact that Josie had someone who loved her so damn much that not only did they pack her a lunch every day, but they actually took the time to write a note on the napkin. I wasn't familiar with that kind of love. It was a kind I didn't even know existed. That day, Josie had opened my eyes to the realization that love wasn't just a bullshit concept. To some people, it was so much more than circumstance and disappointment.

After the napkin had remained in her hand for a few more seconds, she lowered it to my face, holding it just below my nose. When my hand replaced hers over the napkin, she leaned in and kissed my cheek.

"What was that for?" I'd demanded, so shocked I almost leapt out of my skin. That had been my first kiss, at least the first one I could remember, and not the romantic kind a person means when referring to a "first kiss." My mom had been gone for too long to remember if she'd ever kissed me, and the only affection my dad showed me was slowing his fist just before it landed on me. It was the first time I'd ever been kissed, and even though I was only six years old and I had a lot of life still ahead of me, I knew no matter who or how I was kissed in the future, nothing would compare to that one on the bus.

None never had.

"It looked like you needed one," she'd replied before moving back to her seat up front.

Slamming the brakes, I pounded my forehead against the steering wheel. "Fuck me." I'd turned into the bleeding heart, nostalgic chump I'd had nightmares of becoming. What the hell was wrong with me? I'd managed to repress all of those memories and feelings for so many years I'd almost convinced myself I'd forgotten them. Boy, had I been wrong.

So why now? Why those memories? Why couldn't I contain and control them? The longer I thought about it, the more questions cropped up. Loads of questions, zero answers. If Jesse wasn't two states over, I might have raced to his place and forced his ass out of bed to keep me company and get my thoughts off their current track. But no, the pussy-whipped sucker was probably cuddled up beside his girlfriend—correction: *fiancé*—having pussy-whipped sucker dreams about white picket fences and honeymoon destinations. As much as I wanted to tell him he was making the biggest mistake of his life marrying Rowen Sterling, I couldn't. Marrying the woman he loved at twenty-one wasn't a mistake for a guy like Jesse Walker. Shit, Jesse could have married the woman he loved at any age and it wouldn't have been a mistake. Jesse was the marrying, loyal, loving type.

Me? It didn't matter what age I was or how much I thought I loved the woman. Marriage, rings, and vows were not created with people like me in mind.

Other than Jesse, Rowen wasn't bad to talk to, but since she was where Jesse was—spooning two states away—she was out too. There was Brandy, but she and I never did much . . . talking. At one time, Josie had been one of my most trusted confidants. Given she was the one I needed to talk about, not to mention the one I had to keep my distance from, I had to scratch her off the list, too. After that, there was no one. I had three people—well, two—I could talk to about things that needed talking out.

My dad had figured it out twenty-one years ago: I was a good-for-nothing bastard.

Pounding the wheel one last time with my forehead, I was about to punch the gas, hoping that Clay left a few swigs in his bottle before he passed out, when something in the distance caught my attention. A bright ball of color lit up the night. Almost like someone had started a huge bonfire in the middle of nowhere. In the middle of nothing but hundreds of acres of barren land and our trailer. Which meant . . .

I punched the gas so hard my truck fishtailed out of control. I eased off the gas just enough to regain control then tore down the bumpy road, watching that ball of light get bigger and brighter. I was still a half mile back when I saw the actual flames rolling off of the trailer. We had a not-quite-dried-up well, but it was clear by the time I slammed the brakes in front of the lawn chairs that there was nothing left to salvage. The entire thing was engulfed in flames, close to the point of being unrecognizable. Everything was burning. Everything was gone.

"DAD!" I yelled, throwing the truck door open and leaping out. Panic settled in my stomach. Dread soon followed. It was after two in the morning, which meant he was passed out drunk. Since he only left the trailer to restock his liquor supply, he couldn't be somewhere else.

His truck had been repo'd years ago, his license revoked years before that, and no one in our county or the next one over would loan him a car. As much as I wanted to cling to the hope that he was somewhere, *any*where else, I knew exactly where he was.

That was when an explosion rocked the trailer and vibrated the ground below my feet. Probably one of the propane tanks. My body and mind flipped to autopilot and, despite the beating I'd taken earlier, I sprinted toward that trailer like I was good as new. I was still a good ten yards back when the heat hit me. The fire was so hot it scalded my face. The bruises and slashes from earlier probably didn't help any. A few yards closer and even if I wanted to breathe—which I didn't because the air was so hot it burned my nostrils and lungs—I couldn't have. The fire had sucked all of the oxygen out of the air.

As I moved closer, I squinted and covered my nose and mouth with my arm to keep the smoke from hitting me full force. The closer I got, the more I realized nothing was left in that trailer to save. The man I'd lived with for twenty-one years wasn't going to be draped over his chair in the back, snoring and unscathed. I knew that, but the autopilot I was on wouldn't accept it. I couldn't have stopped moving forward even if I wanted to.

By the time I made it to the burning door, I was coughing so hard I felt like I was expecting a lung to come up. I didn't think—I simply reacted. Grabbing the handle, I pulled on it as a scream ripped through my body. White hot pain shot from my hand up my arm, so intense I felt close to passing out. The only time I'd felt pain close to that had been when that behemoth brahma down in Casper had come down on my shin a few years back, fracturing my femur.

The smell hit me next. That acrid, metallic scent was so thick in the air I could almost taste it . . . and I knew what it was. I didn't have to have smelled it before to know that human flesh was the only thing that could smell as unforgettable as that. I reassured myself it was my flesh, my palm, causing the smell. Nothing or no one else.

Setting my jaw, I cried out and charged for the door again, not consciously recognizing why I had to get in. My hand was inches from wrapping around the scalding doorknob again when a firm set of arms wrapped around my chest and pulled me back.

"Garth! What are you doing, son? You're going to kill yourself!"

I struggled, but no amount of fight worked. "Let me go, Neil! Clay's in there! He's in there!" The fight slowly faded from me the farther Neil wrangled me away from the trailer. "My dad's in there!"

Another explosion blasted from inside the trailer. Another propane tank. That's when I realized and accepted that the father I never really knew I'd never know because he was gone. He'd been gone for a long time, but his body had followed the rest of him.

"No, son." Neil stopped pulling me away but kept his hold on me. "He's not in there anymore."

E.R. VISITS HAD been a pastime of mine for as long as I could remember. I was about as comfortable in a hospital bed as I was in my own bed. Since my own bed was nothing but ash and soot, I suppose the hospital bed was even more appealing than it had been before. The fire department had shown up a few minutes before Neil got me into his truck and booked it for the hospital. He was the second person that night to suggest an E.R. visit, and since I was too exhausted and in shock to argue with him, I went with it.

The nurse had fixed up my hand, and the doctor stopped in a few minutes later to pump me full of pain meds. He'd seen me plenty of times growing up. My dad had threatened him when he'd recommended I take the summer off from bull riding after I broke my leg. The doc was a decent guy who seemed that much more decent as the drugs worked their way into my system. I guessed he'd given them to me more for the mental than the physical pain.

The benefit to having perfected repressing stuff was being able to do it again. My dad had just been barbecued inside our "home," and I still hadn't cried a single tear. I hadn't broken down, punched a hole in a wall, or dropped to my knees. I didn't face it; I couldn't yet. So I repressed it. I didn't think about what tomorrow would bring, and I didn't think about what the day after that would. I focused on my bandaged hand, still pulsing with pain, the hospital bed I was curled on which, for all I knew, might be the last mattress my body felt for a long while, and the antiseptic smell surrounding me. Those were the realities I obscured real reality with. Those were the things I centered my attention on when my father's funeral needed to be planned.

I was close to passing out in a drug-induced haze when the curtains whooshed open and a figure slipped inside. "Garth? Oh my god . . ." A sniffling, bleary-eyed person approached.

"Hey, Joze. What are you doing here?" Talking hurt, thanks to the fire singing my throat.

"Neil called Jesse, then Jesse called me . . . He and Rowen are on their way. They were leaving when I was talking to him." She approached the foot of the bed slowly. "I'm so sorry, Garth. And, wow, that sounded as pathetic and petty as I always thought it would."

"It's okay. I get it. You're sorry, I'm sorry, the whole fucking world's sorry. But it doesn't fix anything. Sorry doesn't bring Clay back. Sorry doesn't stop that fire from starting. Sorry doesn't get me to that trailer before the fire started. And sorry sure as shit doesn't make me feel any better."

I wasn't mad at Josie. I knew there wasn't much else to offer than an *I'm sorry* when tragedy struck. I'd already heard it a few dozen times in less than an hour, and I'd hit critical mass. If I never heard another *I'm sorry* again, I'd be good.

Instead of saying something back, Josie came around the side of the bed and crawled in next to me. Her body fit around mine as her arm wrapped around me, holding me close. It was an odd embrace, a foreign one for me, but it felt so exactly what I needed right then that I melted right into her. Screw the drugs.

"Neil told me what happened. About how you were trying to get inside." Her hand wrapped around the wrist of my bandaged hand and gave it a gentle squeeze. "I always knew you'd be one of those people who'd charge into a burning building to save a person. I always knew you were a superhero in hiding."

Josie liked to see the good in everyone, and she'd never let go of the idea that some was still left in me. At

35

one time, I'd believed her. I didn't anymore.

Her embrace became more painful than comforting. "I didn't save anything or anyone, Joze. I don't qualify as a superhero."

"But you *tried*. That's what matters."

"No, that's not what matters. Saving my dad's what would have mattered. The only thing that matters now is that he's dead, my hand is burnt to hell, and I'm home-less." Too bad the doc didn't hook me up with an I.V. Then I could have just kept pumping the drugs into me. I wasn't sure if it was Josie or reality, but one or both of them were forcing me back to a place I didn't want to be.

"You know you can stay with me and my family for as long as you need to." Her hold around me tightened when I tried to squirm away. Classic Josie.

"Oh, yeah. That would be ideal. Absolutely ideal. Because we all know how highly your dad thinks of me. If I was the last living creature on earth, he wouldn't even skin me and use me for his boots, and that's without him even knowing I slept with his daughter under his roof." Josie hushed me. Maybe because I was getting a little loud, but probably because I'd brought up being one of the men she'd been with. She hated that. Probably always would. I hated myself for it. That was one of the few things Josie and I had in common. "And let's not forget your mom, who looks at me like she can't decide whether to pray for me or pray that the ground opens up and a legion of demons drag me into hell where she thinks I belong."

Josie let out one of those long sighs, and the warmth of it crept down my neck. "I just wanted you to know the invitation's there should you choose to accept it."

"Thanks, Joze, and I mean this with sincere gratitude .
. . but no thanks." Truthfully, that she'd even invited me to
stay at her place was enough to choke a man up, but I
couldn't let her know that. There was no way I could let
her know she was probably the only person on the face of
the earth who'd invite me to crash at their place for an
indefinite amount of time. A few minutes of silence passed
between us, long enough so her embrace shifted back from
pain to comfort. Long enough I'd almost fallen asleep
from the drugs.

"Do you want to talk about it?"

"No," I said instantly. I didn't want to talk about it
then, the next day, or never. Talk, kind of like *I'm sorry,*
didn't change anything.

Josie didn't press me. She didn't try to encourage me
that opening up and talking until my vocal chords oozed
blood was a part of the healing process. She knew me, and
while most of the time that was a detriment, right then it
wasn't. She knew I didn't talk about anything I didn't want
to because she'd been around long enough to know my
M.O. Plus, she was the same. Trying to get Josie to open
up about something she didn't want to would have been
about as successful an endeavor as trying with me.

"What are you going to do?" she said a minute later,
her voice soft, almost scared. Josie did scared about as
often as I did, so I couldn't understand where it was coming from. What was she scared about? Scared for me?
Scared of life and its suddenness? Scared of what?

Letting out a long sigh, I said, "I don't know, Joze. I
don't fucking know."

Moving so smoothly I barely felt the mattress shift,
Josie crawled over me until she was laying in front of me,

her face inches from mine. Whatever sadness or fear had been in her voice wasn't on her face. Her green eyes locked onto mine, and if I believed in that kind of shit, I would have sworn whatever peace or certainty was in them transferred to me. For the first time that night—for the first time that *year*—I felt peaceful. At rest. It was such an alarming sensation, I didn't know what to do. Run and duck for cover, or exhale and bask in it.

Before I'd made up my mind, Josie leaned in closer until her lips pressed into mine. My eyes hadn't dropped before her mouth left mine, but the taste of her strawberry lip gloss lingered.

"What was that for?" I asked once I remembered how to speak. Josie was an expert at rendering me speechless.

Sliding off of the bed, she paused before disappearing behind the curtain. "It looked like you needed that."

chapter THREE

HOW DID ONE hold a funeral for a person whose body was gone? Hell, for a person whose ashes didn't even fill an urn? The whole concept was lost on me, but I was about to find out.

A few days after the fire, the chaplain at the hospital offered to do a service after he asked about funeral arrangements and I pretty much scratched my head in answer. Clay died with no money in the bank, and his secret whiskey stash went up with the rest of the trailer. Since I had a whopping forty-two dollars in my wallet, having a funeral service inside of a church was out. So much for not-for-profit . . .

The chaplain had suggested holding the service outside, at a location of my choosing—maybe somewhere I had fond memories of Clay and I being together. When my answer was another head scratching, the chaplain gave up and suggested a spot by the river. Worked for me. So long as it was quick and to the point, I was fine with Clay's funeral being held there.

It was almost one o'clock, and I was going to be late. I'd pulled into the public access parking lot fifteen minutes ago, but I couldn't pull myself out of my truck to make the short hike to where the chaplain was waiting for me. He was already there. At least, I assumed his car was the one with the bumper sticker that read *Don't drive faster than your guardian angel can fly.* There weren't any other cars in the parking lot. It was late fall, too late in the season for fishermen, or campers, or anyone other than a random funeral goer to be enjoying the river.

The chaplain had encouraged me to invite as many family members and friends as I wanted, assuring me the mourning process was so much easier to go through with the support of loved ones. The best I could do after he'd said that was to not laugh. Loved ones mourning Clay Black? Hell, I was his last living flesh and blood, and even I wasn't so hot on the idea of mourning him. How was I supposed to mourn a man I'd hated more days than not? How could I miss a father who'd reminded me every day how he cursed the day I was born? Mourning a person didn't come standard with death. It was an honor reserved for those who lived life right.

Needless to say, I hadn't invited anyone else. No one but me would be there, and even I didn't want to attend. The only reason I finally shoved open that driver's side door was because I knew the chaplain was waiting and he sure as hell didn't need to go out of his way for Clay. So I sure as hell wasn't going to let his good deed be wasted. Adjusting my hat, I made sure the bottle cap was still in my shirt pocket before heading down the trail.

Since the only thing left of Clay was whatever was left inside the shell of the trailer, the chaplain recommended I bring something meaningful to Clay and me. Something that could stand in place of a casket or an urn. Something that encapsulated his forty years of life. It took me a while, but I finally found something that summed Clay Black up perfectly. A token that was more the man my father was than any varnished casket.

The trail made for an easy hike down to the river, but I struggled with every step. My feet had grown concrete blocks, and just when I thought I couldn't go another step, I saw the chaplain. He saw me at the same time, gave me a small smile, and waved. He'd picked a nice spot with the river as a backdrop, and he stood beside a large rock, almost like it was a podium. As expected, we were the only two around.

"Hey, Chaplain. Sorry I kept you waiting." I forced myself to take the last few steps. Once I got it over with, it would be done. Over. I could sweep the whole thing under the rug and forget about it.

"It's fine, Garth. I've just been enjoying the bounty of God's workmanship."

I forced myself to return his smile. The chaplain had drunk way too much of the Kool-Aid in Sunday school as a child.

"How much longer would you like to wait for the rest? Don't worry about me, because I've got the whole afternoon open."

The chaplain and I might have lived on opposite ends of the spectrum, but he was an all right kind of guy. Despite being a little out of touch with reality. "You might as well do your thing because I'm the only one coming."

The chaplain indicated just over my shoulder. "Either fisherman have started wearing formal wear to pull trout out of the river, or you've got company."

My sigh cut short as soon as I saw who it was. "What the hell are you two doing here? This is a funeral, not a wedding."

"Good to see you too, Black," Jesse replied, helping

Rowen over a few rocks in the trail. "How are you doing?"

"I'm fucking on top of the world. Can't you tell?"

"I'm not sure that *fuck*'s allowed at a funeral, Black." Rowen shot me a wink as she and Jesse came up beside me.

"Why not? Clay was that word's number one fan. The profanity and the act." The chaplain looked off into the distance."How in the hell did you two know what was going on today?" I couldn't decide if I was pissed or relieved they'd shown up. I definitely felt a bit of both. I'd seen Jesse and Rowen a couple of days ago, pretty much right after they got in from Seattle, but I hadn't mentioned a thing to either one of them about the funeral.

"You called in sick today," Jesse answered, nudging me. "You've never called in sick before. Not even the day after . . . after . . ."

"The day after the fire," Rowen interjected. Jesse thanked her with a smile.

"You mean the day after Clay was burnt to such a crisp nothing was left of him?" Jesse's eyebrows lifted. Rowen's came together. I wasn't trying to upset two of my only friends. It just went against my nature not to. Truthfully, having them with me made the whole thing less daunting. We were nothing more than a few friends hanging down on the riverbank, saying good-bye to a person I wasn't sure even deserved it.

Rowen said, "You want to take out your anger at us today, fine. Do it. You get a free pass. Today and today only. Tomorrow you'd better find somewhere else to channel your anger."

I waited a moment for her to go into more detail, but none came. "Or else?"

She arched an eyebrow. "Or else."

"I sure have missed your veiled threats, Miss Sterling -soon-to-be-Walker."

"Yeah, yeah. And we've missed your unparalleled goodness, too."

Jesse tried to keep from smiling, but that was about as easy for him to do as it was me to keep smiling.

"So I get that me calling in sick today alerted the dogs to what I had planned, but how in the hell did you know where to find me?" Montana had as many wide open spaces as there were stars in the sky. "Did you go and install a GPS tracker on me or something?"

Jesse stared into the sky while Rowen's eyes locked onto mine. "No. We followed you," she answered with a shrug.

I shook my head. If I hadn't been so preoccupied with trying and failing to spin a brodie in the middle of the road and tear out of town and never look back, I might have noticed Old Bessie tailing me. That truck was such an atrocity it was impossible to miss. "You two are a couple of regular ninjas, aren't you?"

"Hi-yah," Rowen deadpanned, thumping the side of her hand into my stomach.

"And look at you, Walker. Dressed up all fancy in a suit. It almost looks like you're heading to your own funeral." I elbowed his ribs, making him elbow me right back. "Hold up. Aren't you the whipped chump getting married this summer? I suppose that explains why you look like you're heading to your own funeral." I chuckled, ignoring Rowen's impressive glare.

"Two words, Black," she said, all tough sounding. "Or. Else." Lifting her fist, she circled it around.

That, of course, only made me laugh. "I sure am glad I have you two here for moral support. I've never felt so uplifted and surrounded by warm fuzzies in my life."

"We love you too, buddy." Jesse slung his arm around Rowen's neck, the other around mine, and pulled us together for some sick version of a group hug. I was protesting with an exaggerated groan when I heard a few others coming down the trail. It probably shouldn't have surprised me, but it did.

Mr. and Mrs. Walker, followed by their three daughters, made their way toward us. Neil had a solemn expression, Rose had a small smile, and the girls all looked a bit red-eyed. Go figure. Three Walker girls who'd barely even met Clay had been crying, but his own son had yet to shed a single tear. I told myself the only reason they were able to muster up a few tears for him was because they didn't know Clay like I did.

Neil clapped my shoulder as his family fell in line beside him. "It's a hell of a thing, son. One hell of a thing."

I nodded once then indicated the chaplain. I had planned on being wrapped up already, not greeting guests I hadn't invited. Despite not having invited them, I was glad they'd invited themselves. The chaplain had been right—it felt good to be surrounded by loved ones, or as close to loved ones as I had. I'd never openly admit it, but it was the truth.

The chaplain rolled his shoulders back. "We are brought together today by a great tragedy. A life ending before its time. A man—"

"Hold on. Wait! I'm sorry. Just hold on one more minute!" someone hollered from the trail.

My initial response to hearing Josie's voice was to smile. So I went with a drawn-out sigh. When she came into view, I saw what was to blame for slowing her down.

"Damn these heels. Why can't they make a pair more suited for rough terrain?" She glanced at me just long enough to acknowledge me with a smile before going back to watching the ground like it was about to reach out and grab her. With the heels she had on, it was a miracle she'd made it that far without breaking her neck.

Jesse nudged me. I didn't get what he was hinting. Then he elbowed me. I still didn't get it. Finally he sighed and said, "Why don't you go help her before she breaks a heel or a leg?"

Riding in on the white horse and saving the day was Jesse Walker's thing, not mine. That's why I hadn't picked up on his hint. When I stayed glued where I was while Josie hobbled over a few more rocks, Jesse shook his head. Before he'd taken one step toward her, I grabbed his arm. "I got it. Hey, stilts, let me give you a hand before you go and break your neck."

If she wasn't so busy watching the ground, I knew she would have glared at me. "I don't know what I was thinking wearing these things. Where's a pair of boots when a girl needs some?"

I'd seen Josie in a pair of shoes other than boots maybe a dozen times since I'd known her, but seeing her in a pair of heels with the knee-length dress she had on made me wish she'd wear them a lot more.

Unbelievable. I was at my father's funeral and having moderately inappropriate thoughts about a girl's legs. I didn't have many, but I knew I'd had finer moments than that one.

"Yeah, but they sure look nice." I forced my eyes up right about the time Josie stumbled over a rock. Hell, maybe she stumbled over her own two feet. I'd gotten to her just in time. I broke her fall right before swinging her into my arms. We didn't have much farther to go, but I didn't want to wait another decade for her to maneuver her way there.

"What are you doing?" Josie asked, her tone as shocked as her expression.

I shrugged, asking myself the same question. "Blue moon."

Josie's forehead lined. "Come again?"

"You've never heard of a blue moon?"

"Yes, Garth. I've heard of a blue moon." Today's eye roll count: one. "What does one have to do with you helping me?"

"This guy's got the day off from playing the hero." I slugged Jesse's arm after setting Josie down. "I'm filling in." Jesse's and Rowen's expressions matched Josie's. "What?" I was ready to slug him again if he didn't stop looking at me like I'd lost my mind.

"I knew you had it in you all along." Josie planted her feet on a level patch of sand.

"Yeah, yeah. No need to go and spread the word, Miss See-the-Good-in-Everyone, because I'm about to have the reluctant hero inside of me exorcised."

"Too bad. That was the first time in years that I haven't wanted to slug you in the jaw."

The chaplain cleared his throat, and Josie zipped her lips at me.

"Fine, bossy," I muttered.

"Whatever. Hero." She gave me a wide grin before

turning her attention to the chaplain.

"Garth? Are you ready to proceed?" the chaplain asked, still looking like he wasn't in any hurry.

"As ready as I'll ever be." Even the smart-ass tone I'd perfected fell flat.

"Did you bring something to symbolize your father being here in spirit?"

"Oh, yeah. I almost forgot." Digging in my shirt pocket, I pulled out the cap and set it on the large rock beside the chaplain. Want to know how to make a crowd of talkers go so silent it made the air thick? Thunk a Jack Daniels cap in front of them where a casket would be if Clay Black's ashes weren't scattered over acres of barren, rented land.

The chaplain was the first to make a noise, even though it was only a clearing of his throat. "Would you mind sharing how this . . . this . . . signifies your father?" The poor chaplain couldn't even bring himself to say it.

Me, on the other hand, had no problem. A cap of Jack was home sweet home in my world. "Clay liked to drink. A lot. He also liked throwing empty bottles at me when I did something that irritated him. Like brush my teeth before bed. Or eat a package of Saltines for dinner. Or, when I was still dumb and hopeful as a child, ask for a hug before bedtime."

I noticed Rowen take Jesse's hand. It was an easy gesture. Effortless. Almost like her hand had acted of its own accord.

"The bottle that cap came from was the last one Clay threw my way. The one he threw at me the night he died. Right before I left. The last one he'll ever throw at me. I would have brought the bottle, but it was busted to shit.

Totally unsalvageable. But that right there, the cap to a bottle of Jack, meant Clay died with the good stuff in him. That meant it was the first of the month and his disability check had just come in. That meant he had a couple more days of drinking the good stuff out of a bottle before switching over to the stuff out of a plastic jug that turned a person's insides. My dad died with the good stuff in him. That's all a person like Clay Walker could ask from life."

I was still staring at Jesse's and Rowen's entwined hands. The longer I studied their hands, the more I realized I never had and never would have that. Someone to stand shoulder to shoulder with and take on life one day at a time. Someone to know what I needed before I even said it. Someone who loved me without conditions. Hell, someone who loved me even *with* conditions. I'd been with a lot of women, so many women I couldn't tell if it was closer to dozens or hundreds, and never once had I come close to loving a single one of them. They'd come about as close to loving me.

Whatever Jesse and Rowen had, what Neil and Rose had, whatever that was, I made sure to steer clear of it. Most of my life, I'd considered that a blessing. One or both parties falling in love just made things messy. Complicated the good thing going on. But standing at my father's funeral, where a whiskey cap stood in his place, alone and with no one to take my hand before I even knew I wanted it held, felt like a curse.

"So this cap signifies freedom? Your father's departure from this world has freed him from the clutches of addiction," the chaplain said after a while.

"Sure, this cap signifies freedom. *My* freedom from him."

The chaplain's eyes widened—just barely but enough to tell me that I'd said something to shock him. I hadn't been going for shock value; I'd been going for the truth. He was back to being tongue-tied, and the air around me was thick with dead silence, when Josie nudged closer to me. Her hand reached for mine, twisting against it until my fist released, letting her fingers weave through mine. Without realizing I'd been holding it, I could breathe again.

Without realizing exactly what I needed, I suddenly had it. A measure of comfort exactly when I needed it. A silent need picked up on and responded to. It was foreign in the best kind of way. Josie's hand heated mine, its warmth traveling up my arm and spreading until no sign of a chill was left to be found. No sign of the winter I'd lived in my entire life was still around.

"Would anyone like to say any last words?"

The chaplain's words startled me out of whatever hand-holding, dreamy world I'd lost myself in. Good thing because that was a world I couldn't be a part of. Not because I wouldn't accept it, but because it wouldn't accept me. I gave my head a shake to clear my thoughts, but even if I wanted to with all my will—which I didn't—I couldn't free my hand from Josie's. I'd have to make sure the next time she was close by, I didn't let her hand get too close to mine. As good as it felt, it would hurt like hell later when her hand was holding Colt Mason's and mine was running over the body of some woman whose name I wouldn't remember in the morning. Holding her hand was short-lived and would do way more damage than good in the long run.

"I suppose I should send a sympathy card to Mr.

49

Baker, the owner of the liquor store downtown, since his best customer won't stumble through his front doors again. He's probably going to go out of business. Now that's a tragedy." I capped my "last words" with a chuckle, but if I thought the silence had been thick before, I'd been wrong.

The fact that Jesse wasn't shaking his head and muttering *jackass* or that Josie wasn't sighing and elbowing me meant my attempt at humor had been timed badly. Too much, too soon. But how the hell was I supposed to deal with it? How the hell was I supposed to muster up some last words that weren't depressing as all hell or, as I'd chosen, tongue-in-cheek? There was nothing heartfelt to be said. Nothing even moderately endearing.

For the second time in a few minutes, the chaplain looked tongue-tied, positively stumped as where to take the runaway train next. That was when Neil nudged between Jesse and me, making his way up to the chaplain. Like his son, Neil was sporting a suit. I'd never seen Neil in anything besides a pair of jeans.

Clasping his hands in front of him, he searched the sky for a moment. "I know Clay was a man who left a person feeling conflicted most of the time. A man like him is hard to know what to make of." I wanted to mutter *No shit,* but the chaplain was watching me carefully. Probably knew the exact words I was biting back. "But I will never forget the first time Garth and Jesse rodeoed together. It was the summer they were eleven years old. Garth was out there on an ornery, old steer—stayed on the whole time, too—and took one hell of a score. Clay was standing beside me, and he nudged me, his eyes focused on Garth, and said, '*That's my boy.*'" Neil paused long enough to make sure I was looking at him. He nodded, tipping his hat. "That's how I'm going to choose to remember Clay Black. As a man who was proud of his son, as hard of a time as he had of showing it most of the time." Dropping his attention to the whiskey cap, he tilted his hat once more before rejoining his family.

The chaplain took it from there, but if someone had asked me what he said, I couldn't have told them. I didn't hear another word after Neil's speech. To say it felt like I'd been hit with the biggest sucker punch of my life would be an understatement. I remembered that day. I'd taken home my first championship belt buckle, and I'd been so sure Clay had been passed out drunk in his truck like I found him later that afternoon. I'd been so certain he missed one of the few times in my life I actually wanted him to be a part of so he could see what I was capable of and maybe, just maybe, feel a moment of pride. I'd believed he'd missed that moment, along with the few others that might have been worth an ounce of pride in Clay Black.

According to Neil, I'd been wrong. Clay saw me that afternoon. He'd said . . . *That's my* . . .

I don't need this shit. Not now. Not ever. Gritting my teeth, I emptied my head and managed to stay silent and in place until the chaplain was finished. It was one of the hardest things I'd done.

As the chaplain passed me, he offered yet another small smile. "Peace be with you, son."

"Peace has never been a big fan of mine. Or me of it." My words weren't meant to be argumentative but informative. Peace and I resided on opposite sides of the universe.

"But like you said, your father's death has given you a new freedom. Freedom to be and do whatever you like."

51

The chaplain patted my shoulder before heading toward the trail. "Give peace a try. I can guarantee it's not as overrated as you might believe."

"Says the man who says good-bye with *peace* be with you," I muttered. The chaplain was out of hearing range, but Josie's elbow in my ribs confirmed she hadn't missed it. "And what are you doing here, by the way? I thought you had wannabe cowboys to date, and mean ones who picked fights in bars to avoid."

"I'm paying my respects," she replied, refusing to make eye contact.

I huffed. "You hated Clay almost as much as I did."

"I'm not paying my respects to him." Turning toward me, her gaze shifted from the whiskey cap on top of the rock to me. I'd told myself hundreds of times, possibly thousands, that I needed to avoid looking into Josie's eyes at all costs. Every single time she did what she was doing then—staring at me, waiting for me to stare back—I forgot all of my warnings and broke my golden rule: stay away from Josie Gibson. "I'm here to pay my respects to *you*."

My eyebrows came together and, before I could figure out what she'd said and what I should say, she threw her arms around me, gave me a quick squeeze, and hurried back up the trail. But not before kicking off her heels to run up it barefoot.

Jesse came up behind me. "What was that?"

"Women are mysterious creatures bound to make a man crazy if he spends too much time trying to decode their every move."

"Amen." Jesse chuckled. An exaggerated clearing of a certain young woman's throat stopped his laugh mid-stream. "I mean, I don't know what you're talking about at all."

"Having you gone so much this year, I almost forgot what a little girl you've become." Spinning around, I patted his cheek. "Thanks for the reminder."

"I've missed you too, sweetheart." Jesse shoved my chest lightly then tilted his chin down the river. "Wanna talk?"

Jesse had been trying to talk to me for the past few days, but I'd done one of the few things I did best and avoided him. Not because I was avoiding *him* per say, but because I wanted to avoid anything to do with talking about Clay, what happened, and the all important what now? The first two subjects I could navigate if need be. The last one, though—the what now?—I didn't have a fucking clue where to start. So I'd been avoiding, ignoring, and pretty much hiding from Jess.

"Not even remotely," I answered him, nodding my acknowledgement as the Walker family passed me, heading back up the trail. Truthfully, I was touched they'd come, but hell if I could find the words to tell them so.

"Too bad." Jesse kissed Rowen, whispered something to her, and shouldered past me to head down the river. I knew where he was going. We used to go down there and skip rocks as kids. As we got older, Jesse came down to fish during the day, and I brought my girl-of-the-hour down at night. Our favorite rock-skipping spot was a couple hundred yards upstream.

"You're going to be waiting a while, Walker!" I hollered after him.

He kept walking. "See you in a minute then."

"He is a serious pain in my ass," I said as Rowen came up beside me.

"Aren't you two peas in a pod then?" She watched Jesse until he disappeared before angling toward me. "I'm not going to ask how you're doing, and I'm not going to ask if there's anything I could do. I know those are the last questions you want to answer right now, and even if you did answer, your answers wouldn't be honest, so I'll just skip all the standard protocol if that's okay with you."

I smirked at her. "You are a fine woman, Rowen Sterling."

She promptly returned my smirk. "Flattery gets you nowhere with me."

I hitched my thumbs under my belt buckle. "And flattery gets you everywhere with me."

Her mouth opened like whatever she wanted to say was on the tip of her tongue, but she clamped it shut, inhaled, and waited a few seconds. "You know, Garth, if you want to take some time off and get away for a while, Jesse and I'd be happy to have you at our place. It's not much bigger than the cab of your truck, but the couch is yours whenever you need it. Seattle might not be your ideal scene, but there are plenty of bars chock full of women who'd jump at the chance to have a real life cow-boy show them 'the ropes.'"

Ah, hell. That was exactly what I didn't want—people treating me differently because my daddy had burned to death. Everyone tiptoeing around me because who knew when I'd lose it. That Rowen was doing it—the one I was sure would be the last one to treat me like a walking time bomb—was a sobering reality.

"No fair. You didn't warn me that the pity patrol were coming to town." I wagged my index finger and tried to act like Rowen's transformation into sympathetic when it came to me, was anything but staggering.

"That wasn't pity, Garth."

I laughed one hard note. "If that wasn't pity, what the hell was it?"

Rowen stepped forward, her eyes narrowing just enough. "That was one misfit telling another misfit that she's got your back should you need it. That was one misfit telling another that you don't have to go through whatever you're going through alone. That was *me* telling *you* that you've got friends. So lean on them, god dammit. Stop acting like every battle you face is a one-man-war." Clearly irritated, Rowen headed for the trail. "It doesn't have to be Garth Black against the whole world, you know. Give your friends a little more credit." If I wasn't so shocked, I might have thought about replying. She skidded to a stop, turned around, put her hands on her hips, and leveled me with a Rowen look. "And if you don't go talk to him in the next two seconds, I am going to spread some nasty rumors about you on the women's restroom stalls of every public place in the state. Rumors that will ensure the only action you'll get for the rest of your life will be from the soft side of your hand."

Lifting my arms, I started down the river. "How can I say no to a woman who talks dirty to me?"

A smile broke on Rowen's face before she recomposed herself. I flashed a salute at her before continuing upstream. I hadn't been up that way a while, and I'd forgotten how many damn slippery rocks there were. I caught myself from wiping out every other step, and my slick-bottom boots only made a precarious situation lethal.

"I lost the boots fifty feet back! Might want to do the same if you're hoping to not break your neck!" Jesse yelled from his perch on one of the tall rocks dotting the riverbank.

"We wouldn't want the town going and throwing a celebration party if both Black men died in the same week, would we?" I replied, continuing over the treacherous terrain. "Thanks for the tip but no thanks. I'm a cowboy. The real kind. We don't take our boots off, god dammit."

Jesse tossed a pebble my way. "Don't or won't?"

"With me, Jess, they are one and the same." After slipping yet again, I finally made it to the rock Jesse had climbed and heaved myself up. "Nice suit, shithead." The only time I'd seen Jesse in a suit was at a funeral or a school dance. In Montana, men only wear suits for death or dancing. True story.

"Nice lack of suit, dipshit." Jesse shoved me as I sat beside him, keeping a respectable distance so we wouldn't look like a couple of love birds watching the river pass by.

"So . . . now that you've got me out here which, by the way, is so very serene and inspiring"—I swept my arm dramatically—"why don't you just let me have it so I can go get shit-faced like I need to. You don't bury the man who wished he'd never given birth to you every day, you know."

Jesse almost sounded like he mumbled *dipshit*, but I couldn't be sure. Grabbing one of the flat rocks he'd piled up beside him, he flung it out into the river. It skipped five times. Weak. "How are you? What's going on in that depraved head of yours right now?" Points for getting straight to the point. Negative points for getting straight to *that* point.

"I'm living the dream, Jess. Fucking on top of the world." I grabbed my own rock and launched it out into the river. Six skips. I grinned.

"Yeah, you sure look like you're living the dream." Jesse didn't examine the scruff on my face, or the dark circles under my eyes, or the notch I was down to on my belt. His words and tone said it all.

"Yeah, yeah. Bite me. Next question." One down. Knowing Jesse, probably only a few million more to go.

"Do you need anything? Is there anything . . . you know . . . I can do for you?"

I wasn't sure who looked more uncomfortable: Jesse or me. "You know, your fee-an-say knew better than to ask those exact same questions. She basically told me she knew I either wouldn't give her an answer, or if I did, it wouldn't be a straight one. So what makes you think I'll give you an answer or a straight one?" I flung another rock, and it barely skipped three times. The stupid Kumbayah conversation was messing with my stone-skipping skills.

"Because I, unlike my sweet one hundred and twenty pound soaking wet fiancé, can and will happily kick your ass in order to beat the answers out of you if need be." I broke out in laughter. Stomach-grabbing, body-rocking laughter. "What?" Jesse shoved my arm. "What's so funny?"

After forcing myself to calm down, I answered him. "I can't decide what's funnier—you describing Rowen as sweet or being so confident you can kick my ass."

"Watch it, Black. I can put up with you insulting me all the way to the second coming, but I won't tolerate for one fraction of a second you insulting Rowen." He interrupted me before I could say what I was about to. "In jest or not. I'm protective like that."

"Protective? You? No way." As much as I loved giving Jesse a hard time—in fact, it was a favorite pastime —when it came to Rowen, it was only out of habit. "You know I like the two of you at least ten times more than I like myself, right? I might talk a lot of shit, but you know if either of you needed anything . . . *anything* . . . I'd give my fucking life if need be. Right?" I nudged him, making sure he was getting what I was saying. I'd shove him straight off the rock if that's what it took for him to get it. "Right, Jess? You know that, right?"

Jesse's face couldn't have gotten more solemn. Then he grinned. "Are we having another moment?"

I should have shoved him off the rock. "Shithead."

Jesse laughed, sending another rock skipping into the river. I was too pissed to count. "I know. Difficult as you are and as much as I know you'd rather chop off your left arm than show any real emotion, I know you've got Rowen's and my back when and if we need it." He paused just long enough to cue me in that he was winding up to say something big. Jesse loved using dramatic pauses. "You do know, though, that friends-through-thick-and-thin goes both ways, right? You need something, we're a phone call or a five-hundred mile drive away."

"So you shouldn't be the first person I call if I sever my carotid artery?"

"Only if you've got a death wish." That ever-present hint of smile fell clean off of Jesse's face. "Shit, Garth. I'm sorry. I didn't mean it like that . . ."

"Walker, please, for the love of god"—I picked up one of the rocks just so I could squeeze it—"don't start treating me like I'm some nut case about to stuff my head in an oven. Give me enough credit that I'm too self-centered to do something like that because really, I can't take another person treating me like I'm going to implode if they say the wrong thing."

Jesse stared out into the river before nodding. "I can do that. No imploding nut cases around here."

"Ha. Other than the one beside me."

"At least your warped sense of humor is still intact," Jesse replied.

"In tip-top shape actually." The rock I was squeezing was either going to break a few bones in my hand or crumble, so before either rock or hand broke, I hurled it into the river. No skipping that time.

"If you want to take some time off and come hang out with Rowen and me in Seattle—"

I lifted my hand, stopping him. "Again, your woman already beat you to the offer-the-loon-refuge punch. If I wasn't terrified of the permanent damage that would be done to me hearing the two of your freaky mating sounds, I might actually take Seattle and your couch into consideration."

"Green much?" Jesse quipped, unfazed.

"Gloat much?"

Jesse sighed. "Take it or leave it, just so long as you know you're welcome whenever. Okay?"

I nodded my acknowledgement because I knew Jesse wouldn't let it go until I did. Before he could get anything else out, because lord knows, that guy couldn't not talk if his life depended on it, I took the conversation and ran with it. "So, what about you? How's pussy-whipped life . . . I mean ball-and-chain life . . . I mean married life . . . I mean engaged life treating you?"

"Just so you know, if you hadn't just been at your

dad's funeral fifteen minutes ago, your ass would be off this rock right now."

"Fuck, Jess. I thought I told you to stop treating me like a self-imploder?"

He shrugged. "Fine."

Then before I noticed him move, my ass didn't fall off that rock—it *flew* off. It was a damn good thing said ass landed on a patch of sand, or I would have paid back the favor and then some. "I sure have missed you, Jess. Kind of like the girl you screw once and who just won't take a hint that you don't want to slap a ring on her."

"Missed you too, pal."

"This summer, eh? You're really ready to castrate yourself?" I'd almost climbed back on top of the rock when Jesse gave me a warning look. "I mean, you're really ready to tie the knot?"

"I'm really ready."

"My god, Walker. You are insane."

"It's a concept you will never quite grasp, I get it." Jesse slid out of his suit coat and rolled up the sleeves of his dress shirt.

"What? Getting married?"

His head moved side to side. "No, loving a woman enough to even imagine getting married."

"Ouch." I thumped my fist against my chest. "I just 'buried' my father. Take it easy on me."

"I thought you didn't want me treating you any differently."

"So did I," I replied.

"Well make up your mind already." Jesse smiled at me and hell if I couldn't not smile back.

"What's the rush?"

"I was planning on asking you to be my best man, but that seems wrong if you're still under the belief that love and marriage are your arch nemeses. I need a best man who'll support me and have my back, not one who'll try to talk me out of saying 'I do' right up until I say it." I glanced over at him, lifting my brows. "Or talk me out of it after saying 'I do,'" Jesse added with an eye roll. "Not exactly the kind of stuff a guy needs in a best man."

"But you and I both know no one is better suited to throw the bachelor party that would go down in infamy. We're talking get Guinness on the phone because we're going to break every bachelor party record out there."

Jesse pitched another rock into the river. "Yeah, something else I'm really not looking for in a best man."

"You suck the fun out of any and every situation, you know that?" Even though I was masking the whole best-man conversation with humor, I was honored as all hell that he'd even consider me his best man. We'd grown up together, but plenty of shit had gone down between us— thanks to yours truly—and I just considered myself lucky that Jesse still talked to and tolerated me. Never once had I guessed he'd consider me as his best man.

But he was right. I'd make one pathetic excuse of a best man with my ideas on love, marriage, and happily ever after. I could smile and get through the ceremony, but I didn't believe in any of that shit. Kind of hard to when the closest thing to love I'd experienced with a girl had been not wanting to immediately toss her out of my bed in the morning. For Jesse, I got it. I understood why he wanted to marry Rowen. He had it so bad for her, his eyes were about to go crossed. Love and marriage made sense for Jesse Walker. Love and marriage made no sense for me. Arch nemeses may have been an exaggeration, but they were concepts I was definitely avoiding.

Or had they been avoiding me?

"Do me a favor and give it some thought, will ya? I'd love to have you as my best man, but I'll understand if you're not up to it."

I nodded. It was a decision I wouldn't make lightly. "There doesn't happen to be a spot for a 'worst man,' is there? Because I can assure you that's got my name all over it."

Jesse laughed with me. I was about to climb off the rock and go in search of that whiskey—enough heart-to-heart for a lifetime—when his face got all serious again. Shit. "What are you planning on doing now?"

I knew what Jesse was asking, but hell if I was answering. "Getting rip-roaring drunk and finding a woman who can make me forget everything, including my name, for a little while. Or a long while preferably."

He let out a long sigh. "And after that? Then what? Dad said he told you that you were welcome to move into the bunk house with the rest of the hands, but you said you were staying at a friend's place for a while." Jesse gave me a purposeful look. "What friend do you have that I don't know about who'd give you the green light to move in with them indefinitely?"

"One you don't know." I kept my reply short and my eyes forward. Jesse was an expert at sniffing out my lies. Probably because he had fifteen years of experience doing so.

"Name?"

"I've got a name for you." I lifted my middle finger at him.

Jesse looked like he was going to shove me off the rock again but stopped. That, right there, was the defining line between the two of us. Jesse thought first, jumped later. Me, I jumped first and maybe, *maybe*, thought later. I'd make an argument as to which was the better option if it wasn't so damn obvious which one of us was winning at the game of life.

"Fine. Should you ever desire to move out of your 'friend's' place, or should they decide to kick you out, you know you're welcome at Willow Springs, right?"

"As welcome as the clap," I replied.

Jesse let out another sigh. His and Josie's reactions to me were lining up. "I already said I've missed you, right?"

"Yeah, yeah. And I think I forgot to say *fuck off.*"

"It's good to have friends."

I tipped an imaginary beer at him. "Hell yes, it is."

chapter **FOUR**

EIGHT SECONDS OF glory. All a man like me could ask from life.

Clay had beat that phrase into me when most parents were teaching their kids the alphabet. With Clay, it was all about the most important eight seconds of a man's life, the glory to be earned from it, and not resting until I'd given the best ride of my life.

In another life, Clay'd been a bull rider, too. From what I'd gathered in between benders and the few pictures scattered around the trailer, one hell of a rider. He'd even been a part of the pro circle for a while. Then he met my mom, knocked her up with the little bastard known as me, and had his kneecap stomped on by a two thousand-pound, pissed off animal. Clay's riding career had ended that day in the arena a month before I was born, and even though he left it with his life, it wasn't much of one. I'd never known the man he was before the accident, and what I knew of the man after didn't make me want to know who he'd been. Clay could have been the fucking Dalai Lama of Montana and it wouldn't have compensated for the man I'd known growing up. Atonement just wasn't in the cards for Clay Walker.

Other than our looks, Clay and I never had much in common. Rodeo was the one exception. I was trotting on a horse before I could walk, and Clay tossed me up on my first steer the summer before kindergarten. Bull riding wasn't about a father bonding with his son. No, bonding was something Clay reserved for his whiskey. Bull riding was about one man living vicariously through another. It was about Clay living his eight seconds of glory through me.

Eight seconds of glory and a whiskey cap. That's all the man who'd conceived me had left me with. Not even a nickel more. It wasn't a big surprise Clay had never made out a will because, really, what was there to fight over when he died? The macrame pillow coated with years of smoke and whiskey fumes? The single dinner plate I'd glued back together so many times I'd lost count? The trailer I'd been too embarrassed by to invite a friend or a girl back to? No, there was nothing to fight over. Nothing to show for a man who'd lived forty years of life other than a whiskey cap and a son who gave his middle finger to life at every turn. Even if there had been stuff, there was no one to fight with. I was the only family Clay had. Or at least the only family he hadn't severed all ties with. Talk about leaving a legacy behind . . .

The fire department had determined the fire had started thanks to a faulty space heater. My guess was that the main "faulty" part of the fire had been Clay, but I guess even the fire department was worried about me losing it if they told me the whole truth. Oh well. How it had happened didn't change that it had happened.

By the calendar's measure, it had been three months since the fire. By my measure, it felt like a couple centuries. Clay was a distant memory, along with so many pieces of my life. Working at Willow Springs and bull riding were the only pieces of my former life that hadn't changed. I'd cut off contact with most of the people in my life, at least the ones who knew the real me, not the person I wanted people to see when they looked at me.

Well, I'd *tried* cutting them off. Josie showed up at Willow Springs every now and then, trying to get me to 'snap out of it,' but she'd been about as successful as Jesse had. I wasn't 'snapping out' of anything. I was happily snapped in. If they didn't like it, that wasn't my problem.

"Black. You're up."

I lifted my chin and slid into my leather gloves. Since the fire, I'd stepped up my training. I'd linked up with a few other guys who trained every Thursday night with Will Jones, who was basically bull riding royalty. Will was an old timer, probably in his seventies from what I knew of his career, but he still moved and held himself like one of us "young and dumb" types. Will had an indoor arena, a few practice bulls, and a mountain of champion belt buckles. The opportunity to train with one of the best didn't come free. Or even cheap. I was shelling out hard-earned cash in my pursuit of eight seconds of glory, and the longest I'd managed to stay on a bull since the fire was five.

Five pathetic seconds of no glory was all I had to show for weeks of hard training and a boatload of cash. That was about to change.

Climbing the gate, I held in my groan when I saw which bull I'd drawn. Bluebell. A sweet name for an any-thing-but-sweet creature. I was convinced Bluebell had been Attila the Hun in a former life because the bull was merciless and out for blood. In the few months I'd been riding him, Bluebell had drawn plenty of mine.

"All right, Black, try to stay on just a few seconds longer than you stayed on top of your date last night." Jason, whose right eye was still black from when he'd run his mouth last Thursday, smirked. My fist was twitching, just dying to make contact with his other eye, when Will hollered at us from the stands.

"You boys going to sweet talk each other all night, or are you going to ride?"

"I don't know about Jason here, he seems the sweet talking type"—I flashed him a tight smile—"but I'm riding."

Jason laughed. "Is that what you call it? I thought what you did was eat dirt."

If I wasn't already getting into position on Bluebell, my fist would have cracked into Jason right then. Oh, well. I'd just have to give the ride of my life and shut him up that way. Double-checking my grip on the bull strap, I lifted my other arm and gave the nod.

The gate flew open, and Bluebell burst out of it like a devil out of hell who was down on his quota for the month. The one benefit to having ridden Bluebell so many times was that I knew the bull's patterns, how high he jumped, and which way he liked to spin out of the gate. Most of bull riding was sheer determination, training, and luck, but some of it was probability and statistics. I knew Bluebell spun to the right. Not every spin, but always the first spin out of the gate. I felt the bull tighten beneath me, ready to break into a spin after lunging out of the gate. I braced myself, and one millisecond too late, I realized my mistake. For probably the first time in the creature's life, its opening spin was to the left and I was, yet again, eating dirt.

Probability and statistics my ass.

I didn't bother to jump up and flee for the gates. The damn bull knew it could do nothing worse to me than throw me before the eight-second mark. I swear it gave the bull equivalent of a smirk before heading to the holding gate at the other end of the arena. The day Will decided Bluebell was ready to retire, I was buying that damn bull and turning his hide into a pair of boots just so I could have the satisfaction of returning the dirt-eating favor with every step I took. Cursing under my breath, I hoisted myself up and tried not to hobble across the arena. Jason and the rest of the guys were applauding my performance with wide grins. Bastards.

"Impressive performance out there, Black. I think you managed to stay on a whole two seconds that time, which was a whole second longer than your date last night had the pleasure of."

If I wasn't already covered in bruises from our training session, I would have thrown off my gloves and charged Jason. What stopped me wasn't the fear of losing a fight to Jason Simmons. When I did have a go at him, I wanted to be at my best because I wanted him to remember every hit I got on him. If I wanted to just kick his ass, it would have been game on, but I wanted to kick his ass *and* teach him a lesson. With the way I was already beat to shit, teaching him a lesson would have to wait.

I had to spit out a mouthful of dirt before replying. "At least I know *how* to pleasure my date. Unlike your sorry excuse for a dick. And the staying-on-my-date jokes were old five hundred ago. Get some fresh material and get back to me."

"A cowboy who stays on a bull for eight seconds

doesn't have to know how to pleasure his date. He's got a whole line of dates just waiting to pleasure him."

For a cowboy who'd ridden a whopping five rodeos, he sure had a big head. "The only line I see around you is a blank-faced, nose-picking male bunch." I waved toward the other guys we trained with on Thursdays. I didn't know their names because I didn't care to know their names. They only rode bulls for the pussy that came along with it. A real competitor didn't disgrace the sport by riding for pussy. They rode because they were fucking cowboys with dicks, and that's what real cowboys with legitimate dicks did. Fucking posers.

"Okay, boys. I'm calling it a night before someone kills themselves or someone else," Will yelled. Part of his job was training us, and part of it was keeping us from strangling each other. I don't know if he would have taken us on if he'd read that in the fine print. "Pack it up. I'll see to the bulls."

"If you need any tips, Black, give me a call. I know a thing or two when it comes to eight seconds." Jason slid out of his protective vest, chomping his gum and grinning at me. "Oh, hold up. You don't have a phone, right? The cell got cut off due to insufficient funds, and the landline . . . well, the landline was burnt to a crisp like your has-been daddy."

Rage monster, here I come. I'd just torn off my gloves and started marching toward Jason—after what he'd just said, he was going to get his ass beat *and* learn a lesson—when a firm pair of hands grabbed my shoulders and stopped me.

"Bad idea, Garth."

I tried pulling free of Will's hold, but the old timer

was either hooked up to a steroid drip every night or was a descendent of Superman. I might as well have been struggling against a pair of steel vices.

"Save your battles for the arena. Beating him by earning a higher score will shut him up a hundred times faster than any ass-kicking. It'll keep you out of jail too because I don't know about you, but Jason seems like the type who would press charges for battery or some shit." When I stopped struggling, Will let me go. "He's the kind of man—I use that term loosely—who doesn't understand you don't call the cops to work out a situation when a pair of fists does a better job of it."

I'd always liked old Will Jones, but my opinion of him had just jumped a few hundred levels from moderate to severe hero worship. "I'd love to shut him up by giving the fucking ride of my life, but I can't even manage a mediocre ride that hits the eight-second mark."

"When was the last time you stayed on a full eight?" Will asked when I turned to him, after waving both of my middle fingers at Jason and his jackass apostles as they left the arena.

"A little over three months ago."

Will grunted, nodding. I'd never talked about it with him, but it was a small town. Will knew what had happened to Clay, how it'd happened, and when. That he'd never felt the need to bring it up or ask if I wanted to "talk about it" put him that much higher in my esteem.

"I went through a dry spell once myself, too. My issue was a woman. A crazy, vivacious one I couldn't get out of my head. I was so consumed with her that I'd already be out the chute before I realized I was on the back of a pissed off bull that wouldn't think twice about stomping me to death." Will's eyes went somewhere else. "That woman . . ." When he came back, he shook his head and studied the ground.

"Well? How did you beat it? How did you get her out of your head and end your dry spell?" That was the point of the whole segue, right?

Will smiled. "I all but hog-tied her, drug her to the closest church, and married her."

I hadn't seen the marry-the-crazy-distracting-woman one coming. "And marrying her *helped* your riding?"

"I earned my highest score my first ride after saying *I do.*"

"How in the hell did that work?" If a woman was my problem, marrying her would be the worst possible solution.

"Because I'd fallen so completely in love, my mind and body and every other part of me wouldn't rest until I'd made her mine forever, for God and everyone else to know. I couldn't be *some* other man to her when I wanted to be *the* man for her."

The conversation was getting a little too touchy-feely for me. I stepped back in case Will was close to breaking out in tears and needing a hug. I wasn't the person to hug when someone was in the midst of a meltdown. I was the person who shook the hell out of someone and ordered them to get their shit together. "Well, that's a Precious Moments story, but it does me a whole lot of no good because my problem ain't no woman."

"Your daddy?" At least if he was going to bring it up, he didn't beat around the bush and he looked me in the eye.

"Daddy, ashes to ashes, dust to dust—literally—

dearest."

Will didn't blink. I suppose when a person had lived as many years as he had, there was little left to be seen or heard that could surprise them. "And what makes you think your daddy dying is causing you to lose your head when you're up there on a bull?"

"Because he's probably some poltergeist following me around, giving me a ghosty shove when I'm up there, and getting a good laugh in his hereafter watching me eat dirt." Will raised an eyebrow. "Because, okay? I know." He lifted his other brow, waiting. "You're a stubborn one, aren't you?"

"Only about as stubborn as you are. But I've had fifty extra years of experience, so don't you think for a moment your stubbornness can outdo mine. Older men than you have tried and failed."

I got why Josie was such a fan of the eye roll when I was around. Being around someone as bull-headed as me almost made me want to roll my eyes. "The only thing Clay ever said to me that wasn't insulting, derogatory, or slurred in a drunken haze, was that men like him and me—men without land or cattle or a lot of money—could only find glory one way."

"Eight seconds on the back of a bull," Will stated, no hint of a question.

"The only kind of glory men like us could ever hope for." I dropped my hands on my hips and exhaled.

"Well, I can tell you what I think about that."

"That it's a whole load of shit?" I almost hoped Will would say that. Then I'd know one other person in the world felt the same way. Most of the time I accepted Clay's glory axiom, but a few times—moments like those

—I wanted to believe it was the biggest, falsest load of shit to be spread.

Will's hand clamped my shoulder. "That it's a whole load of *sad*. A person's glory doesn't come from trying not to fall off, but picking themselves up when they do. That's the measure of a person's glory." He headed toward the end of the arena. Apparently his confounding work was done and he was calling it a night.

Proverbial whiplash . . . why, yes, yes I am your most recent bitch. "So since I'm covered in a mixture of bull shit and mud, I must be swimming in glory? Is that what you're saying?" I called after him.

"You're not swimming in glory until you find someone to swim with you. Glory isn't glory if you don't have someone to share it with. It's just pride and bullshit on your own."

Unbelievable. Will Jones wasn't only one badass cowboy; he pretty much could have been the love child of John Wayne and Yoda.

"I think I get why you married the crazy one!" I hollered. "You needed someone to keep up with your special brand of it."

Will glanced back for a second, tipped his hat, and kept going.

And I thought the bull had fucked me up good.

chapter **FIVE**

IT WAS ANOTHER Thursday night, and somehow I'd wound up with more bruises and dirt between my teeth than I had last Thursday. The whole "things can only go up from here" concept hadn't made my acquaintance yet. I'd run out of pain reliever a few days earlier and had yet to restock my supply, so I let half a bottle of whiskey have a go at it instead.

My brain still felt like it wanted to burst out of my skull, and the rest of my body felt like it had been tumble-dried with a load of rocks and needles. To say I was in pain was like saying I was freezing. One of Montana's notorious cold snaps had set in, and my breath wasn't just fogging—it was about a degree away from crystalizing. The one positive to the frigid temperatures was that it made my body numb, thus dulling the pain.

Who ever said I wasn't a silver lining kind of guy?

I'd just burrowed down in my sleeping bag and closed my eyes when a loud thump lurched me awake. The sound had come from behind me so, after defogging the window, I gazed out to find the face I'd been trying for weeks to forget about. I'd failed miserably.

"What the hell, Black?" Josie yelled, thumping the window again with her mittened hands. "What the hell is this?"

So much for flying under the radar. Sighing, I cranked down the window and stuck my head out of my truck. "I was in the middle of a sweet dream, Joze."

"That wasn't a sweet dream, you idiot. That was your body shutting down thanks to hypothermia."

At that stage in my life, they were the same thing. "What are you talking about? It's balmy in here." I hadn't seen Josie so pissed in . . . well . . . Actually, I'd never seen her that pissed.

"I bet. That must be why your nose looks like it's about to fall off." She was bundled up in her knee-length down jacket, a hat and scarf coving all of her face but her eyes. If I'd never seen her so pissed and two-thirds of her face was hidden from view, she was close to going nuclear. "You really are a bastard. You know that?" I was about halfway through my nod of agreement when she narrowed her eyes even more somehow. "Your dad burns to death, and his son freezes to death three months later. Isn't that just a goddamned fairy-tale ending?"

She sounded like she was just getting started, so I decided to use the silence while she sucked in a breath. "Did I miss something? Why are you acting like you want to hang me up by my toenails and skin me?"

"BECAUSE I DO!"

Even through my hat, that scream did some permanent damage to my eardrums. "Mind explaining yourself before you scream me deaf?"

I hadn't even said it with sarcasm, and she was glowering at me like she was willing me to die on the spot. "You told me you were staying at a friend's place. You told me you were somewhere with a roof over your head, with running water . . . with a kitchen . . ." Okay, she was starting to break. As much as she was trying to fight them, a couple of tears surfaced in the corners of her eyes. "You told me you were safe . . . and . . . and *warm*." She gestured at where I sat in my truck, close to breaking out in shivers. "And here you are, camped out in your truck in front of your burnt out trailer in the middle of negative degree temperatures. You lied to me, Garth. You *lied* to me." From the looks of it, there was no greater offense.

I had lied to her. Not because I'd wanted to tell Josie a lie, but because I wanted to admit the truth much less. I'd been living out of my truck for months on land I'd essentially been evicted from because I didn't want to burden anyone. I'd clearly been a burden on Clay all twenty-one years of my life, and since I was free of him, I didn't want to pass that burden baton on to someone else. The Walkers or Josie especially. If I was going to be a pain in the ass leech, I sure didn't want it to be on one of my real friend's backsides.

"What do you want? An *I'm sorry*? Because I'm not." The only good thing about arguing with Josie was that it was heating me up. Which brought my Thursday night war wounds back in all their throbbing glory.

"No. Screw *I'm sorry*. You owe me a hell of a lot more than that after what you've been pulling the last couple months." Grabbing the door handle, Josie flung the door open. "You owe me the decency of getting out of that ice box of a truck into mine, and then I'm taking you to my place. You can thaw, eat a warm meal, and figure out what the hell to do next. Because living out of your truck isn't a viable long-term solution."

I inhaled. "Let me make my answer to your suggestions sweet and succinct." I leaned across the seat until my face was in front of hers. "No."

Wrong thing to say. I saw the flash of something go through her eyes that would have had me shaking in my boots if I had any on, and then she grabbed my arms, dug in deep, and pulled. She didn't stop pulling until my sleeping bag and I had fallen in a heap at her feet. I was adding bruises on top of bruises.

"Shit, Josie. What the hell was that for?"

"That was because I asked you once and I won't ask again." Kneeling beside me, she pressed her face so close to mine our noses rubbed together. "Get up and get in my truck. Now."

"What is the matter?" I worked myself free of the sleeping bag and grabbed my boots.

"You. That's what's the matter."

"Me?"

"Yes, you."

"Care to expand on that?" I had to grit my teeth as I stood because, on top of her finding me camped out in my truck in near Arctic temperatures, I didn't want her to know I was probably in need of yet another E.R. visit.

"No, I do not. The only thing I care about right now is getting you in my truck and taking you back to my place."

I managed a weak crooked grin. "Now that's what I'm talking about."

"Leave the dickhead here. I don't care if that part of you freezes to death."

"I'm not leaving any part of my dick here to freeze." I stuffed the sleeping bag back in my truck before closing the door. I wasn't in the mood to argue with Josie, and I could almost feel the heat from her truck cab.

"If you don't stop being 'cute' with me, I'm going to

knee your entire dick all the way up into your throat."

If I wasn't a frozen, pulverized popsicle, Josie getting all bossy probably would have turned me on. But really, being turned on was the farthest thing from my mind right then. "Fine. You win." I followed her as she marched to her truck.

"Whoop-dee-doo. Look at my grand prize." She glanced over her shoulder long enough to run her eyes up and down me in a way that was the opposite of approving. I couldn't figure her out. She'd just threatened my manhood if I refused to go with her, and I was. So why did she look about as thrilled as if she'd just learned she had five minutes to live? Josie had never been a tough one to read, at least not until the past couple of years. Lately, she'd been like a faulty Rubik's cube. There was no figuring her out, but that didn't stop me from wanting to take a crack at it.

As soon as I opened the passenger door, warm air rushed over me. She had the heater cranked so high the cab was almost as warm as a sauna. It felt so good I actually sighed. Crawling into her lifted truck took a little effort, but as soon as I was seated, with the door closed and warm air enveloping me, I could have fallen asleep in thirty seconds flat. Josie threw herself into the driver's seat, muttered a curse word I'd rarely heard her say, and shot another death glare my way. For someone who'd seemed like they wanted to help me, she sure changed her tune after I went along with it. Oh, well. It was late, I was bushed, and all of the warm air was clouding my mind and making me one heartbeat above comatose.

She pulled her downy mittens off, threw them at me, and punched the gas. "I can't believe you did that. You've done some crazy shit since I've known you, but this is beyond your usual brand of crazy shit." The way the woman drove . . .

"Joze," I said, my voice raspier than usual. Probably because of the extreme temperature changes. "Buckle up."

Her eyebrows came together. "Huh?" She was obviously so worked up that my simple request wasn't computing.

Reaching over her, I pulled the shoulder strap across her body and clicked it into place. "Buckle up. The way you drive when you aren't certifiable is scary enough. I don't need to lose another person."

Josie blew out a breath. "Well you keep camping out in this kind of weather, and you won't have to worry about losing another person. Because you'll be dead." She practically spat the last word at me.

"Okay, so back to the crazy shit bit you were saying earlier"—I clicked my seatbelt into place, too—"I'm sorry. I'm not going to pretend to understand why you're so pissed at me, but I know you are. For that, I'm sorry. Me doing what I do isn't meant to make you so upset." It was a vague apology—I wasn't quite sure what I was apologizing for exactly—but it was an apology nonetheless. I issued one about as often as a lunar eclipse.

"You're sorry about what exactly?"

Of course that would be her follow-up question. Burrowing deeper into the seat, I cupped my hands over the heaters and planned my words carefully. *Think before you speak* was something I reserved for times like those. When Josie Gibson was at the wheel, hot on the heels of threatening to knee my dick into the next county. "That I was camped out in my truck—"

"In Arctic temperatures," she interjected.

I nodded. "In Arctic temperatures. I'm sorry for nearly freezing myself into a popsicle-like state. But, you know, maybe if I was kept frozen, I could come back a few hundred years later and—" Another look of death stopped me mid-word. "I'm sorry for nearly freezing myself into a popsicle-like *death*. There. Is that better?"

"It's a start, but you've got a lot to be sorry for, Garth Black, so keep going."

I'd rather eat my boot than apologize to just anyone . . . but Josie wasn't just anyone, so I sucked it up. "And I'm sorry I didn't tell you where I'd been staying."

She kept silent and gave me the *And?* look.

"And I'm sorry I've been avoiding you and not returning your calls . . . *but* I knew if you cornered me, you'd figure where I'd been laying my head every night and you'd do something crazy like this." I twirled my finger around the cab. I'd also been avoiding her because that was the right thing to do and my number one priority in life. Given her current state, I didn't think it best to go into how I needed to stay away from her for all eternity.

Her only reply was that same expectant look. It seemed *And?* was the tone of things right then.

"And I'm sorry you had to come out in this weather in the middle of the night to look for me." I still didn't know why she had or how long she'd been looking before making it to my truck, but again, that wasn't the time to clarify. The more apologies I made, the angrier she seemed to get. Either I was missing something, or she was. Like her sanity.

"And I'm sorry you had to dry up an entire oil field from the amount of gas you went through driving from your place to mine?" Yes, my apologies were starting to tip more the smart-ass scale than the genuine one, but I was running out of ideas.

She gripped the steering wheel so hard, her knuckles blanched white. Okay, what was I missing? What kind of an apology was Josie waiting for? Sure, over the span of the fifteen years we'd known each other, I had a whole universe of things to apologize to her for, but right then, what was the apology she was looking for after I'd lied to her about where I was staying?

Ah, yep, that was it. Since my eardrums were still ringing after she'd gone off about being lied to, I had a good idea what she was waiting for. I twisted so I could look her straight on. "I'm sorry I lied to you, Joze."

Her anger melted off, one layer at a time, until the face of the girl I was used to came back. It took a moment, but when Josie's eyes flashed to mine, I knew the screaming and glaring was past. At least for my latest offense.

"So? Am I forgiven?" I dropped my hand on her shoulder and gave it a gentle squeeze. Even though she had on a cushion of down and fleece, the touch still felt intimate. More intimate than I'd expected, and too intimate for the distance I needed to keep between us. I dropped my hand and made a note not to touch her again if I could help it.

"I haven't decided yet," she replied matter-of-factly, making me chuckle.

"Well what more do I need to say or do to get you closer to a decision?"

She gnawed her lip for a few seconds. "Just try to explain, get me to understand why . . . *why* you'd rather camp out inside your truck than stay with one of your friends. Because that makes no sense to me. None. Actually, as far as sense goes, that makes, like, negative sense."

Of course it didn't make sense to Josie. Someone like her, who'd lived right and said and did the right things, wouldn't have any qualms or guilt about taking a friend up on a generous offer. She would have been invited out of love and respect. Me, on the other hand? I'd been invited only out of obligation. That Jesse, Rowen, and Josie had even thought to extend the invite after Clay's death wasn't something I was spitting on—not even close. They'd been the only people to ever offer help, and I'd never forget it. I wasn't fool enough to believe they'd invited me because they actually hoped I'd move in though. We were friends, but I wasn't exactly a ray of sunshine to be around. They'd issued invitations simply because I didn't have a home anymore. Therefore, those invitations had come out of obligation.

Putting that whole concept into actual words wasn't something I wasn't up to the task of doing, though, so I went with a short, honest answer. "I didn't want to be a burden to any of you." That worked. Short and to the point, just how I liked most everything in life. Save for my johnson.

Josie snorted. "Yeah, because worrying me sick about you for months wasn't a burden. Because driving out there to shake some damn sense into you wasn't a burden. Because being friends with you, Garth, as hard as you like to make it on me, isn't a goddamned burden." She wasn't back to her former anger levels, but being able to flip a switch like that was a rare trait. "Thank you *so* much for saving me all of the effort and burden." She didn't even attempt to hide her sarcasm.

I couldn't grasp why she was so upset. Was she mad at herself that I'd pulled one over on her? Maybe. Did she care about me so much the thought of me living out of a truck for months was upsetting? Unlikely. Josie seemed more to tolerate me than actually like me—but what else was there? I couldn't come up with a whole hell of a lot more.

"You know, I've been working at Willow Springs the entire time, so I'm getting three warm meals, three *good* warm meals, five to six days a week. I wasn't starving on my days off, either, so it's not like I haven't had a solid meal in three whole months, okay?" I wasn't sure if explaining my day-to-day life would comfort her or piss her off even more, but I was definitely hoping for the former. "It hasn't even been all that cold until last night. I had a good sleeping bag, and the cab of my truck is more comfortable than that old egg crate mattress I slept on in the trailer. On the nights Clay actually let me sleep inside instead of out in a lawn chair."

I glanced over to gauge her reaction. Her face wasn't drawn up in angry lines, so I supposed we were making progress. "Even if I had the choice, I'd still take the cab of my truck over the inside of that nasty trailer." That was the truth. A sad one, perhaps, but factual. "Come on, don't be mad. It wasn't bad, okay? It wasn't the Ritz, but it was a far cry from the worst living conditions I've been in. A far cry."

Then a tear slid down Josie's cheek. I would have expected her to shoot lightning bolts out of her eyes before an honest-to-goodness tear. Something kicked to life inside of me then. Something that needed to say or do whatever it took to make her feel better. To make sure a second tear didn't follow the first. It was all very . . . unfamiliar to me. "Please, Josie, don't be upset. I wasn't fighting for my life in horrific conditions, and when the conditions did turn horrifying enough to freeze my toes off, you swooped in to save the day. Everything's okay, so please—*please*—stop crying." I grimaced, anticipating more tears.

Josie sniffed and wiped her eyes. "I've done plenty of it in my lifetime. Crying isn't going to kill me."

"But it might kill me." I wished I could go back in time and clamp my mouth closed before those five words escaped. Not because they weren't true—they were—but because of the way Josie's eyes widened with surprise before her whole expression softened. I'd been trying to calm her down, but not so much that she'd get comfortable enough to lower all her defenses against me. I needed her to keep those defenses up, those walls strong, because as much as I wanted to deny it, my walls had a way of crumbling when Josie was close by. My defenses, my actual ones, skipped off to la-la land when I was with her. That's why I'd fabricated extra-abrasive defenses with her. It was the only way to protect her from the giant mess I was.

"Here we are," Josie announced.

I had to look out the window to confirm it. That she'd managed to cover miles of country in a handful of minutes seemed humanly impossible. Good thing she had family in the sheriff's department. Otherwise she'd have enough speeding tickets to wallpaper her bedroom. Gazing at the Gibsons' barn, I wondered if the cot was still tucked away in the back stall.

In seventh grade, after Clay had landed more hits on me than usual, I'd hitched a ride to the Gibsons'. I was "running away" for good that time. I'd arrived in the middle of the night, thrown some pebbles against Josie's window until I woke her up, and without a word, she led me into the barn. She set up a cot with blankets and a pillow for me. She even had a plastic container stocked with a flashlight, snacks, and some comic books, like she'd been expecting me. Since it was summer break, no one missed me, most of all Clay. A few mornings later, Mr. Gibson found me, ordered me to leave, and pretty much said he'd be waiting with a shotgun the next time I decided to move into his barn with his teenage daughter a hundred yards away. Josie had cried that day too, but Mr. Gibson wasn't swayed by her pleas or her tears. I left that day, never returning to Josie's place until a couple of years ago. That one night . . .

In seventh grade, I hadn't understood why Mr. Gibson wanted as much space between me and his daughter as his shotgun could create, but I figured it out a few years later. He'd figured out sooner than I had that I was no good for his daughter.

"So"—I glanced out the windshield at the dark house—"your dad?"

Josie opened her door, and a rush of cold air hit me. "He's asleep. He successfully got his daughter through her teenage years without her getting knocked up, so he sleeps a lot more soundly. He wouldn't even hear a herd of cattle run through the dining room."

"Does he still sleep with his shotgun under his pillow?"

Josie smiled at me. "Only when he's expecting you to show up."

"Comforting. Thank you." I smiled back before

forcing myself out of the cab. After all of that warmth, the frigid air almost knocked me over. Hurrying toward the barn, I was stopped halfway there.

"Where the hell are you going?" Josie stepped in front of me.

"The barn. Preferably before I freeze my ass off."

Her whole face except her eyes was covered up, but hell if those eyes weren't the most expressive things I'd ever seen. "You're not sleeping in the barn. It's probably a whole two degrees warmer than your truck." Grabbing my arm, she turned me around and steered me toward the house.

"Hey, two degrees can mean the difference between losing and keeping one's toes."

I wasn't fighting her, but she didn't stop tugging on me until we were at the front door. "And seventy-five degrees can mean the difference between chattering yourself awake all night and drifting off into a peaceful sleep."

If Josie thought peaceful sleep was an option for me, she was living in a state of disillusionment.

Putting her mittened hand up to her mouth, she opened the door quietly and slipped inside. I followed her, half expecting to find Mr. Gibson in his favorite chair with his shotgun aimed between my eyes. Like most of the homes around there, the Gibsons' place was an old farmhouse that they'd done a nice job of keeping up. It was more updated and modern than the Walkers' home but just as inviting. Well, inviting for anyone who hadn't been threatened with death if they ever showed their face around it again.

The guest room was on the main floor, across the hall

from Josie's parents' bedroom. The old wood floors creak-ed with every step, and I hoped Josie was right about her dad sleeping heavily. I was just about to take off my boots and continue toward the guest room when Josie shook her head and tugged on my arm again. She wanted me to fol-low her up the stairs. Only two rooms were on the second floor. One was a bathroom. And another was Josie's bed-room. The one time I'd been in her bedroom, I managed to sleep with my best friend's girlfriend. If that was the kind of disaster I could expect from entering Josie's room, I would not be making a return visit. No. Way.

Like the wood floors, the steps creaked, and I didn't stop wincing until we reached the second floor. Josie looked as relieved as I was we'd escaped detection. Keep-ing her hand wrapped around my arm, she pulled me down the hall, past the bathroom, and stopped outside of her . . . I pulled my arm out of her grasp and shook my head. Hell, no. I wasn't going back in that room. Not only because of the bad memories, but because of the good ones, too. That night had been a combination of extreme highs and lows.

Josie rolled her eyes, opened the door, and managed to grab my arm and pull me inside before I knew what was happening. She flipped on the light and closed the door before I could escape. "Afraid of a girl's room? It's not like you've never seen one before."

That was true. I'd been in my and a dozen other men's fair share of girl's rooms. That wasn't what had me all but breaking out in a cold sweat. I was in Josie Gibson's bedroom. That wasn't just another girl's bed-room. "Yeah, um, why don't I just take the guest room tonight?" I hitched my thumb over my shoulder as Josie peeled off the layers of winter wear.

"Sure. Be my guest. But just so you've been warned, expect my dad to crawl in beside you in a couple of hours because that's normally when my mom kicks him out for snoring up a storm." Josie kicked off her boots and waved me toward the door. "Happy spooning."

I pinched the bridge of my nose. "Okay. The barn it is."

"Uh-huh. I thought I already made that clear. I didn't go save you from your truck to let you sleep in the barn."

I pinched my nose harder. "Then where do you want me to sleep?" I knew it was a dumb question, but I needed Josie to spell it out for me.

"Wherever you want, so long as it's on this side of that door."

I silently groaned and let out a string of curses. As miserable as my truck had been, it beat sleeping in Josie's room by a mile. There was hell, and then there was Josie's room. It was the last place in the world I wanted to be.

As rooms go, it wasn't an offensive one. Her room had a lot of white, lots of windows that let in plenty of light, and it wasn't overly girly. She still had that picture of Jesse, her, and me taken at the Fourth of July picnic the summer we were ten. Jesse had that stupid smile on his face, like usual. I had a scowly frown on mine, like usual. And Josie . . . well, she wasn't looking at the camera—she was looking at me. It was the only photo, the only instance, where she'd noticed me when Jesse was close by. I loved that picture.

So the room itself wasn't a problem. It was what had happened inside the room. Right there. On that bed. If I wasn't so damn conflicted, I would have needed a cold shower to calm the memories flashing through my mind.

"If you want, you can take a shower. Dad and Mom will think it's me, so you don't have to worry about that. A hot shower might feel good." A hint of a smile crawled into position as she opened a dresser drawer. "Popsicle man."

"I'm so exhausted I'd probably fall asleep in the shower, so thank you, but I'm just going to pass out if you don't mind."

"I don't mind." After pulling a couple things from her drawer, she looked at me and twirled her finger. "Turn around, please." My forehead lined. She grabbed the hem of her sweater. "I'm exhausted and would like to pass out, too. Being out half the night searching for a certain someone has a way of sapping a girl's energy. But I don't sleep in my clothes like some people. Me, I prefer pajamas."

Oh, perfect. She was about to change with me a whole ten feet away. The situation just kept getting better and better. Yes, that was a whole heap of sarcasm right there. I swallowed and spun around. I cleared my throat and tried to clear my mind of what was happening behind me. "Some of us lost all their pajamas in a fire."

"Oh . . . um . . . do you want to borrow something?" After the fury her voice had held earlier, hearing it soft and quiet was almost as alarming.

"No, thanks. I don't think we're the same size."

When a pillow hit the back of my head, I turned around. Changing time must be over if her hands were free to throw a pillow at me. When I saw Josie, my mouth almost fell open. "I thought you said you were changing into pajamas."

She glanced down and lifted her arms. "These are

89

pajamas."

"Really? Because from a male's point of view, that's lingerie. Pajamas are, you know, the flannel, frumpy things that cover lots of skin that old ladies wear." Shit, I was trying so hard not to check her out, but it was impossible. A man could have held a knife to my throat and told me to stop looking at Josie or die, and I would have been a dead man two seconds later.

Josie gave me an amused look as she finished tossing the mountain of pillows off of her bed. "I'll keep that in mind. When I'm an old woman. But right now, I like this kind of pajamas."

Yeah, I liked them too.

Flipping her hair forward, she worked it into a ponytail before flicking off the light switch. "I thought you said you were exhausted. Are you planning on standing there all night?"

If I got to watch her in my new favorite women's "pajamas," then hell yes, I would stand there all night. The lights might have been off, but those windows and that moonlight didn't exactly make it dark.

What in *the hell* was I thinking? I felt like I'd grown a second consciousness, and the two had declared war on each other. One part of me knew staying away from Josie was priority number one. The other part of me, the one I wished I could locate so I could radiate it the hell out, wanted to be as close to Josie as she'd let me get. Those two agendas didn't align. In fact, they couldn't have been any more at odds. If one didn't roll over and die soon, the battle would split me right down the middle.

Threatening both of my subconsiousnesses with a lobotomy if they didn't shut up, I made my way toward the bed Josie was already crawling into. It was a relief when she threw the covers on. I grabbed a pillow and threw it on the ground. I was just grabbing the blanket draped on the chair when I heard the bed springs groan.

"What are you doing?" She sat up in bed, watching me like I'd tripped a wire.

"Going to bed," I answered with a shrug.

"And the reason you're throwing pillows and blankets on the floor is. . .?" Josie and I were not on the same wavelength apparently.

"Because you've got the bed, which means I've got the floor." It was her room, and even if she'd offered me the bed, I wouldn't let her sleep on the floor. Truthfully, Josie's hardwood floor looked pretty damn close to heaven. It was warm, I had a big fluffy pillow to rest my head on, and the blanket was the softest thing I'd ever felt.

"Since when did you turn into Mr. Chivalrous?" The wire-tripping expression deepened before she patted the space on the bed beside her. "There's plenty of room. No need to wake up with a stiff neck and back."

I stared at the empty space. Fuck, if I slept beside her all night, I'd wake up with something else stiff. "Really, the floor's good." I slid off my hat and set it on her nightstand.

"Oh, please. We've already done the worst in this bed, so you don't have to worry about that. Just get in and get some sleep already."

I knew I shouldn't, but since the invitation had been extended, I couldn't say no. Tossing the pillow back onto the bed, I peeled off a few layers of clothing and crawled in beside her. Josie's back was to me, but her shoulders were so stiff I knew she wasn't asleep. Despite her no-big-deal attitude, could Josie be just as conscious of me beside her as I was of her beside me? The journey to that answer was a road I couldn't take. I already knew the ending, and I wouldn't do that to her. I wouldn't hurt Josie any more than I already had. She deserved better, and she deserved a million times better than I could ever give her.

"See? Was that so bad?" she asked, her back still to me.

I slid my hands behind my head and grinned at the ceiling. I hadn't been paying attention the last time I was in it, but Josie's bed was the most comfortable thing I'd ever been on. "No, Joze, that wasn't so bad."

"Told ya."

My grin stretched wider. "Oh, and you don't have to worry about me crawling into your nice clean bed in the same clothes I worked in all day."

"Why's that?"

I positioned the blanket just below my navel. "Because I sleep naked."

"What?!" she hissed, twisting around. As soon as she saw my bare chest, her eyes widened. At least I could still get a rise out of her. That part of our relationship hadn't changed. She shrieked and covered her eyes. By then, I was laughing. I would have been howling if her parents weren't a mere floor below us. "Garth, please, for the love of god and Montana, please put something on. Anything on."

Josie in her itty-bitty tank top with her hair in a floppy ponytail and her hands clamped over her eyes . . . It was the funniest, sexiest sight I'd seen. "Okay, fine. If you're going to go all prude on me." Sitting up just enough, I pretended to get up to grab some clothes, but I was watching her without blinking.

A couple moments later, her fingers splayed just enough for me to see her eyes, which meant . . .

I flashed my face in front of hers and winked. "Made you look."

Josie's hands dropped from her eyes and went straight to my chest. She shoved me hard enough I almost tipped off the bed. "Nice jeans, asshole."

I laughed again when she threw herself back down, her back to me again. "Nice sneaking a peek there, Secret Agent Gibson. Hoping to catch a glimpse of something?"

Josie gave an irritated sigh. "Shut up, Black."

"Why would I do that when it's so much more fun to tease you?"

"Because you like-slash-love your dick and probably want to keep it."

"Hold up. Are you threatening the very piece of anaomy you were just hoping to sneak a peek at?" I pulled off my socks, left my jeans in place, and laid back down. Josie had been checking me out. I was back to grinning at the ceiling.

"My threat's about to turn into a reality if you don't zip it and go to sleep like I thought you were dying to do five minutes ago."

"Come on, it's no big deal. It's perfectly natural to want to inspect a fine specimen like myself. I'd be happy to give you the whole show—the full monty—free of charge. But only looking, no touching. Or wait, you prefer peeking, right?" Our endless banter felt good. It took me back to a happier time before things had gotten so complicated between us.

"Sleep now or forever hold your peace, Black." I was

working up my reply when she added, "I mean it." From her tone, I knew she was done. She'd hit her bullshit limit.

I'd learned enough to know when to back off. After a few minutes of silence, I was close to falling asleep when I felt the mattress quaking. It was so infinitesimal, I was surprised I'd even noticed. When I glanced at Josie's back, I understood where it was coming from. She was shivering. I didn't think next. I responded.

"You're shivering." I scooted up behind her and draped my arm around her before pulling her close. I couldn't tell if she was cold. The only thing I felt was her body pressed into mine.

She didn't pull away. In fact, she seemed to burrow deeper into my arms. "Yeah, well, I had to go and save this asshole from freezing to death."

I tilted my face into her hair and smiled. "Plus, you're wearing lingerie to bed."

"Plus that." I heard the smile in her voice.

We didn't say anything else for a while. We just lay together until our breathing synced and her shivering stopped. I'd been on that bed with Josie before in the most intimate way a man and woman could be together, but I hadn't felt connected to her the way I did with my arms around her, both of us mostly clothed. I wasn't familiar with that kind of intimacy, but it felt strangely more intimate than sex. I was close to falling asleep, and I was sure she already must have been, when I whispered, "Better now?"

I wasn't expecting a response, but the last thing I heard before letting myself go was a quiet, "Better now."

chapter SIX

I WASN'T A dreamer. Never had been, never would be. That translated into my sleep state as well. I didn't dream at night. Or at least not the kind I remembered when I woke up.

Waking up in Josie's bed, I remembered so many different dreams, it didn't seem possible that much could have run through my brain in only one night. I wanted to discount the new dream phenomenon with sleeping in a warm house, in a soft bed, but I couldn't even bullshit myself into believing that. I knew what had caused the dreams. Or *who*.

A certain someone who wasn't curled up beside me like she'd been all night. Peeling my eyes open, I scanned Josie's empty room. If it wasn't a work day, I wouldn't have minded throwing the covers over my head and passing out for a few more hours. I hadn't slept that great in my whole life. I hadn't woken up feeling so good *ever*. That might have had something to do with not passing out with a heavy dose of whiskey in me, but it also had a whole lot to do with sleeping beside Josie. Falling asleep beside her was so . . . peaceful. So easy. Those concepts— peaceful and easy—were terms I wasn't familiar with. They were ideas I'd never really thought I wanted to become familiar with until last night. Until I felt them so strongly I wondered if my whole life, I'd been doing it wrong.

Unfortunately, a good night's sleep hadn't eased my confusion. If anything, it had only increased. Confusion was the new normal for me, but one thing I had been able to pinpoint—Josie was somehow connected to it all. The confusion, the dual consciousnesses warring with one another, the steady stream of questions, the dry river of answers . . . it all connected to her somehow.

My life had become one giant cluster-fuck all because of a woman. I suppose, given my history, that wasn't so hard to believe. What was hard to believe was which woman had brought it on. The girl I'd grown up with. My childhood friend, my adolescent secret obsession, my biggest mistake. That was a whole lot of screwed up I just wasn't up to working out without a cup of coffee in me.

Rolling over, I sat up. My gaze immediately landed on Josie's vanity mirror across the room. Not because I was so relentlessly vain I couldn't go thirty seconds after waking up without checking myself out—I might have been a cocky son of a bitch, but vain was a stretch—but because it was impossible to miss the red lipstick note taking up the whole mirror.

Stay put until I give you the all clear. I'd hate to spend the summer picking shotgun shell out of your ass.

I couldn't decide what I liked more: the oozing smart-ass in Josie's note or that she'd written it in lipstick on a mirror. Because, you know, a paper and pen were so inconvenient.

My jeans were still in place—something that was as

fortunate as it was unfortunate—so after grabbing my shirt from the floor, I slid into it and stood up. How long would I have to wait before Josie deemed it safe for me to come out? Hopefully soon because my stomach was rumbling something fierce and Willow Springs was, judging from how high the sun was, expecting me at work at least three hours ago. Neil was the kind of employer who was quick to forgive, but I wasn't. He depended on me, and I didn't want to repay that by disappointing him.

"All clear!"

If Josie was yelling at that volume, her parents had to be a state away. I didn't need to be invited twice. Hurrying out of the room, I jogged down the stairs and into the kitchen. Josie finished pouring a couple cups of coffee before sitting at the table.

She motioned at the chair beside her but couldn't seem to look at me. "I made some breakfast. If you're hungry." My stomach answered for me. "Dig in. I wasn't sure exactly what you'd want, so I made a little bit of everything." Josie bit her lip and waved at the spread on the table. I'd been so preoccupied with staring at her that I hadn't noticed what was for breakfast.

"Whoa, Joze. This isn't breakfast, this is a bloody feast." I'd seen that much food at a table before—when I was in the Walkers' kitchen and they were feeding twenty hungry cowboys.

"I know, I know. I overdid it. My mom's a firm believer in having too much food rather than not enough food, so I suppose I picked up that from her."

I came around the table and took a seat. When I was that close to her, it was hard for me to look her straight on, too. "Too much food is having leftovers for the next day.

This . . . well this is having leftovers until next year."
Really, there was so much meat on the table, it was a
miracle it hadn't buckled from the weight. That was just
the start. I saw so many different types of eggs, I couldn't
even identify them all. The pile of pancakes in the center
of the table was a true engineering feat. Fruit, fried potatoes, pitchers of juice . . . It was a damn breakfast buffet fit
for the cavalry. "Did your parents already eat?"

"They left earlier this morning to run some errands in
town. I made this for you." She scanned the table again,
biting her lip even harder.

"For me?"

"Well, for us."

I could recall every last kind gesture a person had
paid me in my life—they were that few—and Josie putting
together a breakfast like that for me, for *us*, just secured a
top five spot. I was momentarily struck speechless. "What
are we doing just gawking at it then? Let's dig in."

I smiled at her, and she returned it. Getting the shy act
from Josie was something I expected about as frequently
as her inviting me to the nail salon. Basically, never. I
wasn't sure how to take it.

I loaded up on fried potatoes and sausage while Josie
went for the pancakes and fruit. After shoveling most of
my first serving down, along with two full cups of coffee, I
gave my stomach a break to process. The food was good,
just as solid as the stuff that came out of the Walkers'
kitchen. Josie knew how to cook. When had that happened?

"So . . . how did you sleep?" I gave her the vocal
equivalent of a nudge.

"Not bad," she answered, lifting a shoulder. At least

she'd thrown on a bathrobe. After last night and her breakfast, I wasn't sure what I would do next. Had Josie still been wearing nothing more than glorified lingerie, the outlook for keeping my hands to myself wasn't good. Lifting her gaze to mine, she lifted an eyebrow. "How did you sleep?"

I didn't even try to dim my grin. "Not bad."

Josie shook her head and laughed softly. At least we were past the shy act. I wasn't sure how to act around shy Josie, but the part-amused, part-irritated one I'd had a decade and a half of experience with.

"So? Parents? Dad? Shotgun? How long before I can expect it to be aimed my way?" Last night I'd been too beat to think about what came next, but after a good night's sleep and breakfast, I was able to form a string of clear thoughts.

"Provided you don't go and steal his daughter's 'virtue' which, hell, you and I know that's two years too late"—Josie shot me a smirk before popping a grape in her mouth—"you should be good. I caught them this morning before they left, explained your situation, and they agreed to let you stay here for a while. In the guest room."

I stopped refilling my coffee cup mid-way through. "Wait. What? Last night was a one-time deal. It was wonderful and amazing and just what I needed, but it's not happening again."

Josie tossed another grape in her mouth. "No need for a recap. I know I totally rocked your world, baby." My eyebrows drew together before she shoved my arm. "Lighten up. Can't take a joke this early in the morning?"

Apparently not when Josie was throwing out sexual innuendos and I was fixated on her mouth. And the grapes she kept popping in there. And the way she sucked one for a moment before biting into it. Holy shit. Proverbial cold shower or face slap or something.

"I can take a joke anytime you want to send one my way, Joze. Bring it." I had to force myself to stop staring at her mouth because apparently I was incapable of talking and staring at the same time. "But by last night being a one-time deal, I didn't mean that in the obvious fantasy you've created of what happened between us last night. Come on, if we're making up fantasies, it was *me* that rocked *your* world." Josie made a Ha! sound. "But hating to have to bring our filthy fantasies to an end and face reality—sleeping in your bed and squatting at your place was a one-night deal. I wasn't planning on moving in with you and your parents indefinitely. I'm not imposing on you all like that. No way."

Josie waited a few seconds. Her reply came in the form of an unimpressed face and voice. "Are you done yet?"

"Just getting warmed up if need be."

"Good for you." She nodded down the hall. "You've got the guest room. If you need anything, let me know."

I exhaled. "Did you hear anything I just said?"

"Yep. Loud and clear. I'm just choosing to ignore it."

Two whole minutes of having the Josie I knew back, and I almost missed the shy version. "Josie—"

"Garth. Stop. Yes, I know you'd rather eat your own boot than accept something that even resembles generosity. I know you'd rather freeze your ass off than sleep in a warm house and bed because of your warped views of making sure you're never in the red in someone's ledger, but this isn't open to negotiation. This is me telling you that you're staying here. Partly because this cold snap is here to stay for the rest of the week, and if you think I'm letting you go back to your truck, you're insane." She looked like she had more to say, but after her mouth clamped shut, it didn't open again.

"And what's the other part?"

"What do you mean?" She was back to looking everywhere else but at me.

"You said 'partly,' which by the laws of parts and wholes, means there's another 'partly' you failed to mention." I tried not to smile at her apparent discomfort. "So what's the other part?"

Josie stalled by sipping her juice. Leaning back, I crossed my arms and waited. After a few seconds, she slammed her juice down and groaned. "There is no other part. None. Nada. No. Other. Part. Got it?" Tilting my head closer to her, I tapped my ear. Her reply was another groan and a shove. "You know, I made all of this food in hopes it would keep your mouth and mind occupied so we could sit in peace for a whole five minutes."

"You mean it wasn't to get my energy stores high so I could give you another world-rocking night later on?" I was just reaching for the fried eggs when I got my second shove of the morning. A few seconds of silence followed, just long enough for me to be reminded of something. "Hey, Joze, would you mind if I borrowed your phone? I need to call Willow Springs and check in with Neil."

"I already called him and explained the situation." Maybe she could explain it to me, because I was still trying to figure out my "situation". "He said to just take the rest of the day off because he's cancelled all of the non-essential work until this cold front lifts."

"Oh . . . okay." I was at a temporary loss. I wasn't used to someone else taking care of my business. It was a novel concept for me, like so much lately. "Did he say anything else?"

"I think he was a little upset you pretty much lied to them about where you were staying. I mean, you know Willow Springs has a bunkhouse for a reason, right?"

"Yeah, I do. It's so the hands who don't have homes close by have somewhere to hang their hats." Plus, my pride might have factored into it as well. I wanted to be able to make it on my own—not take up residence in my employer's bunkhouse.

"Garth, your home burnt to the ground . . ."

"I've got a home, all right?" I hadn't meant to sound so sharp. So hard.

"Where is that exactly?" Josie was used to my regular bouts of acting like an asshole. They didn't faze her anymore.

"Joze," I warned, dropping my fork on the plate. I was done eating if the conversation continued.

"Fine, fine. Home is where the heart is, right?"

"Right."

"Although I was under the impression you didn't have a heart," she mumbled before tossing a grape at me.

"You're just full of witty comebacks in the morning. I've been missing out." Taking another chug of coffee, I studied Josie from the corner of my eyes. "What about you? Since you're still here with daddy and mommy dearest, I'm guessing this is where your heart still is."

Josie shrugged. "I love ranching. All aspects of it. I won't be happy unless I'm living and working on one, and since dad and mom can't do it all by themselves and my brother wants nothing to do with it, this is still where my heart and home are." She shrugged again. "At least until something changes."

I didn't need to ask what she meant—I knew. She meant until some rich rancher's son tossed a ring on her finger. I drained my glass of water to cool me down from the thought of Josie falling in love with and marrying some other guy.

Josie tossed the last grape on her plate into her mouth—*thank* god—and her expression shifted into something not so light. I knew that face. I needed to get up and bail or grit my teeth and strap in, because Josie didn't ask roundabout questions or blunt the truth. That was one of the many things I appreciated about her . . . except when it was directed at me.

"Are you ready to tell me why you've been living out of your truck for months when you didn't have to?" She wasn't easing in with a warm-up question or anything. Straight to game point.

"Partly"—I lifted my finger—"take notes on how a person utilizes the word *partly*." And there it was, my first eye roll of the day. "Partly because I like living on my own. Partly because I've been sleeping in my truck since I bought it—"

"What you and some nameless Jezebel do on the mattress in the bed of that thing is not considered sleeping." Cue the peanut gallery. Josie could hang with the best of them.

I continued. "Partly because I don't like living by someone else's set of rules. Partly because I don't like imposing on people. Partly because I kind of like pissing you off."

Instead of a grape, a wedge of apple slapped against my cheek. "Are you done yet?"

"Joze, I've got so many *partlys* you'll be old and gray if you sit here listening to them all."

"Then why don't you put your parts away before you hurt yourself."

"Myself likes playing with my parts." I smiled at her over my cup of coffee.

"That would explain why you spent most of your teenage years cross-eyed. My mom was right, after all. You really do go cross eyed if you masturbate too much."

"Your mom's a wise woman." I drained the rest of my coffee and set the cup down. If I ate any more, I would have to undo the top button of my jeans. But if I was the kind of person who knew their limits, I wouldn't have drained as many bottles of whiskey as I had and I wouldn't have an army of women plotting my demise.

"So, because I know you, I understand why you didn't want to impose on anyone, you've been living out of your truck for a while, blah, blah, blah . . . But why didn't you just go get your own place or something? Rent an apartment or rent a room from one of the old widows out here? I'm sure you've been making decent money at Willow Springs."

I froze for a fraction of a second. "Neil pays me well, but it's not like I've got mountains of money in the bank."

"What about a mini mountain?" I shook my head. "A molehill?"

I gave another shake. "I believe, at last count, I had a whopping thirteen cents in my account."

Josie's forehead lined. "Where the hell has all the money you've been making gone?" She wasn't asking in a rude way; she was just flabbergasted.

I got it, though. I was bringing home solid cash . . . it just didn't stay put long. I met her gaze and raised a brow in answer.

"Shit, really, Black? You've spent that much money on whiskey and women?" I guess she took my lack of response as a confirmation. "Wow. I don't know whether to applaud you for living it up or have you arrested for grossly irresponsible behavior."

"Welcome to my predicament."

Josie stared at the table. "Wow. Just wow."

"Glad I could wow you this early in the day."

"There's a negative and positive form of wow, you know?"

"Yes. Unfortunately I've become very familiar with one form, but thanks for the reminder." Generally, I didn't care what people thought of me or how I chose to live. For some reason, Josie's face lined with shock and disappointment hit me like a painful blow to the gut. A change of topic was in order. "How did dear daddy and mommy take it when you told them about me and my predicament?"

Josie picked at her scrambled eggs. "Fine. I basically told them you needed a place to stay, we had a place for you, and that was that."

"They just agreed to it? No questions asked? No argument?"

"Pretty much. Yep." Whenever Josie kept her answers short and sweet, she was sugarcoating something. Given she was trying to sell me that her parents just went along with the villain known as Garth Black moving into their house without so much as lifting a finger, she wasn't just sugarcoating. She was sugarblasting.

"And they thought what about me sleeping here last night? In your room?"

Josie took a sip of her juice and threw me a sideways look. "What are you talking about? Your first night here is tonight. In the guest room."

"My, oh, my. Did Miss Josie Gibson tell her parents a bold-faced lie? You did go to Sunday school growing up, right? The whole thou shalt not lie to thy parents . . . that's something they taught, right?" I scooted my chair next to hers and leaned in close until she couldn't not look me in the eye. I grinned.

She scowled. "Since I lied to save your life since my dad has a shoot-first-ask-questions-second policy about guys being in my bed, I figured someone higher up would give me a pass." She grabbed the brim of my hat and shook it before popping out of her chair to take her plate to the sink.

"If anyone deserves a pass, it would be you." I stuffed the last piece of toast in my mouth and carried my plate to the sink. She grabbed a washrag as the sink filled with sudsy water. I turned off the water and blocked her from the sink. "Hey, you cooked. I have clean-up duty. But that starts with getting myself cleaned up, then the kitchen." I tried not to zero in on the triangle of skin just above her chest that popped out of her bathrobe when she threw her hands on her hips. Tried and failed. "Do you mind if I use your shower? Then I'll clean up in here, and then I've got to head over to Willow Springs. Just to check in and make sure Neil really doesn't need me today."

"Be my guest. Just save me some hot water."

"You could just join me, you know. That way you'd be sure to have hot water, and we'd conserve the world's most precious resource."

"You and I both know your idea of the world's most precious resource might be a liquid, but it isn't water."

"Ooo, burn. Nice one." I held my hand up for a high five, but all she did was flick it.

"Away to the shower with you." She sniffed the air in my direction. "You reek."

"Whatever. That's all man you're smelling. Might want to take note of that the next time Colt Mason shows up at your door smelling like eau de pussy." That earned me a shove. And another when I didn't head for the stairs. "Enough with the shoves already, pushy. No more." She gave me a *what are you going to do about it* look. "Or else."

She waved her hands in exaggerated terror at my threat. As far as threats went, "or else" was definitely one of my weaker ones. I was halfway up the stairs when I heard Josie follow me. "What was your plan, Garth? You weren't planning on living out of your truck the rest of your life were you?" She was at the bottom of the stairs, staring up at me with curious eyes.

"I don't know. You know me. I live life day to day, hour to hour. I'm not the guy with long-term goals or a five-year plan. I'm the kind of guy who lives for the moment." I shrugged. "I'm sure if that truck had gotten cold enough, I would have figured something out. I just hadn't gotten uncomfortable enough to make a change."

Her eyes widened. "Garth, it was two below last night, and I found you with icicles practically growing out of your nose. That doesn't make you uncomfortable enough to make a change?"

"Are you trying to say I've got the survival instincts

of a wooly mammoth?" She was trying to say something; that was obvious.

"No, I'm trying to say I don't think you know what's good for you. I'm trying to say you wouldn't know what was good for you if it fell out of the sky and squirmed around on your face. *That's* what I'm trying to say."

I grabbed the handrail. "Okay, this is all a little too much . . . psychoanalysis for one morning. I'm hitting the shower."

"Have a nice shower. I hope it's full of introspection." She waved before heading into the kitchen.

I leaned over the handrail. "The most introspection that will be happening is me deciding whether to soap my junk clockwise or counterclockwise." When Josie didn't have an immediate comeback, I smiled and headed up the rest of the stairs.

"Haven't you heard? Your junk has a reputation for not being discerning."

I hated when she got in the last word.

chapter SEVEN

I STARED AT myself in the mirror until the steam from the shower fogged it up. Again, not a vanity thing. It was a was-Josie-right? thing. Did I not have a clue what was good for me? I'd always believed I was one of the people who'd drawn the short straw in life. I'd accepted that fortune favored the few, and I wasn't in that tight circle. I'd accepted life was a chore some days, a damn obstacle course other days, and out to get me most days. Could twenty-one years of waving my middle finger at social norms have given me a skewed sense of right and wrong? Of what was good and what was bad for me?

Instead of driving my fist into the mirror like I wanted to, I gripped the edges of the sink until my knuckles went white. Up until recently, I'd never questioned anything and everything. I had all the answers. Lately, I had exchanged all the answers for all the questions. I was drowning in an ocean of questions, and even though I knew the answers would eliminate the questions, I was afraid of what the answers would be. I was afraid the answers would do the opposite of set me at peace. So my options were to stay lost in a sea of questions or drown under the weight of the answers.

Yeah, I was fucked. I barely stopped my fist before it pounded through the mirror. Not even a second later, a different pounding sounded. It came from the bathroom door. "Yeah?"

"Unless you want to come out smelling like honeysuckle body wash—which you're totally free to use, by the way—I brought you a bar of soap."

With handful of words from Josie, my mood shifted to a few levels above depressed. "Thanks, Joze. You know how I hate honeysuckle."

"I'm not doing this for you, Black. I'm doing this for your date tonight. I wouldn't want her to crawl into bed with a man whose junk smelt like honeysuckle when she thought she was in for a wild night with Garth Black. That's a way to crush a girl's fantasies."

"You're so selfless." I chuckled before wiping the steam from the mirror with my forearm. "Hey, Joze? You wouldn't happen to have a blade I could use to shave my face, would you? I'm about to turn into Grizzly Adams." I didn't mind a little bit of scruff and, let's face it, neither did the ladies, but there was scruff and there was the monster I was growing on my face.

"Um, yeah, I think so." The doorknob twisted. "Are you decent?" That was a question I didn't need to answer. "Never mind. Most obvious question ever. How about . . . are you clothed?"

I glanced down. "Mostly."

"Given you said you were naked last night, but the opposite turned out to be true, I'm going to go with the same trend this morning and assume that you saying you're mostly clothed means you're bare-ass naked."

The girl's reasoning was solid, but trying to apply reason to me was a huge error. "There are no bare asses in view. I promise. Unfortunately."

"You swear to god and hope to die?"

I smiled. That had been our favorite way to promise things as kids. "I'll even stick a needle in my eye."

"I'm trusting you, Black." The door opened slowly before she slipped inside. Her eyes were sealed closed. "As much as trusting Garth Black is counterintuitive."

I settled my backside on the ledge of the sink. "See? No bare asses in view since it's sitting on your bathroom sink. Only bare fronts in view." Josie's face ironed out in shock before her eyes flashed open. Just as quickly, they narrowed on me. "Made you look." I winked.

"You and those jeans." She tossed the bar of soap at me. "You seem more like the guy who'd be waltzing around in his underwear every chance he got."

I shrugged. "I probably would be, but that would require wearing underwear in the first place. Which I don't. Which you might remember if . . ." *Insert foot here.*

Thankfully, Josie didn't look as uncomfortable as I felt. "Even if I hadn't been so drunk I couldn't remember my name, I'd still repress that night into the darkest recesses of my mind."

"You mean the *Black* recesses of your mind?" The words and smile I'd given her totally deserved a slap across the face, but instead she gave me a look that made me feel half a foot tall. Pulling open a drawer, she grabbed a razor and flashed it in front of my face. "Do I look like the kind of guy who uses a razor to shave my face? A *pink* one at that?"

"No, you look like a guy who doesn't have a lot of options, and unless he wants to go into the rug-growing business, he'll take what's offered. With a smile and a thank you," Josie finished with a sigh. "Besides, if you don't use a razor like this, what do you use? An electric one? I think my mom still has the one she uses—"

I lifted my hand. I did not want Mrs. Gibson's electric shaver—wherever she used that sucker—up against my face. "I use a straight-edge. I've got one in my truck, so I'll just grab it and shave tomorrow."

"A straight-edge? Isn't that one of those things that can slice through a man's neck with just a hint too much pressure?" I shrugged. "Seems a little barbaric given there are modern options and advancements." She waved the pink razor at me again.

I grabbed it and tossed it in the garbage can. "A barbaric tool for a barbaric man." Josie shoved my chest, but that time, I caught her wrists and pinned them behind her back, grinning victoriously at her. She rolled her eyes at me. "I warned you with my intimidating 'or else' threat. What are you going to do now, tough girl?"

She didn't waste any time trying to physically over power me. She didn't go for the cheap shot and knee me in the nuts either. She just stood there for a few moments, focusing on a spot just past my shoulder, as the wheels turned in her head. She was working something out so hard I was waiting for smoke to billow from her ears. A few seconds later, I saw the light bulb go off. Her eyes widened for a split second before a smile so small it could barely be detected fell into place.

And then, her eyes shifted up. They locked onto mine, and something in hers softened something in mine, and I wasn't sure what I wanted to do more: get down on my hands and knees to worship her or throw her up against a wall and screw until we passed out. My breathing picked up, my heartbeat even more so, and she was still a half a foot away from me. When she stepped forward so that her body, and all its curves and bends and soft spots and hard spots, formed into mine, my breath and my heart stopped altogether. My mind was made up. I was one stalled heart-beat away from doing what I needed to do most with her when a door slamming jolted us out of whatever fog we'd been in.

"Josie! We're home, sweet pea."

"Shoot," Josie hissed, breaking free of my hold and rushing toward the door.

I took another moment to break free of whatever spell she'd put me under, then uttered my own estimation of the current situation. It wasn't Josie's PG version either. "I thought you said they were running errands in town."

"They are. They *were*." Josie fumbled with the door-knob like she was hoping a lock would magically appear. A pair of footsteps marched up the stairs. The next thing Josie hissed wasn't a *shoot*.

"What do you want me to do? There isn't a window for me to jump out of, and I'm not a damn gopher who can burrow my way out of here," I said.

"Stop being such a smart-ass."

"Start giving me a little more direction and a little less attitude."

"Josie? Are you in the bathroom?" Mrs. Gibson asked, almost outside the door.

"Uh, yeah, Mom. I am. Just a minute!" Josie powered up to me, and lowered her voice. "Sorry I don't have a lot of experience sneaking guys in and out of rooms. I thought you were the expert on this."

"Sneaking guys out of rooms?" I gave her a look.

"Unbelievable. You still manage to be a comedian

when your life's thirty seconds away from being over."

I never knew a woman whispering could be more intimidating than one screaming, but I made sure to take note. "Fine. Since my options in the escape route department are limited, I'll hop in the shower and hide out there."

"Josie, I have to show you this dress I picked up for you. You're going to love it." The door was just opening when I dodged behind the shower curtain. Who walked in on someone in the bathroom without being invited? *Oh, yeah. This is Mrs. Gibson we were talking about.* She didn't do personal space well—or keeping her thoughts to herself.

"Hold up, Mom!" Josie called, but it was too late. Mrs. Gibson was already in the bathroom. How did I know? Heaps of experience in lying in wait, or hiding from, all sorts of people. Boyfriends, husbands, and lovers mostly, but name a kind of person and a certain place, and chances are I'd hidden from it or in it. I could detect when the air moved inside a room from a door opening or closing. I was just that good. Or, thanks to the things I was doing leading up to finding myself in that kind of a situation, I was just that *bad*.

"Would you look at this? Isn't it to die for?" Mrs. Gibson said, her excitement so extreme I could feel it.

"Yeah, Mom, it's . . . great." Josie's voice bounced around the room, which meant she kept looking over her shoulder. If she didn't cut that out, mama bear would figure out what was going on, and then papa bear would get his gun, and then I would be a Garth-skin rug on display in front of their fireplace.

"I thought you could wear it tonight for dinner. It's

just your color. Brings out the gold in your hair and eyes."

"Sure, that sounds . . . great," Josie said. I sighed quietly. The girl really didn't have any experience hiding a guy from her parents. She was a damn rookie. "But are you throwing some party for dinner tonight I don't know about? Why do you want me dressing up in silk chiffon?"

"Didn't I tell you? Oh, dear me, it must have slipped my mind . . . Your father and I invited Colt Mason over for dinner. He's such a nice boy, Josie, and we haven't seen him around lately. He comes from such a good family, and all of that money . . ." Mrs. Gibson sounded close to fainting from the thought of it.

I was close to boiling over. I did not want Colt Mason over there, sitting around Josie's dining room table, checking her out in whatever pretty dress her mom had picked up for her. The mere thought of him running his eyes all over her made me want to squish his head with my boot until it went splat.

I had a lot of anger. I was working on it.

"That's great, Mom, but tonight is Garth's first night here. I thought we could do a dinner with just the four of us. You know, ease him in before having a bunch of company over."

"It's just Colt. One extra person hardly qualifies as a bunch of company. If you ask me, Garth Black could learn a lesson or two from Colt. Let's hope he takes notes tonight."

Colt Mason was a grade A poser douche. The day I took notes from him was the same one I tied a noose around my neck and pulled the lever myself.

"I don't know. I'm not sure that's the best idea." Josie sounded about as uncomfortable as I was pissed off. "Colt and Garth aren't exactly best friends."

"They don't have to be friends, but they do have to tolerate each other while under my roof. And we both know who would be the first to break that rule."

Yeah, that made three of us who knew that. No matter if I was under the Gibsons' roof or inside a seedy bar or he was heading into that damn tanning salon where he kept a standing weekly appointment—I didn't tolerate Colt Mason.

"Sweetie, were you about to take a shower? Of course you were. I'm sorry. You'd better start warming that water up now if you want a warm shower before lunch. With these frigid temperatures, the water's taking its sweet time heating up. I had to wait a good ten minutes before the shower downstairs was ready, and the water up here takes much longer to warm up."

I glared up at the shower head.

"That's okay. I'm sure it won't take that long." Josie's voice had a nervous wobble.

Mrs. Gibson let out a long sigh. "You are a stubborn one, Josie Belle. Fine. If you don't want to turn it on, I'll do it." A pair of heels only got a couple of clacks toward the shower.

"No worries. I got it." Josie's nervous wobble was gone, but something close to frantic had taken its place. "You're right. I should warm it up first."

Josie's shower was small—old farmhouse small. I was already cramped up as small as I'd go on the floor of the tub. There was no way I could cramp up smaller to position my body away from the shower head, so it looked like I'd be getting that shower after all—minus the warm water. Josie peeked her head inside the shower curtain, an apologetic look on her face. Mouthing *I'm so, so sorry,* she cranked on the water and ducked back out again. The pipes inside the old farmhouse didn't work as quickly as modern pipes. That gave me a few seconds to brace myself.

When the water finally burst out of the shower head, I realized how wrong Mrs. Gibson had been. The water wasn't cold. Not even close.

No, it was fucking glacial.

I had to clamp my mouth closed to ensure I wouldn't let out some sort of hoot, holler, or curse. Once I was certain of that, all there was left to do was wrap my arms around my chest and curl up as tight as I could and wait it out. So much for saving me from the freezing cold. Josie had simply removed the threat of one form and replaced it with one that was twice as severe.

"Do you know what time Garth will be arriving?" The oozing excitement in Mrs. Gibson's voice as she talked about Mason? There wasn't a scrap of it left when she mentioned me.

"Um . . . later?"

Killer answer, Joze. Killer.

Mrs. Gibson let out a familiar sigh. I knew where Josie had learned hers. "I know you and Garth go way back, but you know how your father and I feel about that boy."

"Yeah, Mom," Josie said. The strength in her voice that I was used to was back in place. "And you know how I feel about you two feeling that way about him. All your opinions about him are due to rumors and hearsay."

I was drenched in freezing cold water that was slowly numbing every square inch of my skin, but in that moment, I felt nothing but warmth. Josie standing up for me brought a strange mix of emotions. All of them good.

"They aren't rumors when I'm friends with the mothers whose daughters have had their hearts crushed and reputations ruined by that boy. It's not hearsay when I've seen him drinking straight out of the bottle at ten o'clock in the morning." Mrs. Gibson was working herself up. I could almost imagine her meticulously styled hair standing on end. "Don't let your friendship with him blind you to the person he is. That's not the kind of man your father or me want you hanging around. We're not letting him move in because he's ever proven himself to us. We're letting him move in because *you've* proven yourself to us. You've proven capable of making good choices for yourself, and as long as you keep up that pattern, Dad and me will continue to let you do your thing. Even if that includes inviting Garth Black to be a houseguest." There was some rustling—what I imagined was Mrs. Gibson hugging Josie—before her heels clacked toward the door.

"Just give him a chance, okay? Once you get to know him, you'll see how wrong you are. There's more to Garth Black than everyone thinks. Way more."

"We'll see," Mrs. Gibson answered before clicking the door closed.

A second hadn't passed before Josie threw open the shower curtain and inspected me like she was worried I'd stopped breathing. She reached for the shower lever.

"No, don't," I whispered in case Mrs. Gibson was within earshot. "It's finally starting to get warm."

Josie tested the shower water with her hand. "So? How bad are you?" Her forehead lined as she kneeled beside the tub.

"On a scale of cold to hypothermic . . ." I slid off my

118

hat and tossed it out onto the floor. It was already soaked, so I don't know why I bothered. "I'm a popsicle." I worked a smile into place and almost groaned as the water continued to heat. I broke out in goose bumps it felt so good.

"God, Garth. I'm so sorry." Josie tested the water again and adjusted the dial.

"It's just a little bit of cold water. No big deal," I understated. If I was asked to choose between getting thrown from a bull a dozen times in one night or sitting through another five minutes of glacial shower water pelting me while I had to lay immobile and take it, I'd take the bull without a moment's thought. I wasn't sure if that made me a badass or a baby. Wasn't sure if I wanted the answer to that either.

"Not that. Although I am sorry about the water, too." The sleeves of Josie's bathrobe were getting wet, so she slipped out of it. Leaving on nothing but the pajamas that had the man stamp of approval all over them. "I'm sorry for the things she said. Those weren't fair things to say, and they were hurtful, too. I wish you hadn't heard any of that."

Josie was right. The things her mom said were hurtful, but that's not what I'd focused on. The thing I took away from that mother-daughter conversation was the way Josie had stuck up for me. I hadn't asked her to; I never had and never would. She'd stuck up for me simply because she *chose* to. Just thinking about it brought the same tsunami of emotions I'd felt minutes ago. All of those good ones that were so foreign I couldn't name them.

"Sure, what your mom said might have hurt my

feelings, Joze." She lifted an eyebrow. "And you'd better not tell anyone that I have any. Feelings, that is . . . But what she said wasn't anything I haven't heard before. What she said was fair because—even though I might try to dismiss it and you might try to soften it—it's the truth. I'm not the kind of guy parents want their daughters hanging around. I have ruined plenty of reputations. I don't think twice about getting rip-roaring drunk on a Sunday morning. I'm that guy. You know it, and I sure as hell do, too."

She tilted her head, studying me. "Your point being?"

I sat up to look her straight on. "I know who I am. I'm not ashamed of that person. *Most* days." I gave her a twisted smile. "I don't want you to be ashamed of the person I am either. You don't have to try to paint me as the misunderstood good guy to everyone and their dog."

Her face broke for a moment, but it cleared, another moment later and then Josie did something I wasn't expecting. She crawled over the side of the tub, closed the shower curtain, and tried to squeeze next to me. When that didn't work, she spread out over me. The shower had her clothes and hair soaked in about ten seconds, and if her expression wasn't so serious, I probably would have laughed at the two taking a shower fully clothed. Or I would have been kissing her, sucking every last drop of water from her lips.

"I'm not ashamed of you. I never have been, and I never will be," she said as her fingers skimmed my fore-head, sliding my hair to the side. The touch was intimate without being the kind of "intimate" I was used to. I'd gotten a lot of those innocent intimate touches from Josie lately. "The only reason I paint you as the misunderstood good guy is because that's who you are. You're the guy who shows up on his friend's doorstep in the middle of the night if they call. You're the guy who is one of the first guys at work in the morning and one of the last to leave. You're the guy who played Cupid when his best friend almost lost the woman he loved. You're the guy who would give your kidney to a homeless three-legged dog if it needed one. You're *that* guy, Garth. You know it. And I've known it for a hell of a lot longer."

A woman could render a man speechless one way, a way I was exceptionally familiar with . . . And there was that way. The things Josie had just said, the conviction in the words and her eyes . . . It was all a bit overwhelming. Especially as we shared a shower with her sprawled out on top of me. I wanted to give what she'd said more thought, but that was next to impossible when our bodies were perfectly aligned. Save for a couple pieces of clothing, I was one hip rock away from . . .

Shit. All my attempts to hide that I was turned on went out the window with that vivid thought. I knew that, given Josie's position, she knew. That she knew I was turned on and hard and still didn't get up to leave in a fit of disgust made me wonder why she was hanging around. That question, of course, led to the next . . . Why had Josie hung around my whole life? Why hadn't she left me in the rearview like so many people before her? Why was she staring at me with that look in her eyes, almost like she wanted me to . . . *kiss* her?

I knew that look—that expectant, lidded-eye, flushed-cheek look. I was a pro at creating it and identifying it because that was my so-called gateway. If I could get a woman to look at me that way—to want me to kiss her—I could get her to go along for the rest of the ride, too. It had worked without exception, and I knew that if I kissed Josie, the same would probably happen. Especially when both of our bodies were responding to each other.

I couldn't do that to Josie. Not again. She might have forgiven me for the first time I let my body take the steering wheel with her, but she wouldn't if I gave in a second time. I sure as hell hadn't forgiven myself for the first time, so if I did what I wanted to then, I would probably wake up tomorrow crushed by guilt.

So instead of coaxing her mouth to mine and sliding my hands down her body like they were twitching to do, I exhaled and forced that twisted smile of mine into position. That smile, with that gleam in my eyes, gave off the cool and removed vibe. The one I was notorious for. The one I knew Josie could see through, but the only one I could rely on to keep me from giving into what my body wanted. One part of me hoped she'd slap me for using a façade and march out of there, and the other part of me hoped she'd call bullshit and drop her mouth to mine and leave it there. Again, the two consciousnesses were at war with one another. "Did you just say all of that because you feel bad for the ice shower you gave me?"

"No, Garth. You and I both know you haven't taken enough cold showers in your life when you should have." She smiled at me, combing my hair with her fingers. "I said those things because they're true. As much as I know you'd rather me accept the lie most of the time. But I don't want to. Not anymore. I'm done lying to myself."

Her face inched closer to mine, and the water dripping from her lips fell right onto mine. My heart couldn't take much more. The rest of my body couldn't either.

Josie's other hand ran up my side, stopping on my chest. It was like a rare form of torture. The woman of my dreams was able to touch me, but I couldn't touch her back because once I did, both of our lives would be ruined. One touch, and we were as good as dead. I closed my eyes and tried to compose my thoughts. When Josie's body slid down a bit, then back up, applying pressure in all the right places, composing anything was history.

My god, that woman would be the death of me.

chapter EIGHT

A LOT CAN change in twenty-four hours. A whole life can change.

While mine hadn't changed totally and completely, it had changed significantly from the night before. I had a warm bed and house to sleep in for starters, but that wasn't all. The rest of me felt like it was also changing . . . shifting. Ideas were forming, beliefs being questioned, convictions being challenged. I was in a state of flux, and the catalyst for it all was Josie. She'd been the catalyst for a lot of things.

After slipping out of the Gibsons' undetected, Josie drove me back to my truck so I could head over to Willow Springs. She was silent the whole ride there. Not like she was fuming in an enraged silence, or festering in a shamed one, but peaceful in a contemplative one. She'd only broken her silence to say good-bye, and that was the one word I didn't want to hear from Josie Gibson, despite knowing it was the healthiest word she could say to me.

I put in a half day at Willow Springs helping Neil and the guys get the herd watered and fed. That was about all we could get done because the temperatures weren't lifting. He and Rose both caught me before I left for the day to let me know I was always welcome—more than welcome—to stay in the bunkhouse. That's why it was there. I respectfully declined, and they didn't push the matter. I liked the Walkers a lot. They'd always been generous in a way that didn't feel like they were shoving their generosity down my throat. It was a quality I could appreciate.

When it was time to head over to the Gibsons' for dinner and my "official" move in, I couldn't seem to get there fast enough. I was eager to get to a place where two people were the opposite of eager to see me, and another person was basically my sworn enemy. I must have been really excited to see the one other person left. After that morning in the shower, I realized Josie harbored some kind of feelings for me. Whether it was strictly animal desire or something else, I wasn't picky. Josie could have whatever kind of connection she felt for me. That made me even more conflicted. I'd turned into a giant ball of questions and conflicts and desires. I'd pretty much become my biggest nightmare. I was a rougher version of Jesse Walker. But a better looking one. A *far* better looking one.

As I pulled up to the Gibsons' place, I decided to give all of those questions a rest. Hopefully after a couple days of ignoring them, some answers would magically appear. Yes, I knew that was a whole lot of wishful, naive thinking, but any options were better than no options. Obviously nothing I'd done to try to work them out had succeeded, so ignoring them was as good a solution as any.

Colt's truck was already there, gleaming without a spot on it. People bought trucks for their function. Or at least most people did. Colt didn't group into that "most people" category. He was one of the jackasses who bought a truck because he wanted the truck to label him, not the other way around. It didn't have a scratch on it, and I'd be willing to bet my left ball that he'd never even hauled anything in the bed. I loved my truck and all, but the thing was beat to shit. It was a truck. Beat to shit came with the territory.

As I passed Colt's truck, I resisted the urge to kick the tires. The damn thing wasn't even made in the U.S. Either because of the cold or who was waiting inside for me, I kept my kicks to myself and hurried up to the front door. I was just raising my hand to knock when the door opened.

"You came." There was a faint smile on Josie's lips.

"I said I would, didn't I?" I stepped inside and shut the door. For the moment, Josie and I were alone, but I heard three other voices coming from the dining room.

"Yeah, but there have been plenty of times when you've said one thing and done the other. Especially when you start getting . . . close to someone. Or they start getting close to you." Josie's eyes flicked toward the kitchen when a round of laughter came from it, and I was able to notice other things. Like what she was wearing.

"Damn, Josie. Are you trying to kill me?"

She glanced back my way. "Not particularly right now. Why?"

I didn't even try to stop staring. It would have been a wasted effort. "Because that dress is enough to give a man a heart attack if you come any closer, or break a man's heart if you walk away."

"Now lines like that help me understand why you've got a reputation for being such a ladies man."

"That wasn't even my best one." I slid out of my coat and hung it up on the coatrack while staring at her. I wasn't a dress expert, other than taking them off, so I wasn't sure how to classify hers. It was the prettiest shade of blue I'd ever seen, and it hugged every line and curve I'd had pressed against me that morning. That kind of dress could bring a man to his knee to propose, even if that had been the furthest thing from his mind when he woke up that morning. Hell, it was bringing me close to a proposal, and I was dead set against anything marriage related.

"No? What is your best one then?" She leaned into the wall, obviously not in a hurry to get back to the others. If she wasn't in a hurry, I wasn't either.

"My best line?"

"Your best, *best* line. I want to hear it. Give me the one line that would blow me away and make me a slave to your every want and whim."

Talking about slaves and wants and whims with Josie that close to me made me feel like my heart was about to burst through my ribcage. It also made me feel like something was going to burst out of my zipper. "Sorry, no can do. It's way too early in the night to start talking about my wants and whims. Plus, your innocent ears would never be the same."

"I've known you since we were five. I think my ears stopped being innocent by the time I was five and a half." She gave me a wry smile and crossed her arms.

"Oh, well in that case . . ." I waited until I was sure I'd created enough dramatic pause that Josie was close to snapping in anticipation. "Sorry, Joze. No best line ever tonight. You couldn't handle it."

"I think I can handle one little line from you. I've handled a lot more from you."

"Fine. *I* couldn't handle it. Now, can we change the

subject?"

"What would you like to change the subject to?" She stepped toward me. I would have stepped back if I wasn't already backed into a corner. Literally and figuratively.

"How about me admitting I was an ass this morning and apologizing? I'm sorry for how far things went." For me, making apologies ranked up there with having a bull come down on my foot. But with Josie, it was ten times easier. Possibly a hundred times. It wasn't even painful.

"Are you really? Sorry for how far things went? Because I recall things going way farther between us before and never receiving an apology for that."

Ouch. Josie was bringing it. I'd come in prepared to trade spars with Colt Mason—I was ready for his brand of shit. I had not come prepared to talk about *that* with Josie. "You're right. I never apologized to you for that, but it was for a good reason."

"And what would that good reason be?"

She was waiting for an answer, but all I could think about that night and the dress she had on right then and how I couldn't apologize because . . . "Because I wasn't sorry it happened."

Yeah, I hadn't exactly planned on that coming out. After it did, I saw exactly why I'd wanted to keep it to myself. Josie sucked in a tiny breath of surprise before her whole face smoothed out. Those eyes wouldn't stop staring into mine like she could see everything I wanted and needed to keep to myself. Then she grabbed my hand and lifted it to her cheek. I was a man who, right then, was a slave to *her* every whim and wish.

"I'm not sorry it happened either."

I wasn't sure what was more confusing—that Josie

was touching me when the boy she'd been dating for months was a few rooms away or that she'd just said that. She wasn't sorry for what had happened between us? That was hard to believe. *Impossible* to believe. But she'd said it. At least a dozen questions were on the tip of my tongue. One was just about to come out when a pair of familiar-sounding heels clacked our way.

"Josie? Was that Garth who pulled up in the drive-way?"

I pulled my hand away from Josie's cheek, and she took a few steps backward, smoothing her dress and expression. "Yeah, he's here."

"Then what in the world is taking you so long? You have company waiting for you."

Josie's glanced over at me. "We were just saying hey."

My brows came together. I didn't realize what we'd said and done qualified as a *hey*, but at least the girl was getting better at the whole parental evasion thing.

"Well can't you say hey in the kitchen? I think Colt's starting to wonder if you've run off to Vegas." The instant Mrs. Gibson's eyes fell on me, her mouth turned down and she exhaled. "Hello, Garth. It's good to see you again. It's been a while." Mrs. Gibson had the robot voice down pat.

I tipped my hat and shoved off the wall. "I'm sorry that 'a while' couldn't have been a bit longer, but your daughter's convinced I can't survive a night on my own, let alone the whole winter." Josie received a sideways look from her mom. "Thank you for offering to let me stay a few nights. I really appreciate it." Just because I'd heard exactly how Mrs. Gibson felt about me earlier didn't mean I couldn't muster up some old-fashioned respect and mind my Ps and Qs.

"A few days? Garth, you can stay as long as you want. It's going to take you more than a few days to find a place of your own," Josie said, crossing her arms.

"Oh, sweetie, I don't know. I'm sure if Garth puts his mind to it, he can do anything. Isn't that right, Garth?"

If only Mrs. Gibson knew the things I'd put my mind to . . . "That's right. You never know, Joze, I might go and surprise the hell out of you." Mrs. Gibson cleared of her throat loudly. Oh, yeah. It had been a while since I'd been in the Gibsons' home. "Sorry, ma'am. I meant . . . I might go and surprise the heaven out of you."

Josie pursed her lips to keep from laughing while Mrs. Gibson looked more to be holding back from strangling me. Josie said, "Why don't we head into the kitchen before I tell you to get out and go to heaven?" We laughed, turning Mrs. Gibson a special shade of red. She practically marched back into the dining room.

Walking beside Josie toward the dining room, I nudged her. "Go to heaven? Really, Joze? That was pathetic. That was like kindergarten quality comedy right there."

"It got a laugh out of you, didn't it?" She nudged me back—with her elbow into my ribs. That "nudge" was a Josie favorite.

"A pity laugh, Gibson."

"Nice try. You were in stitches back there. Rolling from your laughter."

"I'll show you rolling in laughter." I pinched her side, and when she tried to slide away, I slid with her and kept pinching until she was an inch from rolling.

Mrs. Gibson did her best to ignore us, but when we made it into the dining room, the others definitely weren't ignoring us. I dropped my hand, but I stayed where I was. Right beside her. That pissed Colt Mason off more than any other opening jab I could have thrown at him. Mr. Gibson and Colt stood up from the table, their eyes narrowing on me. So one person wanted me there. The rest, not so much.

"Good to see you again, Mr. Gibson."

He shook his head. "Since you're going to be staying with us for a while, why don't you cut the bullshit now, Garth? I know you're about as excited to see me as I am to see you." I tipped my head in agreement. "Good. Now that we've got that out of the way, let's enjoy dinner."

"Daddy, no. We do *not* have that out of the way." It was good to know Josie didn't use that tone only on me. "You promised you would be fair and not act like a caveman. You promised to give Garth a chance, and you saying your hellos that way is not giving him a chance." Josie grabbed my arm and tugged me toward the table. I went along because . . . well, where else would I go when Josie was pulling me forward? "You are going to shake his hand and try it again."

Mr. Gibson shifted, not making eye contact with Josie. It was also good to know I wasn't the only male she could make uncomfortable and ashamed at the same time. Once we were a few feet in front of Mr. Gibson, Josie stopped and moved aside like she was playing referee. She pretty much was.

"Well?" She gave me a look and then her dad. When that pointed expression made its way back to me, I sighed and extended my hand.

"It's good to see you, Mr. Gibson." I glanced at Josie, making sure she was taking note. She was definitely taking note, and the way she was looking at me reminded me of what she'd said in the hall about not being sorry about that night, and that got me thinking about . . .

Fuck. All the way to infinity and back. I was about to shake hands with her dad with a hard-on. Not a proud moment.

Mr. Gibson extended his hand with a sigh and shook mine with another sigh. "Good to see you, too, Garth." He gave Josie a look before his eyes zeroed back in on me. I don't know if he knew the thoughts I was having about his daughter and the way my body was responding to those thoughts or if he just downright hated my guts, but that was one look I would take to the grave. "Keep your hands off my daughter. I have no problems going back to prison."

I lifted my eyebrows. "Duly noted."

With a huff, Josie broke our handshake by stepping between us and leveling her dad with a look that wouldn't have only leveled me; it would have obliterated me. "That's your idea of—"

"That's all I'm capable of right now, Josie Belle. I don't hand out second chances just because. If Garth proves himself worthy of me changing my less-than-stellar opinions of him, I will do it with a smile. But until then . . ." Mr. Gibson patted Josie's cheek, the same one I'd just had my hand around. "He's serving his sentence for all the years he's spent building a bad reputation."

I totally got where Mr. Gibson was coming from. If I ever became a father and my daughter hung around a guy like me, I'd be faced with two options: serve a life sentence for putting a bullet into the kid's head or sequester my daughter to her own private iceberg in the middle of the Bering Sea. I'd die before I'd let a daughter of mine get involved with someone like me. Mr. Gibson and I spoke the same language there.

There was a problem, though. Mr. Gibson didn't know Josie and I'd slept together. He and Mrs. Gibson didn't have a clue I'd been the reason Josie and Jesse—their golden son-in-law who could have been—broke up. The three of us had come to some sort of unspoken agreement not to talk about what had happened. We didn't talk about what had taken three best friends and split them apart. He didn't know I'd been intimate with his daughter, and he'd still formed the opinion of me that I was about as worthless as a bull with no buck. If and when the day ever came that he found out . . . well, I would never get a second chance because I'd spend the rest of this life and my next serving time for the first chance I'd *ruined*.

Josie hitched her hands on her hips, and I knew it wasn't a matter of if, but when she got back into it with her dad. So instead of carrying on what I knew to be a stalemate, I turned to the other guy. The one who made my fists ball the instant I looked at him. As expected, he was running his eyes all over Josie. When they stopped on her ass, I stepped forward, and I swear to god if his gaze hadn't shifted right then, I would have hammered him into the ground.

"Colt." I shifted until I was between Josie and his leering gaze.

"Garth." He crossed his arms and stood taller. I still had the douche by two inches. "Looks like your face healed up okay."

As expected, getting in a bar fight with me was the highlight of Colt Mason's life. "What? From those butterfly kisses you gave me? It was like a day at the spa." Instead of refereeing her dad and me together, Josie shifted to trying to referee me and Colt apart. Wasn't happening.

"Don't spa days cost money? Something you don't have any of?"

Josie let out a small gasp. I lifted an eyebrow at him that said *Is that all you've got?* "You know, there are plenty of things you can't buy with money. Like respect. Or integrity. Or a dick that doesn't malfunction."

"Garth," Mrs. Gibson hissed. Of course she'd missed Colt's insult.

Colt stepped forward. "Given all of your conquests that might have a little . . . *mileage* on them, I suppose you know about malfunctioning dicks."

Why was I letting the asshole still run his mouth? Oh, yeah, no reason. I was so close to bringing my left fist around until to smash that stupid little smirk off his face when Josie's hand slipped into my fist. With one touch, she'd diffused a bomb. Her hand didn't stay in mine long—just long enough to calm me down. It slipped out before Colt or her parents saw.

"If either of you boys want to stay around for dinner, you'd better watch your mouths. And your fists." Mr. Gibson gave me a pointed look. I guess he hadn't missed that I was ready to send Mason across the living room with one hit.

"Sorry, Mr. Gibson." Colt turned his back to me and headed to the table. "This guy just has a way of getting under my skin. Along with everyone else's."

"Garth is a guest here. So are you. The better man isn't the one who hits first or the hardest or the most. The better man is the one who uses his head instead of his fists."

I had so many smart-ass responses to that, but I tried something I'd been trying more and more and bit my tongue until it almost bled. Mr. Gibson sat at the table and waited for us to do the same. Mason, the ass kisser, sat next to Mr. Gibson before I'd stepped toward the table.

"Hey, Josie. We're still on for next month, right?" Mason asked.

Two points for knowing just how to push my buttons. My hands were back into fists as I approached the table. He might have sat beside Mr. Gibson to get so far up that man's ass he'd need the damn enema of enemas to get him out, but I wasn't there for Mr. Gibson. I was there for someone else. Sliding out a chair, I glanced at Josie and raised an eyebrow. She smiled. She was still smiling when I sat beside her.

"Josie? Have you gone deaf, child?" Mrs. Gibson set a big roast in the middle of the table. "Colt asked you a question."

Her smile dropped. "I must have missed it. Sorry, Colt, what did you ask?"

He put his elbows on the table and leaned forward. "I asked if we were still on for next month?"

"What's next month?"

Colt's shoulders dropped just enough to make me grin. "The big winter dance and barbecue at Wild Bill's."

I wanted to make like Josie and roll my eyes. Our town and its fondness for seasonal get-togethers at the local honky-tonk. As a rule, I avoided "community" get-togethers since community made me nauseous. The only reason I'd been to a few of them was because there were so many single and willing women at those things, it was like shooting fish in a barrel.

"Oh, yeah. I forgot about that." Josie grabbed the basket of rolls and handed them to me. She knew I'd never met a roll I didn't like. "We'll see."

Colt did not look pleased. Mrs. Gibson looked horrified. Me? Well, I still hadn't stopped grinning.

Mrs. Gibson peered at Josie as she sliced into the roast. "If you promised Colt you'd go with him to the dance, it's only right you keep your word. That's just good manners."

"And lecturing your grown daughter at the dinner table while we have a couple of guests sitting around it is the opposite of good manners." Josie peered right back at her mom as she heaped a couple servings of mashed potatoes on to her and my plates. Josie probably didn't think anything of it—she was too distracted by her flaring temper to realize what she was doing—but no one had ever taken care of me the way she was. Handing me the biscuits even though she didn't take one, dropping a spoonful of potatoes on my plate, giving me only a small portion of peas because I wasn't hot on them . . . I wasn't used to people showing me that level of care and concern.

"Thank you," I said and waited for her to look at me. When she did, I slid my hand beneath the table. I let it rest on her leg, just above her knee. She didn't gasp, she didn't jolt, she didn't even look surprised. The look on her face said she'd almost been expecting it. Then her hand found mine, and our fingers tangled together. I couldn't imagine ever getting tired of holding Josie's hand.

"You're welcome," she replied.

After that, dinner was pretty uneventful. Other than Colt keeping his lips vacuum-sealed to Mr. Gibson's ass and Mrs. Gibson criticizing each of her dishes by what was missing and which ones needed more salt, it was a pleasant dinner. Mostly thanks to Josie's and my hands never separating. Thankfully, Mrs. Gibson's roast was tender. I would have rather picked it up and eaten it with one hand than let go of Josie's to cut it.

Plates were being cleared when Colt cleared his throat and made his move. I knew that look in his eyes. I'd practically invented that look. I didn't like that look when some douche had it aimed at Josie. No, that wasn't quite true . . . I *hated* that look aimed at Josie.

"My mom was just saying as I left tonight that if I didn't bring you home so you two could catch up, she was considering disowning me." Colt wiped his mouth with his napkin and shoved back from the table. "She had the actual disownment paperwork signed and ready to go. So what do you say? Will you come over to my place tonight? Or will I be homeless and motherless tomorrow?"

I hated Colt Mason. If there was any question before, his cheap move confirmed it. I knew exactly what Colt had in mind about bringing Josie to his place, and it had nothing to do with talking or parents being anywhere around.

"I don't know. It's late, it's freezing, I'm tired, and Garth's here. It's his first night." I didn't miss the quick glance she threw my way. Nothing like sharing a secret that would probably get both our asses thrown out if her parents found out about my first *first* night. "Maybe some other time?"

Mrs. Gibson was just about to say something when Colt cut in. "It's barely nine o'clock, coats and car heaters do a pretty good job of taking care of the cold, I'm guessing your mom threw on a pot of coffee to serve with dessert, and Garth's a big boy capable of tucking himself in. Isn't that right, Garth?" Colt glanced at me for a fraction of a second, making it clear I wasn't worth his time or attention.

"I don't know about that. I'd take Josie tucking me in over myself any night. Strictly hypothetically speaking here," I added when Mr. and Mrs. Gibson's heads snapped my way.

"Oh, yeah. I forgot you're used to some woman tucking you into bed, or your truck cab, or the bathroom counter of Brandy's, or beneath the grandstand bleachers, or—"

"The bathroom counter at Brandy's? Have you seen that thing? It's a hazmat team's wet dream. I might not be picky, but I would not choose to be tucked in there." I knew Colt was trying to get to me, to turn me into a cussing ball of instinct. I also knew why he was trying to release my inner Hulk. He wanted Mr. and Mrs. Gibson to have front row seats to the Garth Black Loosing his Shit Show. I wasn't sure what I wanted more: to ruin Colt's baiting me plan or to not let the Gibsons see I was the guy they assumed I was. Both were strong motivators for fighting Colt's traps.

Before Colt could decide what to hit me with next, Mrs. Gibson paused before heading into the kitchen with the tower of dirty dinner plates. "Josie, why don't you head over to Colt's after dessert? You made two pies, after all. You could take one over for his family to enjoy. I know you're tired," Mrs. Gibson added when Josie looked ready to argue, "but I'm sure Colt will get you home before it gets too late. Isn't that right, Colt?"

"Of course, Mrs. Gibson. I'll make sure she's home

by eleven."

Eleven? That would give them at least a couple of hours at the Masons'. That was way, way, *way* too much time for Josie to be at Colt Mason's. Assuming he was the one-pump wonder I'd always believed he was, thirty seconds was too long for Josie to be at his place.

"Thank you, both of you"—Josie stood, her gaze flicking from Colt to her mom—"but I am twenty-one and able to decide *if* I want to go out and what time I want to be back by. But thank you for your efforts to treat me like a thirteen-year-old. Always appreciated." Without another word, Josie charged past her mom into the kitchen. I wasn't sure if I should expect her to start breaking stuff or if she'd come back with a butcher knife in her hands. Based on the blaze in her eyes, I was betting on the butcher knife. Josie and I had quick-flare tempers, and I knew from fighting my own that it was best for me to work it out myself.

That was why I stood up and headed for the kitchen. Josie's words from that morning were on my mind—about how I didn't know what was good for me. If she was right, that meant working my temper out on my own wasn't the best case scenario, which meant leaving her to work out hers wasn't either. Either way, I just wanted to be with her. Mrs. Gibson was setting the dishes in the sink, and Josie had her head in the . . . *freezer*. That was a form of cooling down from a temper high I wasn't familiar with.

"Joze?" I ignored Mrs. Gibson's looks and headed for the fridge. "If you're looking to vent your temper, I've got a whole list of effective ways to go about it without crystallizing your brain."

"Oh, yeah? Do you have a whole list of effective

ways to go about getting ice cream out of the freezer?" Holding out a tub of vanilla ice cream, she closed the freezer.

"You know me, I've got a list of effective ways for doing everything."

"I wouldn't use the work *effective*. More like *creative*." She smirked at me as she grabbed a scoop out of a drawer.

Mrs. Gibson stationed herself next to Josie and tried to grab the scoop. "I've got dessert. Why don't you go back out there and keep Colt company?"

Josie whipped it out of her reach. "I made dessert. I'm serving dessert. Why don't *you* go keep Colt company since you're his number two fan?"

Mrs. Gibson put a hand on her hip and let out a sigh of exasperation before heading back to the dining room. "With an attitude like that, it's no wonder you're twenty-one and still single. You're my only child. I'm counting on you for grandbabies—lots of them—preferably before I'm dead." She stopped just outside the kitchen. "Are you sure you don't want some help with dessert, honey?"

"No, thanks, Mom. Garth's here—he can help." Josie grabbed some plates and set them on the island. "With dessert, and heck, maybe even the grandbaby making. You know, kill two birds with one stone. In five whole minutes, you might be able to enjoy a piece of homemade pie *and* knowing you're going to be a grandma in nine and a half months."

I shifted from the look Mrs. Gibson gave me. She'd probably disown a grandchild if I was the baby's father. "Don't worry, Mrs. Gibson, I'll keep it to the pie." One more head shake and she was gone. "So? How are we going to do this thing?" I headed toward the island where Josie had thrown down what looked to be a cherry pie.

"I'll cut. You scoop." She handed me the ice cream scoop and grabbed a huge knife from the butcher block. I knew Josie would wind up with some huge-ass knife in her hand before the night was over.

"I was referring to the other way you wanted me to help you out. This island here looks pretty solid." I grabbed the ledge of the island and rocked into it. "Brace yourself."

Josie glanced at the island then at the area just below my belt buckle. Her face flushed. "You do realize I'm holding a knife, right? You might not want to go whipping anything out you want to hang onto."

I loved that she was blushing. I loved what she was blushing over. It made me want to throw her up on that counter. Screw the pie. Or . . . *forget* about the pie. "You're right. I've got the scars to prove that seducing a woman who's clutching a knife isn't a good way to go about things. Plus, I did promise your mom I'd keep it to the pie tonight."

"And tomorrow night?" Josie cut into the pie. She was trying so hard not to look at me I almost felt her about to break out in a sweat.

"All bets are off." I stepped closer to Josie so my arm was intentionally touching hers. I knew my touch and words were making her uneasy. I wanted them to. I wanted to see if what she'd said earlier was true. I wanted to see if her actions proved that she wasn't sorry for what had happened between us or if she'd just said it. "Who's Colt's number one fan?"

I wasn't looking to change the subject; that was just

where my mind went next. It was all over the place when I was around Josie. Her eyebrows came together.

"Just now. You told your mom she was his number two fan. Who's his number one fan? You?" I probably would have chucked the ice cream across the room if she said yes, but I had to know.

"This is Colt Mason we're talking about," Josie answered, smiling at the pie. "I think it's pretty obvious that he's his number one fan."

If I wasn't sure she wouldn't slap or knife me, I would have kissed her hard and long for that. Instead, I did the only kind of cartwheel I ever would do—the internal kind—and nudged a little closer. "It's been obvious to me since I set sight on the guy. Glad to know I'm not the only one." I pried open the ice cream lid and put the scooper to work. "Am I to take that as an indication that you will not be going to his place tonight?"

"Garth." Josie's voice was full of warning as she worked on the pie.

"Josie," I mimicked. "He's a douche. You pretty much just admitted that, so I'm also taking that as an indication that you won't be going with him to the hillbilly hoe-down at—"

Josie groaned and wielded that knife in such a way I was inclined to take a few steps back with my hands lifted. "Not you too. I thought you were the only one on my team. I thought if one person had my back and wouldn't tell me what to do, how to do it, and play the goddamned puppeteer in my life, it would be you! Jesus Christ, you're the poster child for being your own person and to hell with the rest of them. You can't give me—*ME*—the same thing?" Josie's face was red again, but it wasn't thanks to a

142

flush from thinking salacious thoughts.

"Two things, Joze." I stepped back just to be safe. "Are you planning on continuing to hack that pie to pieces? If so, I'll get the blender and milk ready, and we'll serve cherry pie milkshakes instead." The corners of her mouth curved up, and she gave the pie one more "hack." "And numero dos . . . I *do* have your back, I *am* on your team, and I *don't* want anyone but you to be the puppeteer of your life. Although strings on you and me playing master sounds like the kind of night I don't want to miss out on." If that comment didn't make her come at me with the knife, I was good to go, so I stepped toward her until we were touching again. We exhaled at the same time. "But all jokes, teasing, and sadomasochism aside, Joze, it's your life. You only get one shot at it, so live it like that."

"Do I want to know how you know about sadomasochism?"

"It isn't from personal experience, if that's what you're worried about." I slid a piece of hair behind her ear and ran my hand down her back. "I haven't crossed that off the bucket list yet. Wanna give me a hand with that?"

"I'm sure your hand's been giving you plenty of help with that."

"More help than I can handle."

Josie gave a small laugh as the anger drained from her face. From hot to cold, breathing fire to soft laughs in five seconds. We were so much alike I sometimes felt like I was dealing with the female me. And yes, I know that being hardcore attracted to someone I felt was me with tits and a vagina said a shitload about my psyche I didn't want to even skim the surface of.

"And that whole on-my-team admission includes letting me decide to do whatever I want or don't want to do with Colt? Like going to his place tonight or to the hillbilly hoe-down?"

"I'm on your team with everything but for one exception. The Colt exception."

Josie plated the first piece of pie and handed it to me. I did my thing and plopped a glob of ice cream on it. "Colt and I have dated on and off for a while. You know that, right?"

"More off than on though, right?" I really didn't want to know anything about Colt and Josie's history, but apparently my carnal need-to-know did.

"More the other way around," she replied matter-of-factly.

"Eh, really? You could have your pick of the litter, and you choose the phony, poser runt who thinks cowboy is a noun, not a verb?"

"And you think if I made a different choice, perhaps with a 'verb' cowboy like yourself, I'd be so much better off?" She plated another piece of pie and handed it to me.

I inhaled. I exhaled. I repeated. I needed to make sure I really wanted to say it. Should I say it? Would she want me to? Did *I* want me to? Ah, hell with it. "There's only one way to find out. There's only one way to know if you'd be better off with someone like"—I swallowed and stuck my thumb into my chest—"me."

When she plated the next piece of pie, she slowly faced me. She wasn't smiling like I'd said something wonderful or glaring like I'd said something stupid. She wasn't doing much of anything other than studying me. I'd been studied by Josie so much in the past twenty-four hours, I felt close to transparent. I didn't even know what she was looking for or what she was finding, but I felt about as see-through as that window behind her.

"Let me get this straight, Garth, because the past couple of days have been a bit complicated . . . and twice as confusing." She tilted her head, staring into depths of me I didn't know were there. "You want me to call off a long-term, stable, supportive relationship—"

"On-again, mostly off-again relationship," I added. If she was about to make some big statement, I wanted the facts straight.

She continued, hardly fazed by my interruption. "You want me to basically stop going down this path I've been on for a while and try out another trail. One that's rocky, and steep, and dangerous. One I'll never know when it will run out and end in a steep drop-off. Which will leave me with nowhere to go besides backward or over the face of that cliff. When and if that jagged, scary trail ends, I'll be abandoned and unsure if I can even make it back to the path I'd been on before."

I didn't blink. I didn't interrupt, or shake my head, or disagree. Everything she was saying was right on. Everything she was saying about the trail she'd navigate if she gave me a chance was right. Except for one thing. If she was brave enough to take that first step, and I was brave enough to let her, there wouldn't be an end. I knew the trail we'd walk together would be a hard one, but I wouldn't ever leave her alone on it. Of course, thinking all of that was one thing. Getting it out in an articulate, heartfelt manner was another.

"You want me to up and change huge parts of my life because we've spent a confusing and complicated and wonderful and terrifying twenty-four hours together?"

I only heard one thing in what she'd just said—wonderful—and it made me smile. She seemed to be done and waiting for me to respond. Given the way she continued to examine me, working up a response took a few seconds. "Yes, that's what I want. But this isn't about what *I* want. This is about what *you* want."

The kitchen was shrinking, the walls were closing in. Everything was closing in around me in expectation of how I would say it and how she would respond. "You're the one who has everything to lose. Let's face it, the only things I have left to lose are my boots and whatever scrap of dignity I have left. You have the world at your fingertips, and I have the weight of it on my shoulders. I know the man I am, and I know that I'm nowhere close to deserving of you . . . But if you feel anything for me like I feel for you, I'm asking you to give us a chance. I'm begging you to give *me* a chance to prove I won't make the same mistake and do you wrong one night and abandon you the next morning. I can and will stay at your side for as long as you want me to stay there."

Josie's eyes went a little glassy, and I couldn't tell if that was because she'd been staring at me without blinking for so long or because I was saying something that was getting to her. "I know how this sounds, but I know how I feel. You're right—it's terrifying and complicated and wonderful and confusing. If it's so confusing that I feel like my head's about to explode, I can imagine it feels the same for you. I'm not asking you to trust me with your life or your heart or your love yet. I am asking you for a chance to prove myself worthy of earning those things. If you can give me that, then let's take it slow and see where this whole thing goes. Inch by inch, day by day . . . let's see if we can be something as great as I believe we could be."

Josie let out the breath she'd been holding. When she stepped toward me, she could have been just as likely about to slap me as she was kiss me. Instead, she grabbed my hand and smiled. "You do realize that 'taking it slow' means not jumping into bed on a first date, right? Not even the second, third, or fourth."

I matched her smile and played along. "I don't know what your definition of 'taking it slow' is, but mine is taking our sweet time in bed . . . after dinner on our first date. And the second, and the third, and the fourth." She squeezed my hand until I winced. "All right, all right. We'll do this according to your definition of 'take it slow.'"

Her face went serious again. "I didn't think you were capable of taking it slow."

"Neither did I."

"And you are now?"

I nodded. "I am now."

"Why?"

That was the big question. "Because you deserve better than my best. You deserve the man I can and *should* be. Not the one everyone else knows."

"And while *we're* taking it slow . . . Where are *you* going? I'm not some girl you just met—I know you. Loyalty and sticking around isn't what you do when it comes to women."

Josie wasn't saying anything I'd never heard before, but because it was her, the words cut through my tough skin. "I'm not going anywhere." I lifted my hand to the bend of her waist. I curled my fingers into her and held on, hoping she'd never want me to let her go.

Her eyes closed, and her forehead lined. "Whose or how many beds will you make stopovers in while we're going slow and figuring this out?"

I winced. All the collective pleasure and satisfaction I'd gained from being with dozens of women was not worth the flash of pain I witnessed on Josie's face right then.

"No one's. None," I answered, lifting our entwined hands back to her cheek. I waited until she opened her eyes. "There's nowhere else I want to be. I'm not going anywhere. I'm exactly where I want to be."

When her fingers gave mine another squeeze, a gentle one, I had my answer. Biting her lower lip, she nodded once. "Slow and steady. Let's see if we can be great together." Then she smiled. Well it was more of a smile-smirk. "Because we've already been not-so-great together, right?"

I chuckled softly. "Whatever. You and I must have different definitions of 'great,' too." I was pretty sure I was going to kiss her. I was also pretty sure it wasn't going to be a short kiss. Then a familiar, and quickly becoming an annoying, clacking grew louder. It was like the woman had built-in radar to know whenever I was about to kiss her daughter.

Mrs. Gibson showed up in the kitchen a moment after Josie and I separated and stood at a distance far enough from one another not to rouse suspicion. A lot about Josie and I would be confusing, but one thing I was not in the slightest confused about? Keeping her parents in the dark for as long as possible. I didn't want to dodge shotgun spray every time I tried to take her to the movies or wrap my arm around her.

"I didn't realize you were *making* a pie. I thought that's what you spent all afternoon doing." The closer Mrs. Gibson got to the pie, the more her eyes widened. "What in the world happened to that pie? And the ice cream? I don't think there's much ice left . . . just cream." She looked inside the carton. It had turned into a sloppy mess while Josie and I worked out what we just had.

Had she really just agreed to give me a chance? The moment was finally catching up to me, and it was causing me to feel a little lightheaded.

"Other than ruining pie and ice cream, what have you two been up to in here?"

I guessed teasing Mrs. Gibson about getting after making her grandchild dreams come true probably would have been humor wasted right then. Josie wiped the pie filling off the edge of the knife with her finger and slid her finger into her mouth. Hot damn. That was not helping the dizzy sensation.

"We were just catching up. Sorry." Josie shrugged.

"You two have known each other since kindergarten. How much 'catching up' do you need?"

"A lot."

"Are you caught up now? Or should I leave and check back later?" Mrs. Gibson could hang with the most sarcastic of us. If I wasn't sure she'd grow horns and breathe fire if she found out how I felt about her daughter, we probably would have gotten along okay.

"What do you think, Garth? We all caught up now?" Josie's face had a hint of a smile.

"I think we covered the important parts. The rest we

can fill in as we go. We've got time. We can just take it slow. Nice . . . and . . . slow." I wagged my eyebrows at her. Josie responded with her standard reply when I was a pain in the ass—an eye roll.

"Good for you both. Glad you could catch up. We weren't really looking forward to cherry pie anyways." Mrs. Gibson cringed when she inspected the massacred pie again. "Please tell me you didn't do the same thing to the Masons' pie."

"Nope. It's still on top of the fridge. Safe and sound."

Not when I got a hold of it.

"Good. Why don't you grab it, *carefully*, and head over to the Masons' with Colt? I'll take care of the mess." Mrs. Gibson wasn't looking at the ice cream. Nope, she was looking straight at me.

Josie looked from her mom, to me, to the pie, and repeated. "Okay." Wiping her hands on a towel, she grabbed the pie off the fridge.

While Mrs. Gibson beamed and hurried into the dining room with a, "I'll let Colt know," a serious frown and a case of what-the-hell hit me. "Did I hear wrong, or did you just say you were going over to Colt's?" I followed Josie around the kitchen as she grabbed a few things.

"No, your ears are working just fine," she replied calmly.

"Okay, then did I just miss something earlier? Something about us talking about giving *us* a chance?"

Josie smiled at me, but I couldn't return it. I was not in a smiling mood. "No, you didn't miss anything. We talked about giving us a chance, and I don't know if anything's changed for you in five minutes, but I'm still planning on giving us a run."

"Then why are you going to Colt's?"

The skin between her eyebrows creased. "Did you miss us talking about taking this whole thing slow? Nice . . . and . . . slow?"

I settled my hands on my hips. When she looked about thirty seconds from heading out the front door with Colt Mason wasn't the time to be making jokes. "No, I didn't miss that. What does us taking it slow have to do with you leaving with Colt?"

"Plenty."

I wrapped my hand around her arm as she covered the pie in plastic wrap. "Explain." As far as relationships went, I had no experience. I'd never had a real girlfriend, but I'd had plenty of girls who were "friends." Josie was the expert in the relationship department.

Josie glanced at my hand on her arm. "Trust."

"The one-word answers are giving me nothing. Trust? What does trust have to do with Colt?"

"Nothing, but right now, trust has everything to do with *you*." She stuck her finger into my chest.

Shit, of course when the one-word bomb from Josie was *Trust,* it would have been dropped with me in mind. "Explain." My new favorite word.

"I'm giving you a chance to prove you have or are willing to learn what it takes to be in a relationship. Paramount in any relationship is trust." She grabbed the pie and turned for the dining room. "This is your opportunity to show you have trust in me."

"I thought I was the one proving you could trust *me*." I was, after all, the man who'd betrayed enough people in my life to make a person doubt I could ever be trusted again.

"It's a two-way street." Josie smiled at me before heading for the dining room.

I dodged in front of her. "I'd prefer this to be a one-way street."

"I know you would. But this isn't about what's best for you. This is about what's best for us."

She moved around me. I slid in front of her again. It was impossible to let her go. "No, Joze."

She could throw a fit, she could slam that pie into my face, she could give me in the silent treatment for a month, but I wouldn't let her leave in Colt's truck and head over to Colt's house where I knew he was already planning to take her to Colt's bed. She took a breath and looked at me. She was as calm as I was flustered.

"Garth, this whole slow and steady thing is a trial period. I need to know that if you don't have it, you're willing to do what it takes to learn how to be in a sup-portive, loving, *trusting* relationship that doesn't center around jealousy and control. I'm here to help you figure it out, but you have to want to figure it out." Her hand formed around my waist, and she stepped against me. "Think of this as the first hurdle in a series of them."

"What's at the finish line?"

"I guess we'll have to get there to find out." When she moved around me again, I let her go. God knows I didn't want to so badly my body almost quivered, but I did it. That was a victory on its own.

Not even two minutes later, I heard Colt's truck fire to life. If trust felt like that every time I had to prove it to her, I didn't doubt it would be the death of me.

chapter NINE

JOSIE HAD GOTTEN home an hour ago. I felt like a third parent when I checked the clock as that sorry excuse for a truck rumbled up the driveway. After helping Mr. and Mrs. Gibson clean up after dinner—something both of them seemed confused by—I'd taken a shower and crawled into bed. I don't know what I was expecting, but I was incapable of sleeping with Josie out where she was. I probably should have just run circles around the guest room. That would have been a better distraction from my thoughts than just lying quiet and motionless in bed.

I was close to throwing off the covers and starting my first lap when Colt's truck pulled up. Speaking of clocks, it was only ninety seconds before Josie came through the front door. A minute and a half wasn't long enough to get anywhere close to hot and heavy inside of Colt's truck, so I exhaled my second relieved breath of the night after Josie left. Being the parents they were, Mr. and Mrs. Gibson were still waiting up. After a couple minutes, I heard a series of *goodnights* as footsteps headed down the hall and one set up the stairs.

I wanted to see Josie. I wanted to talk to her. I wanted to hold her like I had last night. I wanted to kiss her. I wanted so much right then. I don't know if I'd ever "wanted" so much in my life.

Josie's bedroom door closed long before I finally felt sleepy. All of that adrenaline took a while to wear off, but once it did, I felt more like I was drifting into a coma instead of sleep. That was when my bedroom door whispered open so noiselessly I was surprised I noticed it. When I saw who slipped inside, I wasn't so surprised I noticed it. Welcome back, adrenaline. It's been a while. I sat up in bed, rubbing my eyes, and watched Josie approach in a different but similar pair of "pajamas."

"It's not a dream," she whispered, smiling at me. I must have looked confused. "That look on your face? It looks like you're trying to decide if this is real or a dream."

"The past twenty-four hours have felt like a dream. I don't know what's real and what isn't anymore." Josie sat on the edge of the bed, and the moment caught up with me. I could almost imagine a shotgun racking. "What are you doing in here?"

"I can't sleep." She clasped her hands and shrugged.

"Do you want me to make you a warm cup of milk or something?" I wasn't sure how Josie went about falling asleep when she had a hard time getting there, but I was certain she didn't use the same methods I usually did: a woman or a bottle of whiskey. Most nights, both.

"Thanks, but no. I wish a warm cup of milk would work. I'd actually be able to get more than a few hours of sleep every night." She was trying not to look at me— probably because I was half naked and we were beside each other on the same bed. I lowered the blankets a few inches to make it that much harder for her.

"Are you an insomniac or something?" I grinned when she finally lost the battle and glanced at me. Not at my face either.

"I think I get a whole half an hour more sleep than a true insomniac, but I'm as close to being one as I want to get."

"Have you always had that problem?" I didn't like knowing something I couldn't fix was bothering Josie. If a genie magically appeared and granted me one wish, I'd have insomnia made into human form so I could give it a serious ass-kicking.

"No. I used to sleep so hard I could snooze through a fire alarm." She shifted so she was facing me more.

"So when did you and sleep decide to become long lost friends?"

She studied her hands in her lap. "A couple of years ago."

I didn't need her to clarify the month, day, or hour. Because I knew. I knew what event and person was responsible for Josie's insomnia. I wanted to kick my own ass? How was that even possible? I didn't know, but if there was a way, I would figure it out. "Ah, hell, Joze. I'm a piece of shit. I don't know why you're even talking to me. I've screwed up so many things for you."

"Well . . . actually . . ." She bit her lip, acting almost shy. Josie did shy about as often as I did humble.

"Well actually *what*?" I asked eagerly. I'd do anything.

"Last night was the first night in two years I fell asleep and stayed asleep for close to six hours."

When she looked at me again, I got it. I mean, I didn't *get it* exactly, but I knew how to help. I might not have understood why Josie could sleep with me beside her, but I didn't need to know why to fix the problem. Scooting over, I threw open the blankets and patted the mattress. "Come on over. I warmed a spot up for you already."

She didn't need a second invitation. Josie had wiggled and wormed her way under the covers before I realized that, for the second night in a row, I was sharing a bed with Josie Gibson. If the young boy version of me could have expected that, growing up would have been a few shades brighter. "What are your parents going to think? Or do?"

"They're not going to think or do anything because they're going to wake up tomorrow none the wiser."

"You are one devious vixen, Joze." Once she was curled up, I draped my arm over her and slid up beside her.

"Are you still in your jeans?" Her hand grabbed the waist of my jeans and gave it a tug. "Do you ever take these things off?"

I couldn't form thoughts, let alone words, with her hand skimming my waist. When her fingers reached the button above my fly, her hand froze before dropping away. I breathed again. Clearing my throat, I worked up something that I hoped would be coherent. "When you grow up never knowing if you're going to be jerked awake by bottles shattering around you, you keep your pants on and your boots close by. I've spent as many nights sleeping under the stars as I have under a roof." Josie's hand slipped into mine, her fingers lacing with mine. "How was Colt's?" A better man might have kept his mouth shut, but I hadn't gotten where I had by being a better man.

"Uneventful. He didn't lure me into his bed like I know you were convinced he would."

I'd already guessed that, but I still exhaled in relief. "Yeah, but that doesn't mean he didn't *try* to."

"No, it doesn't mean that."

Imagining Colt trying to get Josie into his bed sent me close to the explosion point. The only thing that kept me from jumping out of bed and driving to Colt's just so I could throw his mattress out his window was Josie's touch. It took a minute or two before I was calm enough to form words. "So? Did I pass the trust test?"

"You passed it. With flying colors. I have to admit I didn't think you could do it. I kept looking out the Masons' living room window expecting to find your truck barreling up the driveway."

"I came close. I must have stopped myself from running through that front door a hundred times. But I didn't, and that's what counts." Josie's feet bumped mine, and I practically jolted from how cold they were. She was worried about me getting frost bite? So I gritted my teeth and pressed the tops of mine—which *were* toasty warm—into the bottom of hers. If the girl didn't run around in lingerie in the dead of winter, her feet might not have been mini glaciers with toes.

"You're kind of great, you know that?" She sighed and wiggled her toes over mine.

"I don't know if this is greatness or stupidity, but I'll take any compliment you want to send my way." So, yeah. My feet *had* been warm. Not anymore. But hers were at least. "Since I passed the trust test, mind telling me why you went over to Masons'?"

"I left my favorite sweater over there," Josie said with a shrug. "When Colt finds out about us, I don't want him throwing it in a bonfire."

Yeah, that odd sensation was probably my heart growing three sizes. The next sensation wasn't so odd. It was that flash of fire over what had transpired for her to leave her sweater at Colt's in the first place. "If he ever did that, he'd be the next thing thrown into that bonfire."

Josie laughed softly. "Good to know you're protective of my favorite sweater."

"You, Joze. I'm protective of *you*." I nuzzled her neck and would have tightened my arms around her if I didn't think it might cut off the circulation to her lower body. "Listen . . . I've been thinking"—a new concept for me, I know—"and I don't want you to up and change anything in your life right now. I've ruined so many things for you—I don't want you to change anything until you're certain about me. Not until I've cleared your hurdles and jumped your hoops and whatever else I need to do to prove I'm capable of making this work." That was hard as hell to say. Because it was so difficult and it twisted my insides when I'd been in bed thinking about it half the night, I knew it was the right thing to do. I wanted Josie all to myself and the whole world to know that. That was what was best for me. But . . . it wasn't what was best for her.

"You don't want me changing anything in my life? Colt included?" There was nothing antagonizing in her voice, but I knew she was gauging me and my level of seriousness.

I felt another flash of fire thinking of Colt and her together. "Let me put it this way—if there was an exception to that, Colt would be it." It wasn't the response I wanted to go with, but at least it was an honest one.

"Okay, I'll take that into consideration. Thank you." Her hand squeezed mine again.

"So what's the next hurdle? Since I'm on this whole proving myself path, I'm eager to get to the finish line."

Josie was quiet for a moment before twisting until we were face to face. "Seeing if you're capable of taking things slow . . . *physically*."

I lifted my brows. "That will be a challenge. I'm afraid my reputation indicates I'm not, but I'm eager to prove myself capable of rising to every challenge." With Josie's mouth so close to mine and her chest pressed to mine that way, *something* was definitely rising. Shit. I didn't need that with the next hurdle I was expected to jump. I closed my eyes and imagined Mrs. Westmore, the ancient elementary school librarian, naked on a cold day There . . . problem solved. Mostly. "When do we start?"

Josie's eyes dropped to my mouth, and she smiled. "What do you think part of the reason I'm here is?"

"Cunning little vixen." Since I knew the test was already in progress, I had to revisit the whole naked-old-woman-in-the-cold image for a few more seconds to make sure I wasn't going to blow it. A big part of me wanted to kiss her and touch her and make love to her the way I should have that one time . . . and I didn't need that to be a part of me. Not when I had to show her I was capable of a relationship that didn't center around sex. "Good night, Joze. Sleep good." Kissing the tip of her nose, I closed my eyes and hoped I'd be able to sleep with Josie pressed into me like that. I knew that was a long shot, so I hoped I'd be able to *pretend* I was asleep.

"Good night, Garth." Before twisting around, she planted a quick kiss into my cheek.

Life had changed just like that. People were right when they said it could change in the blink of an eye. Josie had been as far off as a person could get, and now she was falling asleep in my arms, promising to give me a chance to love her the way she deserved to be loved. It was all very . . . "I know I'm going to sound like some pathetic douche, but are you sure this isn't a dream?" If it was, could I expect a dream Josie to answer honestly?

Bringing our entwined hands to her mouth, Josie brushed her lips over my knuckles. I felt that soft touch all the way down into my freezing toes. "This is real."

Even if it wasn't, that was okay. I just wouldn't wake up. When her mouth moved away from my hand, I half sighed, half groaned. "Damn, because a dream would be good right now."

"Why's that?" she asked in the midst of a yawn.

"Because then I could do all the things I'm holding myself back from doing to you and not have to feel guilty or reserved about any of it," I teased. I was only partly teasing.

"I'll take real over a dream any day."

I thought about that for one moment. "With you, Joze, they're the same thing."

chapter TEN

JESSE MIGHT HAVE been the one who took Josie to Homecoming our freshman year, but I was the first one to ask her. Well, I was the first one who'd *tried* to ask her. She didn't even see my method of asking before Jesse showed up after school with his stupid smile, holding a sign at her locker that said something lame like . . . *You? Me? Homecoming? Please?*

I'd been pissed about two things that day. First was that Jesse had swooped in out of nowhere and asked her. I didn't have a clue he liked Josie *that* way. Jess and I had been inseparable for years, so that I hadn't known he liked the same girl I did, the one who was just as inseparable with the two of us, blindsided me. Josie wasn't Jesse's. She was mine. I'd met her first; she'd sat by me on the bus; I'd punched Roy Watkins in the nose when he called her names; I'd chased off Ryan Spitz when he made moves on her in fifth grade. Josie was supposed to go to Homecoming with me, not Jesse. She was supposed to fall in love with me, not him.

I was also pissed that she would never see how I'd tried to ask her. I'd taken hours to make the necklace dangling on her bedpost, and I had to rush over to her place to sneak it back out since she got a date to Homecoming. And it wasn't me. She'd never know I wanted to ask her either. I couldn't tell her because even if she would have gone with me, when she agreed to go with Jesse, I knew—even as a fifteen-year-old—that he was the better pick by a landslide. If Jesse liked her and she liked him, her future was a lot brighter than it could have been with me. That day sucked.

Actually, there was a third thing that had pissed me the hell off that day. Jesse didn't even go to the same school as us. He was home schooled for crying out loud, and he still had the balls to walk through the halls, stop at her locker, and ask her to *our* school's dance. Ballsy. It was the first time I'd wanted to sock Jesse in the nose. Not because he'd done anything wrong, but because I had. By waiting too long and being too big of a piece of shit.

I didn't deserve her, but I didn't need the reminder of what she deserved every time my best friend recapped a date with me. Jesse and Josie took a few years before they made things "official," but I don't know what took them so long. That freshman homecoming dance made it obvious to me and everyone else that Josie was Jesse's and vice versa.

Those were the memories haunting my dreams the past couple of weeks I'd spent with Josie. Those were the images that flashed through my mind while I held her every night. We took turns sneaking into each other's bedrooms, and so far, her parents were none the wiser. I'd managed to be a good boy and do nothing but hold her. Okay, *once* I'd barely brushed her chest. But it was just barely and only once. Keeping my hands, dick, and everything in between to myself was like earning sainthood. At least in my book. I had yet to learn if it had earned it in Josie's, but I hoped she'd give me some sort of progress report. Soon. I was keeping myself together with frequent cold showers and just as frequent self-servicing sessions, but a man could only take so many showers and so much jerking off before he lost his mind.

I was maybe one or two of either away from losing mine.

Last night's dream was that first homecoming dance. Josie had been there with Jesse, and I was there with some girl whose name or face I couldn't even remember. Probably because I'd barely looked at her the whole night. My gaze stayed on Josie. Her smile for Jesse, the pretty blue dress she wore for him too, and the way her arms wrapped around his neck and her hips swayed softly when they slow danced. Every time her gaze shifted my way and she smiled at me, it took everything inside of me to stay where I was and not pry her out of Jesse's arms. Not taking what I wanted when I wanted it went against everything I'd known, but I knew, even back then, that Josie deserved more. So I'd stayed with my date and felt like I was losing a little bit of myself every time Josie danced with Jesse. Every song took her that much farther out of my reach.

The dance had been almost over, the music ending and couples trickling out of the gymnasium. My date was making out in the corner with some guy—not that I cared —and Jesse had just left Josie's side to head to the bathroom, and I saw my opportunity. I knew it wouldn't last, but I'd realized that, from then on, I'd only have Josie in stolen, fleeting moments.

Before I'd made up my mind, I was heading her way. She was leaning into the bleachers, waiting for Jesse. I realized that I'd give everything to have her one day waiting for me like she was him. I made a quick stop at the

DJ's, begged him to play one last special request, and once he'd reluctantly agreed, I went to Josie. I didn't say a word; I don't think I even smiled. All I did was grab her hands and pull her back onto the gym floor as Garth Brooks' "The Dance" started to play.

"What are you doing, Garth?" she'd asked, giving me a careful but a genuine smile.

"Stealing you away," I'd replied.

"Jesse's coming right back." She'd sounded like she was putting up an argument for why the whole last dance thing wasn't a good idea, but her body wasn't. She kept coming with me, her hands planted in mine.

When we'd reached the middle of the floor, I drew her close and looked her in the eyes. "Finders keepers."

That night, that dance, *that* girl . . . had messed me up something fierce. In good ways, but mostly in bad ways. I had to watch the girl I'd grown up wanting be happy and in love with my best friend. The three of us still hung out, but nothing was the same after that dance. For Jesse and Josie, for Jesse and me, and for Josie and me as well. Everything changed in one night, and all I remember thinking was how badly I wanted to go back in time to the first time I set eyes on her on that bus and blurt, *Choose me. Be mine. I know we're only in kindergarten, but promise you'll go with me to Homecoming our freshman year. Be happy and find love with me.*

Those were the thoughts I was lost in when the chute flew open. Bluebell threw me with his first buck out of the gate. At least when I hit the ground, it was on my left side. My right side had already taken so many blows, I would be black and blue. I muttered a curse, sat up, and threw my hat. I'd gone from staying on four seconds last month to barely staying on two this month. Eight seconds of glory was not my friend.

"You spend any more time rolling in the dirt, and you're going to turn into a pig," Jason hollered from his perch on the fence.

I wanted to introduce him and his smiling pretty-boy face to my left hook, but I'd worked too hard lately to ruin it. Jason wasn't worth it. Since I couldn't let my fists do the talking, I let my talking take the jabs. "I thought your mom and sister already told you—I am a pig." I lifted a brow and grinned cockily.

Shooting me a scowl, Jason leapt down and followed the other guys leaving the arena. "Excuse us, Black. The *real* bull riders are going to get a few drinks before getting laid."

"Just so you know," I hollered after him while standing, "your hand and imagination don't qualify as getting laid!"

I knew he heard me, but he didn't reply. Probably because I was right. That guy was getting laid about as frequently as I was lately. Which was a whole lotta nada. When I'd told Jesse how long I'd gone without sex after promising him I was up to the task—mostly—of being his best man, he was silent for a whole ten seconds before breaking into a fit of laughter that went another ten seconds. I guess me going weeks without getting laid was one of the funniest things he'd ever heard, but I wasn't laughing. Neither was my dick.

"You want me to fetch you a bandage? Maybe an aspirin? A tissue?" Will crossed the arena, shaking his head. "It looks like you need all three, but all I really want to give you is a swift kick in the ass."

"Your damn bull's inflicted enough damage, so it's only fair you have a go at me, too. Take your best shot." I patted my ass at Will.

"As much as I'd love to kick it, I'd rather see that ass of yours stay on a bull for a whole eight seconds. Hell, I'd settle for the old four-second routine you had going a few weeks back."

"And I'm paying you good money why? Coach," I added with some sarcasm.

"To make what used to be a good bull rider into a fucking great one."

"Hoorah," I grumbled with a weak salute. I'd been a decent bull rider, but I wasn't anywhere close to "good" anymore. If Will thought "great" was even an option for me, he'd been knocked in the head too many times.

"Son, you can be as big a smart-ass as you want, but it doesn't change the fact that you came to me because you know I can help you be better." I dusted myself off and lifted my eyebrows. Will chuckled. "Well, and you came to me because, in my day, I was one of the best. You don't become the best without learning from one of them, right?"

"It seems the only title I'm capable of winning after training with the best is 'the worst.'"

Will seldom found my humor funny. And by seldom, I meant never. His face ironed out. "Any time you're ready to shut up and let me do what you're paying me to do, I'm ready." I clamped my mouth shut and waited. "You're one hell of a rider. That's as obvious as it is that you've convinced yourself you're not. You come from good stock. Your daddy and his daddy before him were championship riders until a couple of accidents and a whole hell of a lot of booze got in their ways."

"Thank you for bringing up the family tree. Always a thrill hearing about the line of assholes I came from."

Will stuck his finger into my chest and then my face. "The point I'm trying to get through your thick head is that you've got bull riding in your blood. That's a point in your corner these others pretenders would sell their soul for." After tapping me a few more times, he leaned back a bit. "But that's not where your talent stops. You're a hard worker, and you've got an intuition that few people in this sport have. I saw you ride back when you used to still be on top of that bull when the buzzer went off. You moved before the bull did every time, like you knew exactly what that animal would do a split second before he did. You have the intuition. You've got the golden ticket. It's a hell of a shame you seem to have lost it."

My mind went to a dark place. "I have a knack for losing things."

"Listen, son, I don't have a psychology degree, and even if I did, you're not paying me to work on your head. You're paying me to keep you on that bull, but in my professional opinion"—I gave Will a look. *Professional opinion . . .* no psychology degree, my ass. Will tapped my temple—"you need to fix whatever's going on up in there before you'll get back to your eight seconds of glory."

"If I spend all of my time fixing what's wrong up here"—I drilled my finger into my temple—"I'll be dead of old age before I'm on a bull again."

Will nodded, studying me. "It's like you're restless, son. So damn restless you can't even manage to stay in the same spot for eight seconds. Whatever it is or whoever it is that's messing with your head, you either need to let it go or grab hold of it. Once you figure that out, you're going to be unstoppable. You've got what it takes. It's in your blood and you've put the sweat and tears into it, so don't let that God-given and God-taken ability go without a fight. Find that thing or that person that puts you at peace, and you'll remember how to stay on the bull again." Will went from straight-up preaching to turning his back and heading out of the arena.

"Thanks for the gentle, not-at-all confusing words of wisdom!" I shouted. "Doctor Will."

He didn't reply. He didn't stop. He'd said what he needed to and kept going. I was ready to pack up my gear and get the hell out of there so I could get back to the Gibsons'—and Josie's and my bedtime ritual—when a loud rattling from a certain bull that'd worked its way into one of the chutes changed my plans.

After retrieving my hat from across the arena, I marched toward Bluebell with determination and a steely glare that damn bull returned. I didn't know who hated the other more, me or Bluebell, but the hate feelings were definitely mutual. I hadn't made it to the underbelly of life by making good choices. However, I hadn't made it to the underbelly of life *alive* by making really bad choices either. What I was about to do might have qualified as a really bad choice, though.

But right then, I didn't care. All I could think about was me, a bull, and eight seconds.

Someone had left the gate from the holding pen to the chutes open, explaining how Bluebell had made his way into one of them. What I couldn't explain was *why* he chose to go into one. All of the bulls needed at least some —or a lot of—encouragement to slide into the chutes. But

Bluebell . . . hell, the bull had worked its way into one of its own accord, and he practically had a smile on his frothy, ugly mug. Damn bulls. If they weren't part of the deal, I'd want nothing to do with a single one of them.

Sliding my hat on, I climbed the gate and managed to work the bull strap back into position. God, I was an idiot. Bull riding might be an individual sport, but it required a team of people to actually carry out. Mainly because it took everything the rider had just to stay on. Forget about throwing open the gate, prodding the bull out if it needed it, distracting it when the cowboy flew off, and coaxing it down into the holding pen. I'd been told more than once that I had the ego of ten men and the stupidity of twenty. Let's hope the ego was riding that night, not the stupidity.

Bluebell snorted as I crawled on. Once I had a good grip, I grabbed the rope that opened the gate and got ready to pull it. Before I did that, I cleared my head. It took a few seconds, long enough for Bluebell to let out another series of snorts, but finally, my head was empty. No dreams, thoughts, or memories of Josie. I was Josie free. Time to ride. I pulled the gate at the same time I opened my eyes. The first thing I saw when they opened? Josie. The second thing I saw? The floor of the arena.

I hit hard. Harder than the times before, and I'd barely made it out of the gates. I'd gone from bad to being an insult to the sport.

"Holy shit! Please tell me you're not dead!"

I wasn't sure which was more comforting: knowing I hadn't conjured up some imaginary Josie or that I still had use of my legs. "Not dead. Not yet." I spit out more dirt as I sat up.

"Not paralyzed, mortally wounded, or internally

bleeding either?" Josie stood across the arena on the other side of the fence with a look of horror on her face. She'd seen me ride plenty, but riding a bull was a hell of a lot different than cartwheeling off of one.

"Now, Joze, why would you be so concerned about me being paralyzed? Is there something of mine you might be interested in keeping in good working order?" Even giving her a tilted grin hurt. Once I finally managed to stay on that bull for eight seconds, I would eat Bluebell steak for a straight year.

"I can tell you what I wouldn't mind no longer being in such fine working order," she replied with a tight smile. "That part of you you think is a sense of humor. It's not funny. Or cute. Or even ironic. So give it a rest."

Josie and I'd been together for two weeks, or we'd been together trying to figure out if we could make it work "together," and as much as she was a pain in my ass sometimes and I was a pain in her ass all the time, I was glad that part of us hadn't changed. Giving each other a hard time was the only constant in our years of knowing each other. Well, I'd had one other constant, but I wasn't ready to share that with her just yet.

"Whatever you say, Joze." Gritting my teeth, I got my knees beneath me and struggled to a stand. For a notoriously tough son of a bitch, I was sure taking a beating. I felt like one of my ribs might have been cracked, but that was as frequent an occurrence as anyone else stubbing their big toe. Josie must have seen the pain somewhere in my eyes or expression because in one swift movement, she was climbing the fence and throwing her leg over.

"Hold it for one hot second!" I yelled, rushing toward her. Cracked rib be damned. "Would you please think twice before leaping into an enclosed area where the orneriest, meanest bull this side of Montana is wandering around?" I glanced at Bluebell—who was just standing down a ways, not in a hurry to go into the holding pen—staring at me with those black beady eyes. I hated that bull. "Go on! Get going!" I clapped and took a few steps in Bluebell's direction, hoping to encourage him to get going. All he did was stare before tilting his head. On top of being mean, bulls were stupid, too. That's why people ate those critters and didn't keep them as pets. "Go! Come on, get out of here!" I banged on the side of the fence, but it did a whole lot of nothing.

Josie's hand grabbed my shoulder, and she gave it a gentle squeeze. I'm not sure if it had been her intention, but it silenced me. Looking at Bluebell, Josie waved her hand. "Shoo." One sweet word, one soft wave, and that bull did a one-eighty. It jogged down the arena until it ended in the holding pen.

Shaking my head, I headed down to close the holding pen gate. "I didn't know you were a bull whisperer."

"You should have," she replied.

"Why's that?"

"You haven't managed to run me off like you have everyone else, have you?"

I double-checked the gate to make sure it was closed before heading back to her. "And you're saying that's because of your bull-slash-Garth whispering skills?"

"That's one of the many reasons, yeah." She finishing crawling over the top of the fence and jumped down.

"And the others?"

"Too many to list," she said, coming toward me with that concerned look.

"I'm okay. Really," I added when she didn't look convinced.

"I guess this explains how you've been getting so banged up." Stopping in front of me, Josie investigated my face with a grimace. Probably because it was coated with mud, blood, and sweat. "I was starting to worry you'd found a woman to fulfill your sadomasochism fantasy. At least I can put my mind at ease about the other woman part."

"And the other part?"

She ran her eyes down me then back up. The rest of my body matched my face. "The sadomasochism part is pretty obvious, but it's just as obvious the bull is taking it out on you, not some woman." I threw a glare toward Bluebell down in the pen. "What are you doing here, Garth? Why didn't you tell me?" Josie grabbed my hat and dusted if off before replacing it.

"You didn't ask."

"I didn't ask because I assumed you were working late at Willow Springs. I was heading into town just now, and guess whose truck I saw parked outside of Will Jones's bull-training arena."

"You seemed surprised. I'm a bull rider. I ride bulls. Why is it so shocking that I'd be training at a bull-riding facility?" I wasn't upset by her questions, just as she wasn't upset by my responses. We were merely curious.

"I don't know. I just thought with your dad dying, and what happened to him bull riding"—she crossed her arms and shrugged—"I thought you didn't want the same kind of life."

"What does my dad's life and how he chose to live it have to do with mine?" I grabbed her hand and led her toward the chute. I had to get my things, and then I was out of there. I'd seen more than enough of that arena for one night.

"Just that you're twenty-one, riding bulls, and drink like a fish." I lifted my eyebrows, making her shake her head. "You *used* to drink like a fish—all of two weeks ago. I mean, your dad and mom had you pretty much just out of high school, right?"

I nodded before sliding out of my protective vest. They'd been high school sweethearts, minus the sweet part. Well, and minus the heart part, too. They'd been something, and their something had created me. I was a preschooler by the time Clay could walk into a bar and order a beer.

"And Clay was close to your age when that bull busted his leg up, right?"

I nodded once more, tugging off my gloves. I didn't like where she was going. I didn't like being compared to Clay, and while I knew Josie wasn't doing it out of malice, that she was comparing us made me uneasy. I never wanted to be compared to Clay, unless it was to say I was totally opposite. That Josie, the person I cared about most in the world, was comparing us made my stomach turn. "Yeah, you've got Clay Walker's life story down. He was born, he got his girlfriend knocked up, and I was the result. He was a high school dropout at eighteen. A bull over in Bozeman came down so hard on his leg it shattered, ending his bull riding career and, to him, his whole life. Fast forward a couple of decades, and he died inside of a white-trash trailer because he was so passed-out drunk the whole thing going up in flames around him didn't rouse him." I'd managed to keep my voice calm, but I punched the metal gate at the end. Too much emotion charging through me.

Josie grabbed the hand I'd just used to punch the gate and sighed when she saw a couple of the knuckles open and bleeding. "How are you doing with that? You haven't said anything since Clay's funeral. You do know I'm here whenever you need to talk to someone? You know I want to be that person you come to when you have to talk to someone, right?"

Josie dabbed the sleeve of her shirt against my knuckles before I could pull it away. I didn't want to ruin her nice clothes. "I certainly don't miss dodging whiskey bottles or fists, that's for sure."

Josie brought my fist to her mouth and kissed it. "But what about the other things? Isn't there something you miss?"

"There wasn't anything else to miss."

"Garth—"

I gave my head a swift shake. "No. You've known me for long enough to know I'm not the person who likes to talk this kind of shit out. I accept the hand I've been dealt, I deal with it, and I move on. I don't miss something or someone when they're gone. I move on."

The skin between her eyebrows came together. "What about me? You wouldn't miss me if I was gone?" Her voice was almost sad.

Whatever I was feeling made sad look like a newborn lamb. I lifted my hand to her cheek. It was the only clean part of me thanks to my gloves. "I've been saving up all my missing for you."

"Planning on leaving me after all, aren't you?" That she didn't sound or look surprised broke my heart.

"No, I'm certainly not planning on it. But no matter what happens, no matter how long or how far we take this thing, one day we're going to be separated. Whether that's because I did what I do best and screwed things up. Or whether another guy came riding in and stole you away. Or whether death separates us. One day, it'll happen . . . and because I know that day is coming, I'm glad I've saved up all my missing for you. Because I'm going to need every last ounce of it when you're gone, Joze. Every last ounce." I smiled at her, feeling like a damn fool for saying what I just had. It was true, but I wasn't the kind of guy who said that kind of truth.

Josie stepped closer and removed my hat. Lifting her other sleeve to my face, she wiped the muck and blood from it, one swipe at a time. It felt so nice having someone . . . take *care* of me that I didn't step back to save her shirt. "You do realize bull riding is something that only accelerates death separating us?"

My smile went higher. I listed a handful of reasons Josie and I could be separated one day, and the one she picked was death. It was the option I'd take too, but we had a lot of life and living before that day. With my record, going a month without screwing up royally would be considered a miracle—forget about a lifetime. "Bull riding isn't going to kill me."

"No? Because you're about two and a half bruises away from death, from the looks of it, Black."

Whenever she called me Black, I knew she was upset but trying to mask it with cynicism. She'd started calling me Black in eighth grade when she found me making out with one of her friends in the janitor's closet. "Bull riding won't kill me. If it could have, it already would have."

Lord knows it had beat me within an inch of my life lately, but that was an inch I wasn't letting go of.

"How does that saying go when it comes to bull riding?" Josie tapped her chin. "It isn't a matter of if you get hurt, it's a matter of *when* you get hurt."

"That's the one. Did you miss the part where it mentions hurt, not dead?" I unbuckled and worked off my chaps.

"No, but given your ego, that saying applies to you differently." She leaned into the chute fence and crossed her arms.

"Believe me, if I didn't have an ego bordering on insanely unhealthy, you wouldn't want me on top of a bull. A guy with self-confidence issues who still wets the bed won't last a second."

"How long were you on that bull just now?" She bit the inside of her cheek to keep from smiling.

"I'm going through a dry spell; give me a break. I've spent so much time on the back of a bull I've probably logged as many hours as a pilot a few years from retirement." I settled my hands on my hips. "And by bed-wetter-low-confidence boy not lasting a second out there, I meant his life—not an actual second on a bull."

Josie was still chewing her cheek. Obviously she found what I was saying rather funny. "Okay, point taken. As much fun as this is, I didn't come here to argue with you."

"What did you come here for then?" I lowered my voice and stepped toward her.

Josie's eyes rolled. "Not that. A roll in the mud and cow shit is hardly my idea of romance, but nice try."

"Damn," I muttered under my breath.

"I came here to tell you that you don't need to keep this secret from me anymore. I'm not asking you to change for me. All I'm asking is that you be the best Garth Black you can be."

"Oh, that's all. No big deal."

She continued, not letting my commentary stall her. "Bull riding is a part of you. I get that. It might scare the shit out of me, and when I actually watch you ride, I feel like I'm about to vomit, but I *get* it. I don't have to like you doing it in order to support you riding on the back of a two thousand-pound beast that would prefer to stomp you to death than have you on its back"— it was my turn to chew on my cheek to keep from smiling—"I guess."

"Now that right there, Joze, those words were the stuff of romance in my book."

"You have a book of romance?" Her eyes twinkled. "It sure doesn't show." That time, she couldn't keep from smiling.

"Oh, it doesn't, does it?" I teased, pinching her sides until she was laughing. "I can be romantic. I can't believe you'd say that I'm incapable of it."

Josie was still laughing, but she managed to get out some words. "Your idea of romance is buying a girl a cheap beer before jumping into bed with her."

That earned her another round of torture by side pinching. "I can be romantic. Admit it." Neither of us were leaving that chute until she had. I stopped pinching her so she could catch her breath but left my hands on her waist.

"I'll admit it when you prove you're capable of it."

"And you're saying nothing I've done has proven that to you already?"

"Really? Come on. My experience with you has been

having drunken sex with you while my boyfriend was out of town, and these past couple of weeks where the only time you've touched me is when your arms are around me at night. Those are on opposite ends of the spectrum." I lifted my eyebrows. "And not on the romance spectrum."

I dropped my hands from her waist and thought about that. I didn't have to think long—Josie was right. Whatever relationship Josie and I had been mixed up in through the years, romance had never been a cornerstone. Hell, it had never even been a pebble on our path. "Well, shit."

"Just in case you're taking notes, *well, shit* doesn't qualify as romance either." Josie blew out a slow breath and leaned her head into the fence behind her.

Did she really have that little faith that I knew how to be or could learn to be romantic? On my list of priorities in a relationship, romance wasn't high . . . but it obviously was on hers. Which made it important to me. I waited for her eyes to meet mine. When they did, mine dropped to her mouth. Wetting my lips, I approached her, one slow step at a time. Her mouth parted just a bit when I was a step away and, when my chest bumped into her, pressing her harder into the fence, it parted some more. I reminded myself to go slow, to be purposeful—all new concepts to me.

I didn't stop pressing until our whole bodies were locked against one another. The breath coming in and out of her parted mouth picked up its pace. Lifting my arms, I braced them on either side of her head, and when I knew I would kiss her if I kept watching her mouth, my eyes shifted to hers. Her eyes were wide, her pupils dilated— signs that whatever I was doing, I was doing it right. I wasn't used to looking in a woman's eyes. When I'd been with a woman in the past, I kept my eyes closed to pretend I was with someone else.

But I didn't have to pretend anymore, because the girl I'd seen when I closed my eyes was standing in front of me. "Josie?" I lowered my face until it was level with hers—until I could feel the warmth of her breath on my lips.

"Yes?" she said with a breathlessness that told me she felt as close to coming apart as I did.

"I want you to . . ." I lowered my voice and enjoyed the feel of her chest rising and falling against mine. "I need you to . . ." She sunk her teeth into her lower lip and trembled. I would have let myself smile if I didn't have to stay focused. "Can I have . . ." I swore I could feel her heartbeat hammering so hard I was worried it might not be healthy for her. Instead of drawing it out any longer for fear of her going into cardiac arrest—or me doing the same—I glanced down at what she still had gripped in her hand. "My hat." My voice returned to its normal volume and tone. Josie's face went from wide-eyed and flat to glaring and lined in less than a second. "Can I have my hat?" I finally let myself have that grin I'd been holding back.

"Unbelievable," she said with a shake of her head. She dropped my hat back on my head.

"Thank you." I only grinned wider when she thumped the top of my hat, pushing it over my eyes.

"You better hope I don't lock you out of my room tonight."

"But then who would rock you to sleep and warm your feet and give you sweet dreams?" I adjusted my hat and winked at her. She wasn't mad, but she was something. She was something that I was, too. Wound so tight for each other that I didn't doubt either of us would mind if we wound up horizontal and rolling through the mud and cow shit. I took a few steps back.

"I hear a warm cup of milk works wonders." Slugging me gently in the stomach, she headed out of the chute.

I watched her walk away until she was halfway across the arena, partly because I didn't know what to say next, but mainly because Josie had one hell of an ass. When she walked with that annoyed anger, her hips swayed just so. Damn, it was one hell of a sight.

"Hey, Joze!" I called out. She slowed, but she didn't stop. "Taking it slow. I'd say I nailed that hurdle." She gave me a *So?* look over her shoulder. "So what's next?"

She gave a huff. "Not taking it *too* slow."

I'd just driven Josie Gibson wild with want. I'd turned her on in about every way a guy could turn a girl on. If she hadn't been watching me, I might have done a flip. I'd turned on my fair share of women, but Josie wasn't just another woman I was hoping to get into bed later. I wanted to turn Josie on for a million other reasons, reasons I hadn't known existed until I'd seen that look in her eyes and felt her breath catch in her mouth. "So it would be okay if I finally took you out on an official date now?"

"A date? Do you even know what one of those is?" Josie stopped when she reached the fence and turned to look at me.

I shrugged. "I've been doing a little research—asking around. I think I've got the basics, and I was hoping you'd help me fill in the rest." It was true. I was a twenty-one-year-old man who didn't know what a real date or true dating was. It was all new to me, like so much of what I'd experienced with Josie lately. I'd enjoyed every step of the journey.

When Josie had climbed to the top of the fence, she smiled at me. "I can help you fill in the rest."

chapter ELEVEN

JOSIE AND I were on a date. Like a real one. It might have only been in the bed of my truck at the local drive-in theatre, and her parents might not have known about it, and we might not have even kissed yet . . . but it was the best fucking night of my life.

Josie had met me at the vacant gas station on the highway a few miles north of Willow Springs after I got off work. She showed up in that same dress she'd worn the first night I'd stayed with the Gibsons. She'd gone and curled her hair and everything. Josie looked great no matter what she wore or what time of day it was—even at five in the morning when she had bed head and sleepy eyes—but that night . . . Damn, my throat ran dry the instant she stepped out of that huge truck of hers. It hadn't been the first time she'd taken my breath away, but it was the first time I got to put my arms around her right after. It was the first time she hadn't taken my breath away only to slip into the arms of someone else.

It was pretty much the best night ever. And we'd only been ten seconds into it.

The Mountain-View Drive-in theatre was normally only open on weekends in the summer, but they always did a special showing the week of spring break when all the kids were out of school and looking to do something. Also known as looking to get into trouble. The drive-in and I had shared plenty of troublemaking times. Thankfully, the same staff from a couple summers ago wasn't still there. Otherwise, I never would have gotten in.

The movie had been playing for a while, but I couldn't say what was playing or who was in it. I hadn't been able to take my eyes off of Josie. I'd replaced the old mattress in the bed—that had seen its fair share of wear and tear—with an inflatable mattress from the sporting goods store in town. Easier to clean and not so . . . *used*. I figured Josie would appreciate that, even if she never would have said anything about it. It wasn't the first time we'd shared a bed, but it was the first time we'd shared a bed on a date. I knew better than to believe we'd be using my inflatable bed the way I was used to utilizing a bed, but I hoped we'd get somewhere. When all I'd done was hold her hand or have my arms around her, even a small kiss was a big deal. So yeah, I was hoping for a kiss. Not expecting one, but definitely hoping for one.

"The movie's up there you know," Josie said, glancing over at me. She knew I'd been staring at her. That was fine, I wanted her to know. I wanted her to know I couldn't *not* stare at her.

"Why would I want to watch a movie when I've got you right here?" I grinned at her and scooted a little closer. Scooting closer and a grin couldn't hurt a guy's chance of getting a kiss. With my arm running down hers, I noticed something. "Shit, Josie, you're shivering." I'd already given her my jacket, and I'd brought every blanket I could snatch from the Gibsons' house without arousing suspicion, so I sat up and started unbuttoning my shirt to give to her.

"No, don't do that. I'm fine. I don't want to undress you one layer at a time." She zipped my coat up higher and burrowed into it.

"Believe me, I have no problem with that. None whatsoever. You feel free, anytime, every time, to undress me layer by layer until you are warm and satisfied." I unbuttoned another one to prove my point.

Her hand reached out to stop mine. "Keep your shirt on, Romeo."

"Why? When we both know you like me best with my shirt off."

She wiped her hand over my grin, which did nothing but make it grow. "Wrong. I like you best with your ego off. Wanna try again?"

I was about to reply when another shiver ran through Josie. I suppose picking a drive-in movie for a date smack in the middle of March in Montana wasn't wise. *Better luck next time, Black.* Pushing away my hopes for what could-have-been, I got ready to stand. "Come on, Joze. Let's get you out of here before you freeze." I'd be sure to pick somewhere that didn't make my date chatter for our next one.

"No, I don't want to go," she said, shaking her head. "I'm enjoying myself."

My forehead lined. "You're shivering yourself." I wasn't cold, but I was probably too focused on Josie to notice the cold, and I'd likely built up an immunity after sleeping in my truck for a few months. I wanted to stay because I wanted to be with her, but not at the expense of her getting hypothermia.

"I'm not leaving, and that's that. Can we get on with our date now?" She brought the blankets up under her chin and returned her attention to the movie.

I sat there, watching her again, and smiled. Josie wasn't a laid-back, easy-going woman. She had some serious spunk and fight. Some guys might have been intimidated by that, but Josie's spunk was what caught my attention years ago. The fight in her had kept my attention. She was the only thing that had my attention. I needed to do something right then so badly my muscles ached from holding myself back. Taking a deep breath, I bolstered up my courage. "I might not have any more blankets, but there are other ways to get you warm."

Josie's eyes flashed my way. "What other ways?"

I scooted down until I was propped up on an elbow beside her. My heart was already thundering, and I hadn't even touched her. "Well, there are lots of other ways, I guess . . . but I had *one* particular way in mind."

"What 'particular' way is that?" Her voice was a few notes high, and then she licked her lips. She knew.

I leaned in closer until my mouth was just barely above hers. "This way is what I . . ." The fight I'd been battling all night, all month, the past fifteen years, finally became too much. My mouth covered hers, and when it did, Josie let out a small gasp. Shoving my hat off, she weaved her hand through my hair, and pulled me closer.

Oh, dear god . . . Her mouth moving against mine was enough to send me straight through the roof, but then her mouth parted and her tongue pressed into mine, and I almost lost it. Lost whatever I'd been holding on to, whatever had been weighing on me and holding me back. I almost lost it all with one kiss from one girl. If that didn't make a man stop and reexamine his life, I don't know what did.

She continued to kiss me like she was finally letting go of everything she'd been holding back while I tried to keep up and hold on to everything so I didn't let myself go . . . all the way. Because that was the place I wanted to go with Josie. I'd already unzipped the jacket of mine she had on, but I craved more. One hand was twitching, ready to go for the hem of her dress. The other hand wanted to close in on her chest. I drilled my twitching hand into the mattress above her shoulder, bracing myself, but when Josie's body rocked under mine, sliding so she was directly beneath me, my hand trying to reach for her breasts didn't need to try any longer because it was there.

"Shit, Joze," I panted between her unyielding kisses. "I'm sorry. I'm trying to behave." I squeezed my eyes closed, separated my mouth from hers for a moment—just long enough to gain some traction of control—and forced my hand away from a very nice part of her body.

"It's okay. You can touch me." She looked up at me. "I want you to. Just because we're kissing and touching and . . ." Josie's hips rocked gently, and I was fairly certain if she did that again, I'd go cross-eyed. "Let's touch. Let's make out. Let's do all of those things you've held back from us doing." I lifted an eyebrow and held onto my last scrap of willpower. "Okay, so not *everything* everything, but just because we're not ready to go there tonight doesn't mean we can't do more than kiss." Grabbing my hand, she moved it until it covered her chest again. She lowered my other hand until it curved around the outside of her thigh. As if that wasn't enough, Josie's hands slid inside of my shirt, one crawling up my back, the other sliding up my stomach. "Kiss me." Her lips pressed into the corner of my mouth gently. "Touch me." Her hand curled into me, her fingernails digging into my skin in a way that made me gasp. Smiling at me, she added, "Preferably both at once."

I had to give my head a swift shake and pull both of my hands away from the spots she'd adhered them before I could reply. "I'm glad you've got that much faith in your willpower, but I don't have that much in mine." Josie had taken my breath away again, but in a way I liked even more than the first way. "I'd love to keep touching and kissing. Screw the movie . . . But, Joze, I don't know how to hit the brakes once I get going. I don't know how to pull back when I'm supposed to or when you want me to. I don't know how to stop." I hated admitting that to her, but I knew the only way we would make us work was if I was honest with her.

"Well you haven't exactly had a lot of practice, have you?" She smiled and pulled the hand on my stomach out of my shirt so she could cover my cheek.

"Try *no* practice." I knew I should probably roll off of Josie and go ice my nuts, but the way she was threading my hair through her fingers as she studied me with that playful look in her eyes made it difficult. Actually, it made it impossible.

"You want to get some?" Josie asked. My immediate response was a wide grin to which she gave a sigh. "Practice. You want to get some *practice*."

"And this practice entails . . .?" I didn't really give a damn as long as she stayed right where she was and kept running her fingers through my hair.

"Touching. Kissing." She lifted her eyebrows. "Fully clothed."

I exaggerated a grumble, but I was anything but

disappointed. I'd wanted to touch and kiss Josie Gibson for so long, I didn't care if she told me I had to do it wearing Saran Wrap. The one time I had touched her intimately, I hadn't fully enjoyed it. She might have been drunk, but I wasn't. I knew what I was doing, and I knew the girl I was touching wasn't mine. The girl I wanted to love loved someone else. My best friend.

"I would love to kiss"—I dropped my mouth to her neck and skimmed my lips down it until her skin erupted in goose bumps—"and I would love to touch"—my hand combed into her hair, my fingers trailing through it and giving it a light tug that made her gasp—"you as long and as much as you'll let me." Moving my face over hers, I felt the skin between my brows crease. "But you're right. I don't have a lot of experience knowing when to quit. Or how to quit. These past couple of weeks, I've taken things slow because I kept my hands and mouth to myself, but now . . . Now that I'm touching and kissing you, it won't be as easy to take things slow. I'll need you to tell me when to stop. And you have my permission to knee me in the balls if I don't. I want to make this work, but I need your help." Saying all that when my breathing was already erratic should have earned me some sort of award.

"You've got my help," she said. "Now would you stop worrying so much and kiss me already? I've been waiting weeks for you to finally cross that line, and now that you have, I'd like to get back to it please."

Letting one hand slip under my bulky jacket, I formed it around her waist. "You know I can't resist you when you say please."

She winked. "I know." Tossing the covers over our heads, Josie's mouth reconnected with mine at the same time her hand returned to my stomach. Her fingers traced patterns into my skin as her mouth played with mine, sucking and nipping and smoothing and all of the things I didn't know could make a person's toes curl. Before, a kiss had been nothing more than a prelude, a stepping stone, a necessary evil. A means to an end. I'd never paid attention to a kiss because it had never been anything more than a segue to sex.

But that kiss, with that girl . . . that was something else entirely. If a person could only choose one memory to take with them into their next life, that would be the one I'd take. That would be the one I'd carry through all of my lifetimes. I didn't need to have lived them all to realize that memory I was making with Josie was the thing men sold eternities for. It was the thing I'd sell mine for.

I managed to keep my hands on her waist and in the bend of her neck, and as each second passed, it became easier and easier to keep them from straying into new-found "danger" zones. A few weeks ago, those areas had been my primary targets. Now they were danger zones. Irony was really making me its bitch.

When Josie's fingers trailed along my belt line, skimming just below the surface, I let out something between a sigh and a groan before returning the favor. She might have been in a dress, but fingers skimming the area just south of the navel packs a powerful punch even through clothing. When she moaned around the kiss we were tangled up in, I came close to hiking up her dress, lowering my fly, and making her moan again and louder. Then, like she knew the internal war I was fighting, Josie's mouth slowed and her hand moved away from the sensitive skin. She knew what she was doing. She knew how to "make out" and when and how to tap the brakes. That was a relief since everything inside of me was dying to punch the gas. A minute ago, I'd been in control. Thirty seconds and one moan from Josie later, I was utterly out of control. Right then, I was back to having a grip. I was returning her slow, soft kiss when something thumped the outside of my truck, jolting us.

"Hey, Black, why'd you pay to come to a drive-in if all you were going to do was fuck your date?"

Josie froze as my eyes narrowed. "Watch your mouth, Mason," I ordered, peeking my head out from beneath the blankets just enough so he could see my murderous expression without catching a glimpse of Josie. I didn't mind Colt finding out about Josie and me, but I wasn't sure if she was ready yet. Even if she was, that probably wasn't the best time.

"What? It's not like *fuck* isn't your second language and we all know that whoever that girl is beneath you is a far cry from a lady, so don't tell me to watch my mouth again, asshole."

I was ready to jump out of the back of my truck to see if Mason had such a loud mouth when I stood toe-to-toe with him, but Josie grabbed my belt buckle and tugged me back down.

"Hey, sweetheart, you do realize you're with Garth Black, right? The guy who wouldn't know commitment if it crawled up his ass and took residence."

Josie gave my belt buckle another tug, and I could almost hear her thoughts—they were that strong. *Why would you want to go out there with him when you can be in here with me?* Exactly. No reason I'd rather go flick Colt's hat off his head when Josie's body was beneath

190

mine and keeping it warm. "At least that's not what's shoved up my ass most nights of the week."

Colt raised his middle finger at me as he tapped my truck again. "Way to go all out and get your truck washed for your date tonight. This thing used to be black, right?"

If Colt thought he could teach me a thing or two about trucks, he must have forgotten which state was listed on his birth certificate. "I'll get around to washing my truck, Mason. When it rains." Josie was still covered and quiet, but when Colt took a few steps closer, I shifted. In addition to the blankets, I was blocking her from his view. "It's a truck, god dammit. You don't have to wash it and wax it and tweak its headlights to get it to perform."

"Whatever you say, Black. Whatever you say." Colt shook his head and walked toward the concessions. "Enjoy your night."

I watched him until he was out of sight before twisting around and sliding the blankets back. "I really hate that guy."

Josie wore an amused expression. "You don't say."

"Why in the hell did he have to be here tonight? My night was about perfect until he showed up with that overly white smile and tanned face."

"I didn't know he was coming, but he said a couple of his brothers would be in town for the weekend. Given the limited choices for entertainment, I suppose it's not a huge surprise we'd all end up in the same place." Josie hadn't let go of my belt buckle, but instead of tugging on it forcefully, she was tugging on it playfully. "Do you want to talk about Colt the rest of the night or would you like to get back to what we were doing?"

Damn, there was a special place in heaven for a girl

who could tell you what she wanted without a hint of shame. "Colt who?" My hands found places on her as I shifted back on top.

Then she shoved my chest away and pivoted on top of me. Josie's eyes gleamed before she lowered her mouth to mine. "My turn."

chapter**TWELVE**

IF A MAN could die from making-out exhaustion, I figured I was close. I didn't know some of the things Josie had taught me could be done with a mouth. I also didn't realize that having a woman basically hold me captive and have her way with me could be so freeing. With the addition of a bit of boob fondling and a whole bit more of Josie rocking her hips into mine, we'd had a successful, insanely-sexy-without-actual-sex make-out session. Josie was showing me all sorts of things I could do that I never would have thought possible.

The second movie had already been playing for a while when I simply had to come up for air. Or hydration. Or sustenance. Something. "Are you warm now?" I cupped her face with both hands. She certainly felt warmer. Actually, she almost looked flushed.

Her lips moved to the corner of my mouth. "I'm definitely something now." Her lips moved to the other corner. "But I wouldn't say warmer is the first thing on my mind." To prove her point, her hips slid down mine again.

I wasn't sure who, but one of us was close to giving in. An intermission was in order. Plus, the clothed grinding was nice and all, but my dick had to be close to being rubbed raw. I needed a few minutes to calm my shit down, rehydrate, and tend to my wounds. "Come on. Break time." I checked to make sure Colt wasn't in sight then grabbed Josie's hands and pulled her up.

"I thought we had one of those when you took a breath ten minutes ago." She grinned at me as she finger-combed her hair and straightened her dress.

After zipping my coat back up on her, I redid all of the buttons she'd managed to get undone on my shirt and tucked it back into my jeans before leaping over the side. "You're right. I'm weak. You are the making out champion." Josie grabbed my hands to steady herself before jumping out of the bed. "But whatever you just did to me in there, I flew past warm straight into hot. I need one of those slushie things to cool down, and I need the sugar before I go into hypoglycemic shock." Making out with Josie burned a hell of a lot of calories.

"You'd better get two so you'll have reserves." Josie grabbed my hand as we headed for the concessions. Everyone else had gotten their drinks and snacks during the real intermission, so it was mostly quiet inside. That was part of my plan. I still didn't know how Josie felt— well, after that make-out session, I knew how she *felt*—but I wasn't sure if she was ready for us to be a public item yet. As much as I wanted the whole damn town to know we were together, I also knew we would give the rumor mill enough fodder to keep its channels busy into next year. The hometown sweetheart hooks up with the trailer-trash bad boy. I didn't want Josie at the center of a bunch of malicious gossip, and the only way to protect her from that was to keep us a secret.

I opened the glass door to the concessions and let her pass through before following. "So? Since you seem to be the making out pro, how would you rate my skills? On a scale of okay to mad." I wrapped both arms around her as we wound through the concession gates.

She tapped her chin and glanced back at me. "Let's see. Your lips are swollen. My lips are swollen. My hair's a mess"—she lifted my hat for a moment—"and your hair's a huge mess."

"It's always a mess. Why do you think I rarely take that thing off?" I mumbled as we continued weaving up to the cashier.

Josie laughed then unexpectedly arched her back so her backside curved into my . . . "We stopped making out five minutes ago, and you're still . . . *excited.* And either I wet myself, or you made me just as excited."

My mouth dropped open. Josie slid her fingers beneath my chin, pushed it closed, then planted a kiss full on my lips. The pubescent male cashier looked like he was about to bust something. That made two of us.

"Damn, Josie. Saying stuff like that is not helping cool me down."

Since we'd finally made it up to the gaping cashier, Josie lifted onto her tiptoes and moved her mouth to my ear. "I don't want you cooled down. I want you back in that truck and on top of me."

A shudder ran down my back. Leaning into the counter, I locked eyes with the cashier—whose eyes were locked on Josie. "Do you sell slushies by the gallon?"

The cashier fumbled with a few cups. "This is the biggest size we've got."

"Perfect. I'll take two." One to drink and one to ice my balls with. Josie giggled and went to grab a couple of licorice ropes. "What are you so happy about?"

She was beaming. Her face was practically glowing,

and I wasn't sure if she was walking or floating. "You. Tonight." She motioned between us. "This. Everything. There's a lot to be happy about right now."

Josie. My Josie. For the first time, I felt like she actually wanted to be mine and, contrary to popular belief, I hadn't done anything to royally screw it up. I grinned back. "There's a hell of a lot to be happy about right now."

The cashier cleared his throat. "That will be twelve-fifty."

"Did you get the licorice ropes?" I asked the cashier. He nodded. "I didn't think you liked licorice, Joze."

"I don't," she replied, winding one around my wrist. "They're not for eating."

Holy shit. As if my dick needed to get any harder. The cashier was back to gaping at Josie like he was close to throwing himself at her feet and worshipping her. Get in line, jackass. The sooner I got the Josie-worshipper paid, the sooner I could figure out what Josie had in mind for us and those licorice ropes. Pulling out my wallet, I opened it and found. . . nothing. "Shit." I double-checked all of my pockets to make sure I hadn't misplaced the cash I'd gotten earlier.

"Double shit," Josie said. "I left my purse in your truck."

"I wouldn't let you pay anyways. Besides, I had money earlier . . . I just must have misplaced it." I triple-checked my wallet. The cashier shifted and gave me an impatient look when the concessions door opened and someone else filed into line. Too bad. They'd have to wait because I needed my slushies *and* licorice ropes.

"Hey, it's okay. I'm good," Josie said, setting her hand on my forearm.

"No, it's not okay." I almost threw my wallet on the ground when it came up empty a third time. Where the hell had the cash gone?

"I got it." A fifty-dollar bill slapped down on the counter as Josie froze and my jaw set.

"I don't think so." Picking up the fifty, I held it in front of Colt's face and dropped it at his boots.

"Hey, no need to be ungrateful and throw money around. This is a fifty-dollar bill." Colt picked it up and spread it out in front of my face. "I know the last time you saw one of these was when your mama was still home and turning tricks to put beans and bread on the table."

I shoved his hand and the money out of my face.

"Colt!" Josie hissed, shouldering up beside me. I was keeping it in, holding myself back, but just barely.

"Josie, what the hell are you doing here with this piece of trailer trash?" Colt crossed his arms and looked from me to her. "Oh, wait. I forgot his trailer went up in flames. Let me rephrase. Josie, what the hell are you doing here with this piece of trash?"

"Colt, so help me God . . ." Josie turned on her glare and aimed it his way.

"Just answer the question, and I'll leave you two alone." Colt took a couple of steps back as Josie glared at him.

"Answer the question? How's this for answering the question?" Stepping shoulder to shoulder with me, her hand slid inside of mine.

Colt studied our entwined hands, his face shadowing. "I thought we had a good thing going."

"It wasn't a bad thing"—her voice was cool and removed—"but we weren't *going* anywhere."

197

Colt shook his head and made his way back toward the door. "And you think that wherever Garth Black's going to take you will be so much better and farther?"

"No, I don't think that. I *know* that." Josie flashed him a big smile.

He paused with his hand on the door. "It's too bad you're going to end up another knocked-up piece of trailer trash. I thought you'd be different than the rest of these small-town girls."

Josie didn't flinch, but I sure as hell did. Leaping over every rail Josie and I'd just wove through, I didn't stop until I was a foot from Colt's face. The guy had the sense to look fearful for his life. "You'd better shut that big mouth of yours, turn around, and leave now, because I am holding on by a thread, Mason." I was trembling, but I didn't touch him. "A fucking thread."

Colt shoved the door open then glanced back at Josie. "When you're done with this guy, you know my number."

Josie made her way to me as the door slammed in my face. I glared at Colt's back until he jumped into the bed of his fancy truck where a few other guys were camped out.

"Garth?" Josie stepped in front of me with a concerned expression. "How are you doing?"

I exhaled a heavy breath and forced my fists to unclench. "I've been holding back so much tonight, I'm about to snap. That's how I'm doing."

"Yeah, you look pretty close to snapping, too. Let's get you out of here." She pushed open the door, waved a quick *sorry* at the cashier, and we walked toward my truck. Josie slipped her hand in mine, and a portion of the rage boiling just below the surface vanished. "Better?"

"Better," I replied, watching Colt's truck as we

passed it. He was with his brothers. From the way his hands were moving and his pissed off expression, he was informing them of what had just happened. When a couple of his brothers leapt up, looking outraged, I pulled Josie a little faster. I knew what hot-headed guys like the Mason brothers would do because I was hot-headeder than them all. They were going to come kick my ass for "stealing" their brother's girl.

That was fine. Whatever, they could kick my ass into the next millennium. Big whoop. What I cared about was not Josie getting mixed up in the middle of it. They wanted to teach me a lesson? Fine—they could do that when Josie wasn't anywhere around. I'd take a hell of a lot more than a serious beating to get to be the one Josie crawled into bed with at night.

I opened the passenger's side door for her and closed it behind her. "Are you okay if we head out now?"

"Since a certain someone kind of put a damper on it, yeah, let's go."

I crawled in beside her. From the rearview mirror, I saw Colt and his brothers motioning at my truck. If Josie wasn't with me, I would have thrown open my door, marched toward them with my arms out, and shouted some sort of challenge and profanity at them. But Josie was with me, and that made all the difference. I fired up the engine and shifted into drive.

Josie's hand rested above my knee as she scooted across the bench toward me. "Thanks for the . . . movie."

I waited for her to fasten her lap belt before moving. "That was the best damn movie I've ever seen." Checking my rearview to make sure the Mason brothers weren't tailing us, I headed for the exit.

Josie leaned her head on my shoulder. "You know what Colt said back there was a bunch of bull, right? You're not a piece of trash, and if he says that to you again, it will be me shouting about hanging on by a thread."

I gripped the steering wheel harder, trying to vent some of my pent-up anger on it. "I know what I am, and I'm okay with that. I know to the Colt Masons of the world, I am a piece of trash. I give a shit what he thinks about me. All I care about is that the Josie Gibsons don't think I am." I wrapped an arm around her shoulders and drew her closer. "At least not anymore."

"I never thought you were trash. Never." She shook her head against me. "I might have thought I hated you for a while, but I never thought that."

If that was true, she was one of the only people who didn't associate the Blacks with trash. Poor, redneck trash that found all of life's answers at the bottom of a bottle of whiskey. I kissed the top of her head because that was the only response I was capable of.

"Do you remember that party we had at my place the summer after sixth grade? The one where we played Spin the Bottle?"

My forehead lined. Going from me being or not being a piece of trash to reminiscing about the summer we were twelve was a sudden topic change. "Yeah. That was the night you dumped orange soda down my new white shirt."

"Spilt. I *spilt* it," she clarified. "And I apologized a thousand times. Are you wanting another one?"

"It was a nice shirt," I said, faking insult.

"Fine. I'm sorry. For the one thousandth and first time."

"And for the one thousandth and first time, you're forgiven."

Josie laughed and played with one of the buttons on my shirt. "It really was a nice shirt."

"Damn straight it was. There were girls at that party, we were playing Spin the Bottle, and Clay felt moderately guilty since the night before he'd clocked me pretty good with an empty bottle of Jack." My mind drifted back in time. I'd been a whole hell of a lot more hopeful at twelve than I was at twenty-one. Even the hardened me had to admit that a few weeks with Josie was changing that though. Not totally, but enough. Hope didn't feel like such a sham anymore . . . It seemed almost *plausible* again for someone like me, with a past like mine. "But after that orange-stained mess, I gave up on color and decided black was a safer option. At least when you were around."

"I'm flattered. Thank you," she said dryly. "But do you know why I was so upset that I 'accidentally' spilled orange soda on you?"

I turned onto the highway and shrugged. "You felt like it?"

Josie grumbled something I couldn't make out. "For a solid week, I'd been practicing Spin the Bottle in my bedroom where I knew we'd be playing it."

"Hold up." I glanced at her for a moment. "You actually practiced spinning a bottle on the floor? I didn't realize that was something that required practice. I kinda just thought you put your hand on the bottle, gave a twist, and voila, there was your kissing partner."

"I wasn't practicing how to spin the bottle. I was practicing how to get it to stop where I wanted it to," she said, totally unfazed by my sarcasm.

"And why were you so concerned with perfecting your bottle-stopping skills?"

"Because I wanted it to stop on a certain person." Her fingers stopped playing with my shirt button and dropped to my leg.

Jesse. She'd been hoping it would stop on him. I didn't realize I was gripping the hell out of the steering wheel until my knuckles turned white.

"Garth"—Josie sat up to look at me—"that person was *you.* When I spun that bottle, I wanted it to land on you." My eyes flickered back to hers, but they couldn't stay there long. Dark country highways were dangerous enough with a person's full attention on the road. "So all I had to do was figure out where Megan Phillips would sit in the circle, and that's how I knew where to practice stopping the bottle."

"What does Megan Phillips and where she sat have to do with me?"

"She had the biggest boobs of all the girls who'd be there that night, so I knew you'd sit right next to her. Since Megan and I were pretty much sworn enemies even back then, I knew she'd sit across from me, as far as she could get."

I played that night out in my head. I hadn't thought about it in years, so the memory was a bit foggy. Whenever Josie was involved, I'd managed to make a memory of it. I might not have had any picture albums, but I did have memory albums. On every page was one of Josie. "But, Joze . . . I didn't sit by Megan that night."

She shook her head. "No. You didn't. You sat by me." She paused, looking like she was reliving the memory as well. "So when I spun the bottle, it landed on

Ben Clovis and yours landed on Megan Philips, and that's why I—you're right—*dumped* orange soda on your brand new shirt." That was coming at me fast, and I couldn't keep up. Why had Josie wanted the bottle to land on me? Why had she wanted to kiss me? Why had Josie wanted . . . *me*? "You know, I wasn't even all that put out that I had to kiss Ben Clovis and that you had to kiss Megan Philips. I was upset because I knew that would probably be the only time I had an excuse to kiss you. The only time you'd have a reason to kiss me back."

We were just pulling up to the old gas station, and even though I had dozens—possibly hundreds—of questions on my mind, I couldn't seem to ask a single one. So instead, I slid my hand behind her neck and pulled her close. "But now you get to kiss me whenever you want." I kissed her gently, and she kissed me back just as gently. After our serious make-out session, it was a welcome break.

"No bottles required," she said, smiling at me.

"Thank. God." Opening my door, I slid out and helped her crawl down. "Why don't you head on home now? I'll hang out here for fifteen or twenty minutes before I leave. Just so your parents don't have anything to be suspicious about."

"No, don't wait around. Just follow me," Josie said, fishing her keys out of her purse. "Besides, now that Colt knows about us, it's only a matter of time before someone tells my parents."

"He better not or that thread I've been hanging on by is going to snap."

Josie wound her hands around my waist. "What's the big deal? I want my parents to know. I don't want to keep us a secret any longer. You've proven that you're ready for this."

"I've proven myself? Joze, it's been three weeks." I tipped my hat back a bit because, from that look in her eyes, we were going to be lip-locked pretty soon. My lips had had a solid half-hour break, so we were good to go.

"And you're saying that three weeks aren't like three lifetimes to you, Garth Black?"

She always had a point. She always seemed to know me that much better than myself. "You've made your point—except three weeks are more like three millennia for me."

Josie laughed, coming closer until she'd rested her head against my chest. "I want to tell them. I want them to know you're the person I want to be with. I want them to know you're the person I've—"

The sound of screeching tires and flying gravel made us both whip around. A jacked-up, shiny, and expensive truck slowed as it approached, its headlights shining direc-tly on us.

"Hope we're not interrupting anything!" someone shouted from the truck.

I spun around and locked eyes with her. "You need to get in your truck and get home. Now."

"Is that Colt and his brothers?" Her eyes were taking longer to adjust than mine. "What in the hell are they doing here?"

That Josie had to ask demonstrated just what opposite kinds of lives we'd lived. When a full truck of guys barrel-ed toward me in an abandoned parking lot late at night, I knew a serious ass kicking was on the horizon. Josie saw the same thing and thought *I wonder what they want?* The way we Montana boys figured things out was: You took my girl. I kicked your ass. We were square. It took a hell of a lot of balls and maybe not a lot of brain, but we settled matters the rough-and-tough country way. We didn't sue or knife tires—we kicked ass. That the Mason boys had left enough of their hippy California roots behind to bring it like true country boys earned them a smidgeon of respect in my book. Mason's truck had rolled to a stop, and I heard doors opening.

"Josie, baby, please . . . your truck."

Her face went soft as her eyes shifted from the truck to me. "That was the first time you called me baby."

Kissing her quickly because I couldn't help it, I led her to her truck. I heard the Mason boys' boots crunching gravel our way. "Unless you get in your truck and leave *now*, that baby will have been less a term of endearment and more a reference to the way you're behaving."

"Stop." Josie pulled her arm out of my grip. "If you think I'm leaving you alone with the Masons after what went down earlier, you're the one rationalizing like a baby."

"Joze—" I wasn't above begging.

"I'm not going anywhere." She crossed her arms and held her ground.

From the footsteps, we were out of time for her to escape anyway. "You are so damn stubborn."

"I learned it from you." Glancing over my shoulder, her eyes narrowed. "Colt, what the hell are you guys doing here?"

"We followed you," Colt replied, standing in the center of his four brothers.

"No one was following us." I'd checked my rearview

the whole drive, half expecting the encounter.

"We didn't have to tail your truck to follow you," one of the older brothers, Finn or Frank or Fart or hell, Filly, said. "All we had to do was follow the stink of trash."

Josie lunged, and I just barely stopped her. I knew enough about the Masons to know they weren't there to hurt Josie—that was about the only point I could give them—but that didn't mean I wanted her within arm's reach of any of them. She didn't fight me like I'd expected.

She said, "Those are awfully tough words coming from a guy who studies managerial accounting on the East Coast and orders a Blue Hawaiian in a bar."

I couldn't help it—I smiled. Literally seconds away from having five grown men jump me, and all I could do was smile at the firecracker in my arms.

"And those are mighty judgmental words coming from a girl who cheats on a good man with this piece of trash."

Josie wiggled in my arms. If she didn't stop fighting me, I would be worn out before I got to the actual fight. "Since your dad basically bribed the county prosecutor to have a DUI dropped from your record, I'm putting it on record that your ideas of what a good man is are a tad skewed."

The F-named Mason's face went murderous. When he took a few steps our way, I moved Josie behind me and lifted my hands. "Not another step, Filly. Not another fucking step. I know why you're all here, and that's all fine and dandy, but you'd better wait until Josie is out of harm's way before charging us again. So help me god, I might not be able to hold all five of you off, but I will kick those pretty white teeth straight down your throat if you keep coming at me with Josie right here."

He slowed, but he didn't stop. Colt and one of the younger brothers had to block his way. "You call me Filly one more time, and it's your teeth getting kicked out."

The testosterone was really starting to zap to life, and I think the moment was catching up with Josie. It felt like she was trying to herd me into her truck with her. "I don't know your name, big guy, sorry. I'm just keeping with the family tradition of naming one son after a barnyard animal and running with it." I pointed at one of the brothers still trying to hold Filly off. "Colt," I stated, moving my finger to the next one. "Horses's Ass." And another Mason. "Jackass." On to the youngest Mason. "Dumbass." Ending on the oldest Mason—whose face had miraculously managed to get a shade redder. "Filly."

Yes, I was stirring the hornet's nest, but that's what I did. If I was going to get into a fight, I expected my opponent—or in this case, opponents—to hit me like they meant it. No shots just because. There'd better be some intention and hate behind each hit or else that was just an insult to the fight. "By the way, just so we all have our facts straight, Josie didn't cheat on Colt. It's hard to cheat on someone when they're not even your boyfriend." Another Mason came for me, the one a year or two younger than Colt.

"Harrison, wait," Colt ordered. "Garth's right. Not until Josie's out of here."

"I'm not going anywhere, so all of you just stop trying to make me!" Josie hollered.

Colt and I both sighed. He said, "You might see things one way, Black, but Josie and I have been together, on and off again, for close to a year now."

"Emphasis on the 'off!'" Josie piped in.

I had an urge to kiss her again. Thankfully, I repressed that urge because I don't think Colt could have taken me kissing the girl he was rather convinced had been his for the past year.

"Fine, you see things your way, and I see things differently, but all of that's beside the point. You all came here with one thing in mind." I unsnapped my cuffs and rolled up my sleeves. It looked like another new shirt would be getting ruined. "And we all know it wasn't to talk this out."

"There's nothing to talk about when some trailer trash piece of shit thinks he can take one of our girls."

All of the Mason boys looked like they'd been drinking, but I could smell the alcohol on Filly's breath. In a fight, alcohol was a tricky deal. If a man had consumed a few shots, he was more dangerous because he still had full control of his motor skills, but his inhibitions were lowered. However, a man who had consumed a few shots past the point of drunk was an easy target—as I'd proven that night Colt had beaten the shit out of me. No motor coordination and too temporarily brain dead for a logical train of thoughts.

Filly looked to be the only one who fit that drunk-as-a-skunk profile. The rest were all varying degrees of dangerous drunk. I was one tough son of a bitch, but up against five big guys who had everything from a baseball bat to an empty glass bottle, I knew the best outcome I could hope for was to leave the fight standing. I wasn't walking away the winner, but hopefully I'd still be walking. I would make sure most of the Mason boys woke up tomorrow groaning. Clearing my throat, I stared down Filly. "You got that wrong, big guy. It's you rich California posers who think your shit doesn't stink thinking you can take one of our girls." *My* girl, I added to myself.

"I can't wait to rub your face into the gravel with my boot." Filly tossed his jacket aside.

"Okay, enough comparing dicks here. Time to show what they're actually capable of."

One of the older brothers held out his arms. "Ready when you are."

"Joze"—I glanced over my shoulder—"time for you to leave."

She shook her head hard. "You boys need to get back in that truck and get the hell out of here. We were minding our business until you came along, so why don't you go mind your own business and leave us alone."

A couple of Colt's brothers chuckled, but Filly, of course, was the one to reply. "You made this our business when you cheated on our brother with this waste of space."

Before I knew she'd moved, Josie braked to a stop in front of him. "The only thing that's a waste of space around here is you, Finn." Josie slapped him hard across his cheek.

And that's when things started getting ugly.

Finn grabbed the wrist she'd just slapped him with. The second he put his hands on her, I went into action. I rushed toward them and drove my fist into his jaw as soon as I was within reach. That made Finn let go of Josie, but since the first punch had been thrown, the rest of the Masons were closing in. Right as I was about to wrap my arms around Josie and drag her back to her truck, something shattered against the back of my head. It wasn't the first time I'd had a bottle cracked over my skull, but it was the first time Josie had been around to witness it. She screamed, her eyes widening as I fell to my knees. The bottle had rung my bell, but I wouldn't stay on my knees long. Especially with Josie still out in the open and five guys getting ready to unleash hell.

"Look who's the tough guy now." Finn lunged at me, his fists ready. Just as I was bracing myself for the hit, someone leapt in front of me.

"Josie, no!" I yelled, trying to push her out of the way, but Finn's fist got to her before my hands did.

The punch hit her across the cheek, sending her flying back into me. I caught her before she fell to the ground. Even though she hadn't cried out in pain and she looked more pissed than hurt, I felt murderous rage flood my veins. If a gun pointed at Finn had magically appeared in my hand, I wouldn't have thought twice about pulling the trigger. That's how blind with rage I was.

"Josie, baby, are you okay?" I ran my hand down the side of her face he'd hit. It was already swelling.

She nodded, her eyes finding mine. "Now that *baby* was a term of endearment." She managed a small smile and tried getting up.

"What the hell, Finn?" Colt charged his brother and shoved him hard in the chest.

"She got in the way." Finn motioned at us, not look-ing the slightest bit sorry or ashamed. "If she's going to try to protect this piece of shit, that's what she deserves."

The thread I'd been hanging onto had snapped when Finn's fist connected with Josie. But fuck the thread. *I'd* snapped. Once I'd scooted Josie up against the wheel of my truck, I formed my hands around her face. "Are. You. Okay?"

"From that little bitch slap? Yeah, I barely felt it." She lifted her hand to her cheek, glaring at Finn.

I would do a hell of a lot more than glare at him as soon as I made sure she was okay. "Please stay here. Let me handle this."

She shook her head. "Sorry, Garth. If I liked hanging out on the sidelines, I would have been a cheerleader."

"Fuck the cheerleaders—"

"You certainly did back in high school."

I was fighting two battles: one with my fists with the Masons and one with my words with Josie. "I'm not asking you to stay here because I want to keep you on the sidelines forever. I'm *begging* you to stay here so I can keep you safe." How was that not clear? Five moderately to severely drunk guys were looking to turn me—and anyone else who got in the way—into their human punching bag.

"We're waiting, Black. But we're not going to wait much longer."

Josie's eyes narrowed into slits. "Why don't you go buy a fruity drink and make out with a guy like we all know you want to, Finn?"

A few of the Mason boys' mouths dropped open, Finn's mouth clenched closed, and Colt tried not to smile. Me? I laughed. Hard.

Lifting his finger, Finn took a few steps our way. I braced, ready to pounce on him if he came another step closer. "As soon as I'm done teaching this piece of trash some manners, I'm going to hold you down and sew a red A on that cheap farm-girl dress of yours, you ungrateful, cheating little—"

Yep. That was it. My rage containment threshold. Letting out a grunt of outrage, I drove my shoulder into Finn's stomach and tackled him to the ground.

"Are we finally going to fight?" Finn yelled at me, dodging my first fist. He didn't dodge the second one quickly enough. He grunted when my fist cracked the same spot he'd hit Josie.

With the reminder he'd laid his hands on Josie, a whole new level of rage bubbled to the surface. Phase two of Garth Black losing his shit. "No, *I'm* going to fight." I cracked him in the other cheek. "You're going to lay there and take it." Before I could get in a third punch, Finn's brothers piled on me. A couple grabbed my arms, and the others pulled Finn off of the ground. He was barely up before he came at me, throwing a solid fist into my stomach. And then another. And another. I lost count a few punches later. When I curled over and coughed up a bit of blood, Josie came charging toward us. Well, she came charging for Finn.

The guy had her by a hundred pounds, and she was coming at him with nothing more than sheer determination and gusto. If I wasn't so terrified of what would happen next, I would have been bursting with pride. Right before she got to Finn, Colt leapt in front of her, stopping her from going any farther. She tried ducking around him, but he dodged in front of her. She tried again, and she almost got by him. Finn was back to turning my insides into gelatin when I sighed.

"Jesus Christ, Colt. Hold her back and keep her out of this," I said.

Josie flashed me a glare like I'd betrayed her. If

betraying her meant keeping her from getting any more hurt, that was what I would do. When Josie made another run at Finn, Colt didn't hesitate. Cinching his arms around her, Colt dragged her away from his four brothers and me. That was the first positive mark in Colt Mason's corner. Josie struggled, and I'm pretty sure she stomped down hard on his toes, but Colt was a strong enough guy. I had a beating from him to attest to that.

Okay, Josie was safe. Time to kick some ass.

As Finn was winding up for another round of Liquefy -Garth-Black's-Internal-Organs, I jumped off the ground and kicked out just in time to send Finn and his fists flying backward. The sudden motion surprised the Mason boys holding my arms, so I was able to twist my arms free. I didn't waste any time pouncing on Finn. I might not have had any issues with the Mason brothers—other than Colt dating Josie—but after what Finn had said and done . . . They'd just secured the number one spot on my most hated list.

The two of us rolled across the gravel, each landing hits as we struggled to gain the upper hand. Finn was a big guy—bigger than me even—but I was a bigger badass, so that made us about even. Even through Finn's and my grunts and curses, I heard Josie crying out, yelling out, and finally, cussing us out. I'd lose the fight right then and there if I could go back in time and keep Josie from seeing it, but since time travel wasn't a skill I'd honed yet, I hit harder and hoped it would be over soon.

Finn and I were a pretty even match, but his three brothers threw themselves at me as soon as I managed to pin Finn. Boots flew, fists connected, and before I knew it, I was on my back, curling into myself and hoping at least a few of my vital parts were still intact when they were done. My dick being the most vital of them all. I made sure to cup both hands over that piece of my "vital" parts.

Josie's screams of protest quickly changed to pleas to stop. She hollered her lungs out begging them to stop, threatening to call the cops, promising she would kick all of their asses. Then her shouts turned to sobs as their kicks and hits only picked up speed. I was close to passing out, no longer able to feel what parts of my body were and weren't working when her weeps turned to choking whimpers. That right there—hearing Josie falling apart and being unable to fix it—was the most painful blow I'd been dealt that night. I'd no sooner convinced myself of that and then Finn grabbed the baseball bat. Shit, that would hurt like a mother.

His first swing hit me in the lower back, his second a bit higher. By the time he'd moved on to his third and fourth, I was passing out. His brothers yelled at him to stop. Their hits and kicks had stopped as soon as Finn took the bat to me, but from their voices, they were scared of the same thing I was: Finn wasn't going to stop swinging until I'd stopped breathing. It took all three of them to pull him away from me. Even then, he was still swinging that bat.

"Colt! We're out of here, man. Get your ass in the truck, and let's go." One of the twins, Dufus or Dipshit, called out.

As the trio continued to wrestle Finn toward Colt's truck, he never stopped glaring at me. "Don't mess with me. Don't mess with my brothers. Don't mess with our women," he ordered. "After tonight, you'll have learned your lesson."

I was beat to shit, more broken than put-together, and I had to spit blood before I could say something, but I wouldn't let Finn think he'd beat me. He hadn't. I hadn't come so far mucking through life's shit it only to be beaten by a few pairs of fists, a baseball bat, and Finn Mason. "You call that a lesson? Come back over here, and I'll show you a lesson."

It was true—I really didn't know when to shut my mouth.

Finn lunged against his brothers, but his adrenaline was fading since he wasn't using me as a human piñata. His brothers had no problem tossing him into the back of the truck and keeping him there. "I'm going to kill you, Black!"

I blew a kiss his way. "Have fun with the boys, sweetheart."

That sent him into another fit of rage, making his brothers look like they were considering using the baseball bat on him.

"Colt! Today!" one of his brothers shouted.

Colt finally let go of Josie, and as soon as he did, she spun around, slapped him so hard it echoed, and raced toward me with a look of terror. From the looks of it, she must have thought I was about to die—or was already there. Once she reached me, she fell to her knees and draped her arms around me. Actually, it was less of a drape and more of a grab.

I grimaced. "Hey, Joze? You know I love you touching me, the more desperate the better, but right now . . . less is more, baby."

Her arms instantly loosened. "Oh my god. Please don't die. Please. Don't. Die." She was such an emotional wreck, it looked like she didn't know whether to laugh or cry. She wound up going with the latter.

I managed a smile, despite it hurting like hell. "Okay, fine. I won't."

Colt was heading for his truck, glancing at us like he wasn't sure what had happened or what to do about it. Just when I was sure he was going to keep on walking, he paused. His whole face lined as he studied Josie and me spread out over the gravel. "You want me to call an ambulance or something?"

Josie shot him another glare.

"Or something," I huffed, slowly rolling onto my back. I stretched out one limb at a time, one inch at a time. Nothing felt broken—at least no bones were. Colt slid his phone out of his pocket. "Thanks, but I'm good. If I called an ambulance every time I got in a fight, I might as well just buy the company because it would be cheaper."

Colt shifted. "You sure?"

"Just get the hell out of here!" Josie shouted at him, eyeing the bat.

"We're good. Do as the lady says." In my state, I wouldn't have been able to stop Josie if she did decide to pick up that bat and take swings at a flock of Masons.

"Okay." Colt nodded and started for his truck. "I guess I'll see you . . . around?"

Josie snorted and wiped at my face with the sleeve of my jacket she still had on. I stroked her cheek. It was still swelling and already bruising. Another flash of rage.

"Colt?" I didn't wait for him to acknowledge me. I knew he heard me. "Tonight, you were my ally because you kept Josie out of all this. Come tomorrow"—I managed to lean up on my elbows to look him straight on—

"you'd better steer clear of me. If I run into you, I'm treating you like any other Mason who did this to her." My eyes scanned her face before shifting back to his. When Colt inspected her face, his eyes closed in a wince. He nodded once before leaping into his truck and peeling out of the parking lot faster than they'd peeled into it.

"Man, Josie. I don't know who took it out of me more tonight—you or the Masons." I cupped her other cheek and worked up another smile. It was done. The Masons had done what they'd wanted to, were gone, and we were both okay. I might need a good night's sleep and a few Tylenol, but I'd had it worse. Unlike other fights, I hadn't had anyone to sit beside me afterward, stroke my hand, and look like they were suffocating in their concern for me.

Concern . . . it was a fairly new concept to me. Once I was sure was overrated and a bunch of bullshit. As I laid there spread over the gravel, blood pooling in my mouth and every square inch of my body throbbing in pain, I realized how nice it was to have someone concerned about my wellbeing. Someone concerned about *me*. Someone cared whether I was still alive come morning, and that gave my life a meaning and purpose that had been absent. She depended on me, and for right then, she wanted me in her life. It was a sobering reality. One that would take a while to figure out.

"Say something. Please," she sniffled, wiping her nose with the same sleeve she'd used to wipe my face with. It was dotted with blood. "I don't know what to do. I don't know what to fucking do right now."

"It's okay. I'm okay." She looked as close to hysterical as I'd ever seen Josie, and despite the pain coursing through my body, seeing her so undone caused the most pain. "Why don't you help me up and over to my truck so I don't get blood all over yours, and then let's just get back to your place and figure out the rest when we get there. Sound okay?"

"Are you sure you don't need to go to the hospital? You look bad, Garth. Really, really bad." She bit her lip as a tear slipped from her eye.

That tear was like another baseball bat slammed into my back.

"No hospitals. They're sick of me anyways even if I actually needed one. Which I don't." She looked like she was about to start screaming for an ambulance. "Just get me back, get me to bed, and I'll wake up tomorrow good as new." Nothing I was saying was calming her down. If anything, every word seemed to be working her up more. Gritting my teeth, I sat up so I could be face to face with her. Maybe that would reassure her I wasn't about to be drug off to hell after taking my last breath. "Look at me, Josie. In the eyes."

She sniffed and shook her head. "I can't. They're swelling shut." She choked on another sob but managed to keep the rest of them back.

That explained why I couldn't see anything more than a sliver of her. "Hey, hey," I said, trying to soothe her with my words, my hands, with *anything.* "Where's that brave girl who just issued the slap heard around the country? Where's my strong girl who just took a swing at a guy twice her size?"

She fretted with my shirt, laying the rips and tears back together, buttoning the buttons that had come un-done. "A lot of good me being brave and strong did to save you."

I adjusted my head until the sliver I saw of her was her eyes. Mine might have been swelling shut, but she could still stare back at me. "You have no idea how much good you've done to save me, Josie Gibson. Don't you ever doubt that."

Josie let those words simmer for a moment, then she rolled her shoulders back, wiped her eyes, and wove her arm through mine. "Let me help you up."

"Thanks"—I shoved off the ground, letting her guide me up—"because I don't think I'm capable of doing it on my own."

When I was up, Josie wrapped one arm around my waist and lifted my arm over her shoulders. "Was that you admitting you need help and actually accepting it?"

"It just might have been," I admitted, shuffling beside her as we made our way to my truck. Being vertical and moving doubled the pain, but Josie's arm around me, supporting me the whole way, dulled it somewhat. When we made it to the passenger door, she opened it and guided me inside. After shutting the door, she hurried around to the driver's side and leapt inside.

Firing the engine to life, she glanced over at me with an expectant look. "Buckle up, buttercup." That made me laugh. Which made me wince. "I'm serious. I'm not putting this truck into drive until you put your seatbelt on. We didn't make it this far for you to die all because you refused to buckle up."

If she wasn't so dead serious, I might have laughed again. I reached for the belt and snapped it into place. I attempted something that was meant to be a *Happy?* expression, but given my face probably looked like a team of plastic surgeons had gone to town on me, I don't know what I managed. It made Josie smile. So fuck the rest. Making her smile, that was my new life calling because really, what else mattered?

"Thank you." Shifting the truck into drive, she peered over at me. "Buttercup."

I snorted. "After taking that beating from the Masons, I feel like a damn buttercup." God damn, where was a morphine drip when I needed one?

"I'm sorry, Garth. I should have seen that coming. I shouldn't have been so stupid. I know what those boys can be like when they get together. Then mix alcohol . . . and *you* into the tornado, and that's like the perfect storm right there." Josie pulled out onto the highway slowly, carefully. The last time she'd driven slowly was when she was *never*. She really was worried fate was about to deal us an unfair hand.

"Don't apologize for them. If you spend your whole life apologizing for other people's actions, you're going to wake up and realize you didn't get to do anything on your own to apologize for. Live *your* life. Don't waste it apologizing for others."

Josie glanced at me from the corners of her eyes, keeping both hands firmly on the ten and two position on the steering wheel. It was kind of cute how careful she was being. Concerned. There was that word again. "You just took a few hits to the head, and you're capable of that kind of profoundness?"

"Was that profound?" One of the few serious questions I'd asked in twenty-one years.

"Deeply."

"For me, right? Deeply profound for Garth Black,

who is known for being so deep he dries up the instant the temperature rises above eighty."

Josie rested her hand above my knee. Gently. "Deeply profound for anyone. I know you want to deny it, but I know there's a whole lot more to you than a big, black hat and an even bigger ego."

"I don't know, Joze." I covered my hand with hers, but when I noticed it was caked with both dried and fresh blood, I pulled it back. I'd made a big enough mess already.

"But I do."

"Yeah, you sure do," I whispered, twisting in my seat to stare at her. My eyes were swollen, my body wrecked, my brain weary, but in that moment, I needed to do only one thing. One thing I needed to *say*. I knew that even if I wanted to keep it back, I couldn't. Besides, I'd been holding it back for long enough. "Josie?" I cleared my throat and reached for her hand again. Yes, I might cover it in blood, but I'd clean it for her later. I'd fix my mess.

"Yeah?" she asked, her eyes focusing on something in the distance. I was opening my mouth to finish what I'd been meaning to say for years when she groaned. "Ah, crap. The lights are all still on." She looked at me. "My parents are up."

The disappointment of biting back what had literally just been on the tip of my tongue was painful, but how could I follow *My parents are up* with what I needed to say? Yeah, I couldn't. I had to close my eyes to focus and shift gears. Josie's parents. Up. Late. Me. Her. Blood. "Do you want me to sneak in or something? I could just wait outside until you all go to bed and then sneak in."

"What? No. Way." She snapped her head back and

forth, slowing the truck a bit as she headed up the drive-way. "I've got to get you inside, cleaned up, fixed up, pain reliever'ed up, and to bed. That's the priority, not evading my parents and their questions."

I took a breath. I hadn't been planning on explaining any of the night to the Gibsons. The drive-in earlier or the gas station parking lot later. "What do you want to tell them?"

Josie's hand reached for mine. "The truth."

I smiled right before I frowned. "I'm not sure telling your parents that you and I are together right after I walk through the door looking like a herd of cattle ran me over is the best timing."

"I want to tell them. I'm sure now." As we approach-ed the Gibsons', she parked right outside the front door to give the newest member of the gimp club a break.

"You're sure of me now?"

"I'm sure of *us* now."

That right there was all the fix I needed. Josie looking me in the eyes and admitting she trusted me enough to give us a chance. I'd been waiting for that moment for a while. It left me speechless. Josie opened her door and rushed over to help me get out, but I clenched my jaw and slid out on my own. I didn't want the minute before Josie told her parents that I was her man to involve her having to wait hand and foot on me because I'd taken a serious beating.

Instead of draping my arm around Josie for support, I grabbed her hand. "Let's not tell them it was the Masons. Let's just tell them I got jumped and go with that."

"What? Why in the heck don't you want to tell them it was the Masons?"

"Because I don't want anyone getting in trouble. At least not the sheriff kind of trouble." Me on the other hand? I would be happy to show them plenty of trouble for a long, long time.

Josie gave me a look, knowing there was something else. "And?"

I sighed. Might as well go with the theme of our crazy-ass night. "And even if I did tell them the truth, do you really think they'll believe me? Do you really think they'll believe that their precious, perfect Masons would do this? They're not going to believe the truth, so I might as well give them a watered-down version of it."

"They better believe it when the same story comes from their daughter's mouth because so help me—"

I caught a glimpse of Mrs. Gibson peeking through the lace curtains in the living room. "I don't want them thinking I've influenced or corrupted you so much that you'd lie with me. If we go in there with the whole truth, that's what they'll think. That I've manipulated and ruined their daughter."

"Garth . . ."

"Please, Josie. *Please*." We started up the stairs, one step at a time. She didn't have a chance to reply because the door flew open when we were climbing the last step.

Mrs. Gibson's face blanched. "Oh, dear sweet Jesus, what happened?" Tilting her head back, she hollered, "Harold! Harold! Get in here now!"

Super idea. Why don't we just wake a sleeping bear? Rousing Mr. Gibson in the middle of the night almost worried me more than Clay when he jolted awake at night.

"Mom, it's okay. Calm down. Don't wake Dad up if he's already in bed," Josie said, helping me through the door.

Mrs. Gibson scooted back, staring at me with wide eyes. I hadn't seen what I looked like, but I didn't need to. The way I felt told the story. Mrs. Gibson looked between the two of us. "Josie—"

"What the hell happened?" Mr. Gibson finished his wife's sentence as he lumbered down the hall. Given Mr. Gibson was a big guy and had one hell of a grumpy expression, we really had woken a sleeping bear. "Well?"

Josie peered at me, then answered, "Garth was attacked."

They must have been so preoccupied with gaping at the train wreck I was that when Mrs. Gibson finally glanced at her daughter, she gasped. "Josie, your face." Mrs. Gibson rushed toward her, examining it more closely, before covering her mouth and shaking her head. "My poor baby. He drug you into this, too?"

At first I thought she was talking about Colt—since he and his brood were the ones responsible—but when I saw her eyes look my way with accusation, I knew she was talking about me. As expected.

"No, I drug myself into this when I got in the way of a fist," Josie replied in a heated voice. "Garth did everything in his power to keep me out of it and safe."

Mrs. Gibson didn't need to say it, her eyes bled it—*Sure, he did* with a heavy dose of sarcasm. "Let's get some ice on that, baby."

Josie exhaled loudly. "Mom, no. Look at us." She waved her hand between her and me. "I'm not the one who needs ice. Or a little human decency, for Christ's sake."

"Josie," Mr. Gibson broke in, "you might be twenty-one and an adult now, but you are still under our roof and that is your mother you're talking to."

Josie's hand grabbed hold of mine as she stared at her dad. I don't know how he managed to keep his shoulders high, let alone keep looking her straight in the eye, with the way her eyes were leveling him. "And this is my boyfriend you're talking to. I'd appreciate it if you'd show him the same amount of respect you show everyone else."

I don't know whose face looked more shocked: mine or Mrs. Gibson's or Mr. Gibson's. Wait, I take that back. Mrs. Gibson definitely won the most-shocked-face award. From the way she looked, Josie might as well have just told her she was going to jail for life.

Having me as a boyfriend . . . Going to jail for life. . . I supposed to Mrs. Gibson, they were one and the same. Mr. Gibson, though? He just stared at our entwined hands with a vacant expression, seeming at a loss. That made two of us.

"Yoo-hoo? Earth to Dad and Mom?" Josie snapped her fingers a few times. "There's a man bruised and bloodied in your foyer. This isn't really the time for open-mouth gawking. Since it looks like I won't be receiving a lot of help, I'm going to get him fixed up."

We didn't make it two steps before Mr. Gibson stepped in front of us. "Josie, time to go to bed."

Josie's face went red in barely two seconds time. "I'm not going to bed when there's a person under our roof who's in need of serious medical attention." I gave her hand a squeeze, trying to calm her, but she wasn't having any of it.

"I need to have a talk with Garth. Man to man."

"Then you can talk with him in the morning," Josie argued.

225

"It can't wait until the morning." Mr. Gibson crossed his arms, looking as determined as I knew Josie was.

It might not have been the best time, but he was right. Mr. Gibson and I needed to talk. I'd imagine a father like him had plenty to discuss with me. Especially when I came through the front door hand in hand with his daughter after midnight looking like I was walking death. Turning to Josie, I tried to smile reassuringly at her, but my mouth wasn't working quite right.

"It's okay, Joze. Why don't you get some ice on that cheek, head up to bed, and your dad and me will talk. I'll see you in a little while. A little while as in the morning," I added when Mr. Gibson's eyebrows raised. "I'll see you soon. In the morning." As expected, Josie whipped her head from side to side. "Please?" I lifted my hand to her face. "You know how hard it is for me to say that. One please every decade ought to be worth something."

She sighed, still shaking her head. "Fine. But not until you're bandaged up and changed."

"I don't think that's necessary. Garth's a tough guy—he's a bull rider after all. He's used to a few bumps and bruises," Mr. Gibson said. "I think he can wait fifteen minutes before having his boo-boos fixed up. Isn't that right, Garth?"

If the tension in the air hadn't been so thick, I might have chuckled when the word *boo-boos* came out of Mr. Gibson's mouth. "This is nothing." I gave a dismissive wave. "I'm fit for a full day of ranch work right now, so a little manly conversation will be a walk in the park."

"I'll wait for you on the porch." Mr. Gibson stopped in front of Josie and studied her face. He stroked her cheek gently then kissed the top of her head. I didn't miss the sideways look he shot me as he headed out the front door.

"I'm fine," I said as Josie opened her mouth. "If I was in his shoes and my daughter came through the door with a bruise on her face, I sure wouldn't be talking to the guy who was responsible for her." I pressed closer to her and stroked her cheek with my thumb. "I'll see you later, okay?"

Her eyes met mine as a silent exchange passed between us. "Thanks for the date."

I laughed a few notes. What a date it had been. It had to rank up there with the most extreme dates ever. "Thank you for letting me take you on a date."

"I figured it was about time." Her hands rested on my chest, and she let a smile come out.

"You figured right." Leaning in, I pressed my lips into the corner of hers. Mrs. Gibson shifted and looked away. I inhaled, breathing Josie in, then let her go. I had a concerned father waiting for me—who hopefully wasn't waiting for me with the barrel aimed and trigger cocked. When I turned to close the front door behind me, I found Josie in the same spot, watching me with sad eyes. It took everything in me not to rush back to her and fix whatever was troubling her.

Mr. Gibson was waiting for me just outside the door, leaning into the porch railing with his arms crossed. No shotguns in sight. "It's obvious to me you want nothing but the best for my daughter," he began as soon as I'd closed the door, "but you and me both know that you're not capable of giving her that."

Shit. And I thought I was done taking hard blows for the night. "So we're just diving straight into this?"

"I took you for a man who doesn't like to bullshit

around the point, kind of like me. If I've got that wrong, then please correct me and we can do some ice-breaking by talking about the weather, or what the Farmer's Almanac is predicting for rainfall this summer, or how the new cafe in town serves piss poor coffee."

"You're right. Let's get straight to the point." I moved beside the rocking chair across from him, but I didn't sit in it the way my body was aching to. I would stand like a man in front of Mr. Gibson and whatever he was about to throw at me.

"I knew your daddy way back. Your mama, too." Mr. Gibson wasn't wasting time, and I couldn't blame him for that. Sunrise was only a few hours away. "She was a good woman, and he was a well-intending man, but you of all people know how that worked out." He paused, letting that sink in. Letting all of the memories and images I did a decent job of repressing flood back into the forefront of my mind. My pain shot up a few levels. "The only difference between your dad and mom's situation and you and Josie's is that Josie has a protective and concerned father. I like you, son—you're a decent enough kid who I know cares for my daughter—but it wouldn't matter if I loved you so much I'd profess you my new religion. I won't let my daughter fall victim to what your daddy, and his daddy, did to the women they claim to love."

I grabbed the back of the porch chair to steady myself. "I wouldn't do that to her. I'd never hurt her. I care about Josie."

His eyes ran down me, taking me in. A person who'd lived through cycling around in a tornado wouldn't have come out as tore up as I looked. "You might not intend to hurt her, but there's nothing about being with you—past, present, and future—that won't hurt her."

My hands gripped the rocking chair so hard my fingers shook. "Since you and I don't know each other all that well and we've never exactly taken the time to get to know each other well, let me explain something to you. On my list of priorities, number one has to do with never hurting Josie. It always has been, and it always will be. Number two on that list is protecting her from whatever or whoever else might hurt her."

Mr. Gibson's eyebrows lifted. "Kind of like you protected her tonight?" That was the verbal hit equivalent of the baseball bat hits I'd taken. "I don't doubt those are your priorities, but here's the thing, son. How can those be realistic priorities? You and I both know you've hurt her plenty in the past, and if it isn't you in the future, someone or something is going to wind up doing much worse than that grapefruit-sized bruise on her cheek tonight."

I wanted to argue, to deny I'd ever done anything to hurt her, but that would be one of the biggest lies I'd ever tell. Mr. Gibson was right—I'd hurt Josie in ways I'd kill another person for doing to her. Even though I wanted to believe I'd learned my lesson, I wasn't sure if that was reality. Mr. Gibson was right again—I might have known my priorities, but were the realistic ones? I didn't have the answer to that question. I hung my head between my arms and focused on breathing. I didn't know what to say next. I didn't know what to do next. Life was closing in on me, and I didn't feel strong enough to hold the walls back from crushing me.

"Life isn't fair, Garth. That is one lesson I learned a long time ago." Mr. Gibson's voice wasn't quite as harsh. Probably because he knew he'd beaten me down so much I couldn't fall any lower. "I'm an aging rancher running a fifth-generation ranch with one son who wants nothing to do with ranching and one daughter who can't run it on her own. You drew the short straw as to what family you were born into."

I squeezed my eyes closed. "I wasn't born into a family. I was born into a dysfunctional fucking mess." That right there was getting straight to the point. A minute or two of silence passed between us. I expected he was waiting for me to say something, but there was nothing I could say to explain myself. There was nothing left to say.

"I know you would never try to drag Josie down with you, but it's inevitable. It's kind of like a person with a cold. They might not mean to spread it, but they can't do anything to stop it either."

I finally opened my eyes. Had he just said what I'd known for so long but tried to ignore during the past few weeks with Josie? "Are you saying I'm a virus?"

Mr. Gibson's silence was all the answer I needed. "I'm saying I'm going to do whatever it takes to keep my daughter healthy and safe."

"I am, too." I let go of the chair and tried to stand tall, but it wasn't happening. I was too beat down, physically and mentally.

Shoving off of the railing, he approached me until only a foot of cool night air separated us. "Can you look me in the eye and promise me, as a man, that Josie wouldn't be better off falling in love and settling down with someone else? Can you look me in the eye and guarantee me that the best life she could expect to lead would be one with you?"

Yes! I wanted to shout. *Absolutely!* But what I wanted

and what I knew were two very different things. Confusion hadn't only settled in; it had taken over.

Mr. Gibson waited for me to respond, but when a minute passed with nothing from me, he patted my shoulder and headed for the door. "Do the right thing. I'll give you until morning to do it yourself, or I'll do it for you. This ends come tomorrow, you hear?"

Having a person order me to stay away from the one thing that seemed more essential to my life than oxygen didn't settle well with me. "I'll leave, but you won't be able to keep Josie and me apart. Fifteen years and you've never been able to keep us apart. I want her, and she wants me, too. That's something you're just going to have to deal with."

Mr. Gibson's hand stayed on my shoulder, and he surveyed me with almost a . . . pitiful look. "She doesn't want you. She wants the idea of you. The idea of the lost and lonely boy from her past that needs saving. Nothing more. I promise when you leave tomorrow and you stay away, she'll be just fine."

I had to unclench my jaw before I could reply. "Josie's never been able to just 'get over' me, and she won't be able to now. I know how she feels because it's the exact same way I do about her."

"You've never given her a chance to get over you. You two have gone through so many ups and downs I can't keep it straight." Mr. Gibson shook his head and dropped his hand from my shoulder. "Give her space, give her time, and she'll move on. She'll move on to the life she deserves. The life even you know she deserves." Our to-the-point conversation apparently done, Mr. Gibson slipped inside the door and closed it behind him.

Just like that, I'd been locked out of her life.

chapter THIRTEEN

IT WAS MY last night sleeping under the Gibsons' roof. I hadn't yet decided if I'd remove myself or if Mr. Gibson and his shotgun would have to do the removing, but I held off sleep for as long as I could realizing tomorrow night, Josie wouldn't be a mere few rooms away.

After Mr. Gibson's and my conversation, I'd stood out on that porch for a while. I heard Mrs. Gibson all but force Josie up to bed when she headed for the front door to find me. I waited another hour after all the lights in the house had gone out. I was cold and I'd been beaten within a few inches of my life, but I felt numb. Everything inside and outside of me felt anesthetized. Everything but my heart. It ached so badly I almost convinced myself I was having a heart attack.

What Josie's dad had said was right. All of it. I might have made a solemn vow with myself never to hurt her and to keep her protected, but I seemed incapable of either. While I knew I couldn't assume the trend would carry into the future, I couldn't guarantee it wouldn't, and until I knew for sure that I wouldn't hurt her, I couldn't be around her. Not after what had happened. Josie would wear a fist-sized bruise on her face the rest of the month because the shit that followed me at every turn had caught sight of her and decided to share the wealth.

So I was leaving. I wouldn't make Mr. Gibson throw me out. I'd pack my bags and leave until I figured out what needed figuring out. Which, when it came to me, was like saying I needed to figure out everything. I hadn't decided what I'd say to Josie yet, or if anything I could say would explain it all to her. How could I express to her that I was leaving her for *her* own good? Especially when I knew neither one of us would feel good about it. That was the question I was stuck on when my body finally gave in and gave up to sleep.

It wasn't the dreamless kind of sleep either . . .

A couple summers ago, Josie's brother was turning twenty-one. Jesse was out of town at some rancher's convention with his dad and had asked me to tag along with Josie and keep an eye on her. Not because he didn't trust her—because he was Jesse Walker and he gave trust like it was in limitless supply—but because he knew there'd be alcohol and a bunch of Luke's frat brothers who had a thing for his little sister. Even if Jesse hadn't asked me to hang with Josie at the party, I would have. I didn't trust those U of M frat boys as far as I could throw their hillbilly deluxe trucks.

The party was at Luke's frat house. After Josie had drained a couple of shots, every time I turned around, some other frat douche was handing her another. I don't know how many she had total, but I'd counted seven when I finally called bullshit. I shut the music off, climbed up on a table, and warned the next son of a bitch who slipped her a drink that he'd leave there with my boot up his ass. The drinks slowed, but they didn't stop. Thankfully, she stayed glued to my side unless she had to go to the restroom, which I stood outside of and guarded like a fucking

Rottweiler. Luke drank himself into a mini coma halfway into the night, so I was literally the only guy in the room not trying to lure Josie into some dark room. It got old. Fast.

I was about two seconds away from driving my elbow into a guy's jaw—the one who kept grinding up against Josie when we weren't anywhere close to the thrown-together dance floor—when Josie threw her arms around my neck, looked up at me with those green eyes of hers, and grinned.

"Ever since that first dance we had back in high school, I've always dreamed of dancing with you again." Before her words had registered, she tucked her head beneath my chin and swayed against me. "Tonight, I finally get to live that dream."

I'd been conflicted in my life plenty of times and to varying degrees, but that dance with that girl . . . there was no word for how conflicted I felt right then. Conflicted didn't even come close to describing it. I knew my arms didn't belong around her, and I knew my body didn't have a right to respond to her the way it was, but my head and heart never aligned when I was with Josie. I danced with her. That first dance, and a second, and a third. After the fifth one, I lost count. Dance after dance didn't make it any easier to drop my arms and let her go. She'd wandered into them of her own accord, and I wasn't sure I could ever let her wander out.

The party was in full swing, and everyone was plastered enough that it wasn't just a roomful of lowered inhibitions—it was a roomful of no inhibitions. The only thing more on my mind than never letting our dance end was protecting Josie. I was about to finally let her go so I could get her out of there when her mouth moved just outside of my ear.

"Take me home," she whispered, her breath warm against my skin.

Grabbing her hand, I led her out of that frat house, lifted her inside of my truck, and didn't touch the brake until we were in front of the Gibsons' house. Her parents were at the same rancher's convention as the Walkers, but the fact that Josie and I had a big, quiet house all to ourselves wasn't even on my mind when I helped her through the front door and carried her to her bedroom when she tripped over the first step. The most I'd seen Josie drink was a couple of a beers, and the girl had a low tolerance. Given the number of shots she'd had, it was a miracle she was still able to talk.

After getting her laid out on her bed, I'd told her I would run and grab her some water and pain reliever to help with the morning-after effects. I fumbled through her parents' medicine cabinet for a while to find what I need-ed. By the time I returned with the pills and water, I expected her to be passed out and snoring. I certainly didn't expect to walk in and find her dress on the floor and her standing in front of an open window wearing nothing but her underwear and bra. She held a frame with the pic-ture of her, Jesse, and me as children. Her thumb circled my scowly face. I dropped the glass of water, and it shat-tered when it hit the floor.

Josie had spun around in surprise, but when she saw it was just me, she smiled. Josie being next to naked and smiling at me as the moonlight streamed onto her skin . . . that would have been enough to drop me to my knees if I wasn't already moving in her direction.

"You dropped something," she'd said, setting down the picture.

"Joze?" I'd swallowed, knowing I should look away. *Knowing* but not able to. "Why are you in your underwear?"

My throat had already felt dry, but by the time she stopped in front of me and pressed against my body, it went something else entirely. "I told you. Tonight, I get to live my dream."

I'd smelled the alcohol on her breath and I saw it blurring her eyes—I knew she was in no condition to make decisions—but when her hands worked the buttons of my shirt loose, I basically said *Fuck it,* shut my brain off entirely, and went with what my heart and body were telling me to do.

Once she'd peeled off my shirt, Josie unfastened her bra. When she pressed her bare chest into mine, I had to bite my tongue and close my eyes to keep from coming right then and there. I'd been with plenty of women, and plenty of women had shoved their chests up against mine in a similar way, but never, *never* had I almost fallen apart when one did it. Not that I needed the reminder, but Josie's touch did things to me I'd never experienced before.

I don't know who was the first to kiss the other. All I remembered was that when it happened and whoever had made the first move, I knew I wouldn't make the last one. I wouldn't be the one to ever stop kissing her because I simply couldn't. When I laid her back onto her bed, while I was busy unfastening my fly, she slipped out of her panties. Just as I was about to lower myself into her, that picture on her dresser caught my attention. From across the room, a smiling blond boy watched me. I'd muttered a curse, and just as I pulled back, Josie wrapped her arms and legs around me and pulled me to her.

When her eyes locked onto mine, she smiled, then whispered, "Finders keepers."

Whether it was her hips that took me in or my hips that took her, I knew one thing—things would never be the same.

They never had been.

THAT WAS THE dream I bolted awake from. While I didn't consider it a nightmare because of what had happened that night, it became a nightmare when I realized that was possibly the first and the last time I'd experience Josie that way. I'd had that dream before, but until Jesse and Rowen had gotten together, I'd burst awake from it drenched in sweat and guilt.

Before long that night, Josie and I had been digging our fingers into the other's backs and screaming each other's names, but unlike Josie—who'd fallen asleep immediately after—sleep never found me. Instead, I went from staring at the girl I'd always wanted and now *had* to the boy in the photograph. What we'd done that night was the ultimate betrayal. Jesse was a good man, the best man I'd ever known. That he openly admitted to being best friends with the town drunk's son was something I'd never felt worthy of. That night, I understood why.

I *wasn't* worthy of his friendship. I sure as hell wasn't worthy of the girl lying next to me with a peaceful expression on her face. I'd taken Josie from him, and even though I'd felt exactly that way back in high school when he asked her to Homecoming, I'd never planned on repaying him. Especially not by having sex with her while he was out of town and he'd asked me to watch out for her.

I'd been worried all night about other guys putting moves on her, but I should have been worried about myself. Mr. Gibson had been right: I was a virus. I didn't mean to spread my sickness, but I simply couldn't help it. I'd infected my two best friends in the world that night, and before the sun had risen the next morning, I was on the phone with Jesse explaining what had happened. Of course that did nothing but further alienate me from both of them. I turned into the even-harder shell of a person I'd been until Josie had catapulted back into my life.

History was pretty much repeating itself. I'd moved in on her when she'd been with someone else, giving no thought to what was best for her—only what was best for me. Given the way she looked at me and the intention in her touch, I'd practically convinced her that I was what was best for her, too. But I wasn't what was best for her. How could I be when the only roof I had over my head was the cab of my old truck? How could I be what was best for her when I didn't even know what was best for myself? How could I love her the way she deserved to be loved when my parents hadn't shown me an ounce of it?

The answer to those and the other questions streaming through my head was simple—I couldn't. That answer made me throw off the covers, jump out of bed, and pull my duffle bag out of the closet. I had to go. It would be hard for her, but unlike me, Josie would recover. She'd dry her eyes one morning and wake up to find the sun a little brighter and her future more hopeful without me in it. She'd live the life I'd always wanted for her. It just wouldn't be with me.

Stuffing the first thing in my bag was the hardest. Once I got past that, the rest went in quickly. I'd made up my mind. The sooner I was out of there, the easier it would be for both of us to move on. Or in my case, pretend to move on. I was sitting on the edge of the bed to pull on my boots when the doorknob twisted. I froze, but as hard as I tried, I couldn't get my heart to follow suit. I needed my heart frozen to say good-bye to Josie. I needed it frozen to make it out that front door and leave her behind. But the instant that door opened and she slipped inside, I knew my fight to freeze anything was over.

She had a playful smile on, and then she saw the full duffle on the bed and the boots in my hand. All playfulness fell from her face, along with the smile. "Where the hell are you going?"

I closed my eyes to keep from having to look into her eyes. "I don't know. I'm just going."

"Is this because of something my dad said to you?"

I shook my head once. "No."

"Is this because of what happened earlier? Are you feeling guilty because I've got a little bruise on my face?" Josie was whispering but just barely. If the conversation got any more heated, and I knew it would, she would wake up the whole house soon.

"I'm going because I have to go."

"No, you don't," she snapped.

I pinched the bridge of my nose. "Yes, I do. You know it, and now I finally do, too."

"No, I damn well don't know that, and you don't either, Black. So do me a favor and stop playing the martyr." Her voice wobbled over a few words, but she still sounded more pissed off than anything else.

"Joze, I'm going." Grabbing a boot, I started sliding my foot into it before she flew across the room, grabbed it, and tossed it into the corner.

"You're not going anywhere."

What I wouldn't have given to have a heart made out of ice so I wouldn't have to feel the throbbing deep in my chest from the desperate look on her face or the tears about to release from her eyes. I wanted to be a shell of a man. I wanted to be the person I'd always let everyone assume I was. I sprung up and threw my hands behind my head to keep from pulling her close. "Fine, Joze. Fine. Give me one goddamned good reason why I shouldn't go now. Why I shouldn't leave now instead of later because you know I've got to leave someday. I can't stay here and pretend you and me are going to live happily ever after. So tell me, how much longer do you want to live this temporary fairy tale? How much longer do you want to keep convincing yourself that you want me for the rest of your life? Give me one good reason why I shouldn't walk out that door now."

"Because I love you." That time, her voice didn't waver. In fact, those might have been the strongest words I'd ever heard her say.

I collapsed on the bed, dropping my face into my hands. My whole life I'd waited to hear those words from her, and their timing couldn't have been worse. "No, Josie, you can't. Don't love me. You get to choose who you love, so please"—I grabbed her hands and kept my head bowed into them—"please don't waste it on me."

"Don't tell me who to love, Garth Black. And don't you dare tell me it's a waste to give it to you." Josie kneeled beside me. I knew she was waiting for me to say something. Anything, probably, but other than good-bye, there was nothing else to say. "I just told you I love you."

"No." I shook my head, keeping it buried in my hands. "Please, Josie, just please stop."

"I love you," she repeated.

Those words hit me hard. Mostly because of the person saying them, but also because they were the first time I'd ever heard them. The first time those three words had been applied to me. Someone loved me. Not just anyone—Josie loved me. Fuck. What I wouldn't have done to be the man deserving of that love. I would have given anything . . . but I had nothing to give. I couldn't produce a diamond when I was made of shit. "You don't love me. You can't."

"I can and I do." She inhaled slowly. "Some part of me has always loved you."

Hearing the exact things I'd wanted to hear for so long, moments before I was going to walk out that door and leave Josie behind, was becoming physically painful. "When you and Jesse were together?"

"Yes. It might not have been the kind I feel for you now, but I loved you."

I shook my head into my hands. Yesterday, I would have killed to hear the things she was saying, but right then, those words were killing me. Because I had to leave.

"When you were mean to me when Jesse and I first got together and you said some hurtful things, I loved you then. And when you dated all of my friends, leaving a trail of broken hearts in your wake, avoiding me like I was one exception to the who-meets-Garth-Black's-belt-notch-standard, I loved you then, too."

All I could do was keep shaking my head. "And what about when you did become one of the girls to crawl into bed with me? What about when you woke up alone the next morning to not so much as a note or a good-bye? What about the months I said horrible things to one of the people I cared about most because I was taking out my anger on her? My anger at failing her, my anger at ruining a good relationship she had with a good man, my anger for failing at everything. What then, Joze?" I couldn't holler the words like I needed to, and somehow, their quietness was ten times more piercing.

"I wanted to hate you after that. I tried so damn hard it hurt." Josie paused. Maybe it was because she needed to wipe away a tear or maybe she was simply at a loss, but I couldn't look at her to find out. One look and my resolve to leave would be gone. Josie had a way of upending my whole world in one moment. "But even then, I still loved you. I realized that if I couldn't find some way to weed out the love I had for you after that, it wouldn't go away. Ever."

"No, Joze . . ."

"Garth Black, I love you." Josie slid onto my lap and slowing pulled my hands from my face. Once she had, her eyes met mine. If I hadn't been about to break down already, I was then. "And I know you love me too."

"Josie—"

"It's okay, you don't have to tell me right now. I know it's hard for you . . . I know it's hard hearing the words." Lifting the hem of her nightgown, Josie pulled it up and over her head. She wasn't wearing anything beneath it. "Just show me you do. *Show* me you love me, and we'll work on the telling part later."

I wanted to squeeze my eyes shut. I wanted to pull my hands away and lock them behind my back to keep them from sliding around her waist like they were. I wanted to keep from looking into her eyes. But I couldn't. I was a strong, stubborn man save for one thing: Josie Gibson.

Pushing on my chest, Josie laid me down. Having her on top of me, looking down at me with so much love in her eyes it practically suffocated me, I almost slipped. I almost said it. Those three words I'd been choking back for years. And years. And years. I almost said those words, but I didn't. I knew if I did, good-bye would be impossible. If I ever let Josie know how I truly felt about her, she wouldn't let me go. I wouldn't let myself go.

Her eyes explored me, inspecting each bruise and bandage, before she leaned over and kissed each and every one. Her hair skimmed my chest, creating goose bumps. When her kisses moved from my chest down my stomach, I stopped breathing altogether. When Josie's mouth had touched every hurt on my body, her mouth moved a bit lower.

"Josie," I sighed in a strained voice, tangling my fingers through her hair.

I felt her smile curve into position before her tongue pressed into the spot just above my button fly. The willpower it took to keep from throwing her on her back and slamming inside of her two seconds later was the kind of thing men only knew of in legends. Stories told around a campfire about a man who was able to lay still and resist the woman of his fucking dreams naked and straddling him as her tongue explored the skin a whole inch north of his hard dick.

My hands slid down her waist until they had a firm

hold of her backside, and when my fingers moved a bit lower, it was painfully obvious she was as ready for me as I was for her. And still, the legendary willpower stood. My idea of restraint had always been slowing down enough to roll on a condom, and there I was, still half dressed and promising myself I'd stay that way.

When Josie's mouth had made the return journey, her face lifted above mine. Her smile and playful eyes were back. "Sorry, I missed a few spots." Slowly, she kissed every bruise and gash on my face as she had my body. The only part she missed was my lips. When her lips slid from my jaw to my mouth, they paused. "I love you, Garth."

It was as painful as it was overwhelming to hear those words. "Josie, no. Don't—"

"Too late," she replied right before her mouth covered mine.

She kissed me until I'd forgotten why I needed to say good-bye—I almost forgot my own damn name. She kissed me like she'd waited a lifetime to do just that, and I kissed her back like I'd have a whole lifetime to live without ever kissing her again. It was surreal in a way only a person who'd loved another their whole life could understand. Josie and I kissed for so long I almost forgot she was naked and ready above me. *Almost.* When her lips skimmed past my jaw and down my neck, her fingers trailed down my stomach until they tugged on my fly.

Oh, shit. I knew I needed to stop, I *knew* that . . . I just couldn't remember why. Once my fly was open, Josie's hand gripped me, moving steadily up and down until I was gasping. When my gasps turned into loud moans, Josie's mouth moved back to mine, silencing my cries of pleasure and pain with her kisses. I might not have been able to remember why I needed her to stop, but knowing I needed to stop it was enough. That made what should have been pleasurable, painful and what was painful, pleasurable. It was a fucking train wreck of pain and pleasure and touch that I never wanted to walk away from.

As Josie's hand moved faster, I had to grit my teeth and move my hands from her ass or else I would come right then. If I was going to come with Josie, it wouldn't be in her hand.

In one seamless move, I had her on her back. I braced myself over her, my hips locked so closely together with hers, one small movement would put me inside of her. Exactly where I didn't only want to spend the rest of the night, but the rest of my life. All the possible conquests in my future didn't hold a candle to the way I felt being so close to Josie, knowing she loved me and I fucking worshipped her.

Kissing her once more, I leaned back just enough to stare at her. I wanted to look into her eyes, and I wanted her to look into mine. She wasn't drunk, she wasn't with Jesse, and it wasn't strictly a moment of reckless abandon. I wanted to look into her eyes when I took her so I could see exactly what it felt like to know she was making love to me just like I was making love to her .

It would be a first, and one I knew I'd never forget.

Then, almost like a spotlight, a beam of moonlight broke through the window and illuminated Josie's face. Where the bruise taking up one whole cheek was darkening. My stomach twisted right after it clenched. I remembered what happened and *why* we couldn't do it. Now. Or ever. I might not have directly caused it, but Josie wore that bruise because of me. I moved to roll off of her, but her legs wound around me and didn't let me go.

"What? What is it?" she asked.

I closed my eyes so I didn't have to see what my shit-poor luck had done to Josie, but then I forced them open and made myself look so I'd never forget. So if I ever got the tiniest inclination to throw myself back into Josie's life, I'd remember the image of her bruised face below me then. "It's just . . . what happened . . ." The skin between her eyebrows wrinkled. I lifted my thumb to the wrinkle, trying to erase it. "Mason. I can't stop thinking about what—"

"Colt and me?" she interjected. "Is that what you're worried about? Colt and me and what happened between us?"

I took a moment to figure out what she meant. "Well, shit . . . No, that wasn't what I was thinking, but now I am." I'd never asked Josie about her and Colt's relation-ship for two reasons. One, because it was none of my goddamned business. And two, because I didn't want to know a goddamned detail. Even thinking about Colt Mason's hands running down the same areas mine just had or about his . . . inside of her . . . I punched the mattress beside her head, trying to get the image out of my mind.

"Garth, stop. There's no need to get all worked up." Her hands formed around my face, and she waited for my eyes to shift back to hers.

"No need to get worked up? Another man being with you . . . Another man being . . . intimate with you . . . It's a lot for me to process, okay? Let's just leave it at that and forget about it. Forget *forget* about it." Truly, if I never had to experience the image of Colt naked and braced over Josie the way I was, that was just fine by me.

"There's nothing to get worked up about and nothing to forget"—she shook her head when I raised an eyebrow—"or forget *forget* because nothing ever happened."

I know I was one flex and slide away from being buried inside of Josie, but I liked to think my brain didn't strictly run off whatever my dick was doing—or almost doing. But what had Josie just said? Surely she couldn't have meant . . . "Are you saying what I think you're saying?"

"I don't know. Are you asking me what I think you're asking?"

"Okay, I was confused before, but now I'm positively dumbfounded." I slid Josie's hair back from her forehead and waited.

"Colt and I never . . ." Biting her lip, she shrugged.

"You and Colt never slept together?" Because I needed it spelled out—especially when it came to the topic at hand.

Josie shook her head. "No."

If my body hadn't been beaten to a pulp earlier, I would have attempted a back handspring. "Then who was the last guy you slept with?" I skimmed through my memory banks. Other than Jesse and Colt, I couldn't recall Josie being with anyone else. I couldn't remember her being with anyone but . . . I arrived at my conclusion the instant before she replied.

"Well . . . *you* were."

That had been two years ago. The last guy she'd been with was me, and that was forever ago. I felt two emotions: pure and utter elation that I was the last man inside Josie and . . . pity. "*I* was the last guy you slept with? Damn, that sucks for you." It certainly didn't suck for me, but it did for her. "At least the first guy you slept with was Jesse fucking Walker. That has to even it out somewhat. Jesse, first. Me, last. Think you could call it even and we cancel each other out?" Damn. I'd slept with so many women over the course of two years I didn't even want to consider tallying up that number. Especially realizing Josie's tally was a big fat zero.

"Jesse and I never slept together either." Josie's hands stayed planted on my face, and her thumbs stroked my cheeks. It was a soothing gesture, but I should have been soothing her. She hadn't slept with Jesse, the guy she'd been with for two years, the guy she'd started dating when a teenager's libido is in full force . . . Which meant . . .

"Fuck," I muttered as my head became too heavy to hold up. Even with her hands braced around it, the weight was too much. "Are you saying I was your first? That that night was your"—I swallowed and hung my head farther —"that was your first time?"

"You were my first. And you were my last."

I'd had some heavy bombs dropped on me in my lifetime. Being parentless, penniless, and living out of a truck confirmed that. But Josie admitting I'd been the one to take her virginity in a night of drunken haze and recklessness . . . Not only that, but it had been the first and last time she'd had sex . . . Well, that was the fucking atom bomb of mind-fucks right there.

"Please, Joze, please, please, please, don't tell me that's true. I can't even . . . I don't even know . . ." That was the truth—I didn't even know. How I felt, what that meant, how to proceed, and what to do next. *I don't even know* became my newest marching beat, and I felt certain it was there to stay.

"There's one more thing, Black. Since you seem to be taking this so well." Josie peered up at me with confusion before continuing, "I don't just want you to be my last right now. I want you to be my last forever. I want to live my last day with you being the last man I've been with."

I muttered one more curse before shoving off the bed hard. I was able to break free of her legs and put the distance between us I needed to think somewhat straight again. After buttoning my jeans back up, I turned to the side in an attempt to stop staring at her naked body still spread out on the bed. "I can't do this. I can't fucking do this."

"Can't or won't?" she asked, sitting up. "And are you referring to having sex with me or having a relationship with me?"

"Those two things are one and the same for me."

She huffed. "Says no one you've ever fucked, and since you've never had a relationship with anyone but yourself, no one's able to offer their opinions on that."

"Excuse me for not clarifying. What I meant was that having sex and having a relationship are one and the same when it comes to you, Josie. *You*."

"Says the guy with his bag packed and tugging on his boots like he can't get out of here fast enough."

I pulled on the other boot before grabbing my shirt. I'd been clouded by Josie's words and her body, but I'd remembered what I needed to do and why I needed to do it. I couldn't get away from there quickly enough. I couldn't linger with her for long enough either. One. Giant. Mind. Fuck. "I need to leave. You know it, and I know it. It's going to happen one day, and a day sooner is better for both of us than a day later."

"I know that? I *know* that?" she huffed again, then tossed a pillow at me. "Stop telling me what I know and don't know and give me a straight answer. Why are you leaving, Black?"

Minutes ago, she'd been kissing me and making me feel things I didn't know could be felt. Then we were throwing pillows and words and breaking each other's hearts. I hated myself, somehow, even more than I ever had. "There are a million reasons I'm leaving. All of them a reason for why we can't or shouldn't be together and why it never could or would work out if we tried."

She swung her legs over the side of the bed and was either issuing the glare to end all glares or was trying her damnedest to keep from crying. "You know what you need to do? Stop focusing on all of the reasons we shouldn't be together and start accepting the reasons we should be." Josie slid her hands through her hair, shaking her head. "You could take the most perfect couple God ever had the audacity of creating, and if they only focused on the small handful of reasons they shouldn't be together, I guarantee you they wouldn't make it. And we're a long, long shot away from being a perfect couple, so why don't you cut the glass-half-empty routine and give us a fucking chance. Give us the chance we've both been waiting for."

A chance. That was all I could ask for with Josie. But to give someone a chance, there had to be a probability— small as it might have been—of things turning out okay. We didn't have even a minuscule probability of turning out all right if we gave us a try. I couldn't give her a chance because I didn't have one to give. "It's too late."

"You're a fucking liar." Another pillow flew at me. "You're taking the coward's way out, and if you do this, if you walk away because you're afraid of hurting me, or messing things up, or whatever it is you're so terrified of, I'll never forgive you. You leave me again, and I'll hate you for the rest of my life."

I grimaced as pain flooded me. I wanted nothing more than to gather her up in my arms and fall asleep together like we had the past few weeks together. That was all I wanted. "That's okay, Joze. I understand. Hate's a good thing. It will help you heal quicker. It'll keep the wound from going too deep and the scar from being too obvious. If hating me'll make this easier for you, you've got my permission to hate me for all of eternity." Damn, I needed some whiskey. Bottle after bottle after bottle until I'd had enough I forgot her name, and the red cowgirl boots she'd been wearing the first day I met her, and the way her hair lightened every summer, and every one of the billion fucking memories I had of Josie Gibson. She wanted to hate me, but I wanted to forget her. Forgetting her was the only way I could survive without her. It wouldn't be much of a life, nothing more than survival, but I wouldn't even be able to manage that if I couldn't find some way to erase her from my mind.

"I'm not asking for your permission," she snapped. A moment later, her face fell as she slid off the edge of the bed. Josie looked as broken as I felt, and the worst part was not being able to comfort her. "I don't want to hate you. But there's no other place to put this love I have for you. It doesn't just go away, you know? I can't just flick a switch, and Poof! it's gone. I can't just build it one day and dump it the next. It's always going to be a part of me. If I can't love you, those intense feelings will morph into something just as intense, but the total opposite. My love for you will have nowhere to go but hate. I'm going to hate you . . . and that breaks my heart." She started crying, and if I wasn't so resolved, that would have been my tipping point.

I took one last look at her—curled into herself and crying on the floor. That would be my last memory of my Josie. The girl I'd made a silent vow to always protect, always take care of . . . and she was destroyed thanks to me. The ball in my throat was close to suffocating me. I grabbed my bag and opened that door realizing one thing—Josie would move on to live a happy and full life. Maybe not tomorrow, and maybe not next month, but eventually. She'd find love and protection and consistency in the arms of another man.

"But at least you've still got a heart left to break, Joze," I whispered before leaving the room, the house, and the girl all behind.

chapter FOURTEEN

DAYS TURNED INTO weeks, and weeks turned into months. I could finally look in a mirror without wanting to slam my fist through it. That first month after leaving Josie, I couldn't count how many shattered mirrors I left in my wake. Looking in a mirror and hating the person staring back at me wasn't new, but what had changed was that the eyes staring back were the same ones Josie had looked into as she admitted her love for me. She'd looked into those eyes and said it again and again and again before they had turned away and betrayed her.

I'd hated myself for so long it didn't feel like hate anymore, but that . . . ? I didn't have a word extreme or intense enough for how I felt about myself. Utter self-loathing was the closest I could get, but that seemed way too cute for how I really felt.

After leaving the Gibsons' that night, I'd headed east. I didn't have any plans. I just went until my gas tank was empty and I felt as physically exhausted as my mind did. I was in Billings. Even though it was my first time there and I didn't know a thing about it, I moved into a motel room I could rent by the month or the hour and made it home. I didn't know a single person in or around Billings. It was perfect. I didn't want to know anybody, and I didn't want anybody to know me. I found work at an old man's ranch just outside of town, a place to practice bull riding, and tried to purge my mind of all things Josie. I watched the sunrise that morning after I left her, knowing she would wake up hating me. She was right—that kind of love didn't just shrivel up and die. It ran too deep and had weaved too far inside of us to just fade away. It was imprinted on our very cores. That kind of love couldn't be weeded out, so it changed and darkened and morphed into what Josie said—hate. I felt it, too. In my case, it was extreme hate for myself, not for her. So the good thing we had—the best thing I'd ever experienced—I'd managed to twist and break and transform until it turned into thick and heavy hate. I really was a virus.

A month had passed when I recognized one of Willow Springs's seasonal ranch hands walking into the feed store in downtown Billings. I headed straight back to the motel, packed my duffle, got in my truck, and didn't stop driving until it was empty again. I wound up in Baker, about as far east as a person could go and still be in Montana. I wasn't sure I even wanted to stay in the same state I'd grown up in. The same one my mom had fled from, my dad's charred ashes were blowing through, and where the girl I'd loved and destroyed was. Nothing was behind me but a mountain of bad memories, so if I hadn't been about empty on gas and money, I would have kept going until I'd crossed into North Dakota.

I worked at another ranch, I rode bulls at another arena, and another month passed. I knew, in theory, my life was going on, but it felt like it had stagnated. Most of it I'd left hundreds of miles west. I'd even left behind two of my favorite pastimes: whiskey and women. I hadn't had a single sip or felt a single woman beneath me since I left the only home I'd ever known. I knew part of the reason for my newfound abstinence was because I just felt numb. I didn't need a drink or a woman to help me get there because that was my steady state anymore. The other part, the main part, was doing it for her. She'd never know, but I couldn't let the love she'd given me and all that she'd sacrificed to be with me be for nothing. I wanted to stay changed, even if we couldn't be together. I wanted her sacrifice to be matched by one of mine. I wanted her love to leave me changed forever so, somehow, I'd always carry it with me. Saying no to the Jack and the girls was the only way I could honor the love she'd given me. It was all that was left of it because her love had turned to hate.

So I cut off all ties with my old life. Since I didn't have a cell phone, no one from my old life could reach me. It would only be a matter of time before I ran into some-one or someone tracked me down, but I was too busy living in the moment to think about the future. Even five minutes into it.

It was a Friday night, and I was competing in a small-time rodeo just outside of Baker. I didn't know why I bothered to enter. I still hadn't managed a single eight-second ride in practice, so I had no reason to think riding in an actual competition would be any different. I suppose, as time had proven again and again, I was a glutton for punishment.

I was up next, and when the guy before me flew out of the gates, I crouched down to scoop up a handful of dirt. Cupping it, I shook my hand and let the dirt sift between my fingers. It was the first time I'd done it, but I'd seen it done plenty of times. When Clay made it to my rodeos, he could always be found staggering around, sifting a handful of dirt between his fingers. I guess it was something he'd picked up from his dad and used to do as a bull rider himself. I asked him once why he did it, and he'd answered—well, he'd *slurred*—how could a man expect to stay on top when he didn't know what was below him? It hadn't made sense to me then, and it still didn't make sense to me. But back in his day, Clay Black had been a bull riding legend, so I figured if shaking some arena dirt through his fingers had worked for Clay, I wasn't above trying it. I'd tried everything else—might as well.

The guy ahead of me managed to stay on a full eight and earned a decent score. Lucky bastard. When my name was called, I dusted off my hands, climbed the chute, and got into position. I didn't know anything about the bull I'd drawn. I didn't know anything about the rodeo, or the people competing, or the people in attendance. The only thing I knew was that I had to stay on the back of that damn thing because that was all I had left in life. Bull riding and eight seconds. Those were the last things I had to look forward to, the only things left to aspire to. Sad and pathetic, but the truth. So I weaved my hand through the rope, lifted my other, and emptied my head.

I should have known better. As soon as it was empty, she leapt into it. Josie always had a way of doing that—sneaking up on me when I least expected it. The image of her below me, holding my face and telling me she loved me, rushed into my head. It wasn't in a hurry to rush out. It stayed until I didn't see or hear the arena. All I heard and saw was her and those three words. The image was so painful, I winced . . . and the chute flew open. I remembered where I was a moment too late. That bull bucked before hurling into a spin, and I caught so much air

I might have been suspended for eight seconds.

But I'd barely made it one on that back of that bull. When I hit the ground, I landed on my chest. My face hit next. I knew what the dirt felt like, and I knew what it tasted like: cow shit and failure. Shoving to a stand, I spit out a mouthful of dirt and chucked my hat across the arena. I didn't notice the crowd, and I didn't turn around to make sure the clowns were doing their jobs. I stomped out of that arena swearing if I never saw another one or another bull, I'd be just fine.

Once I'd leapt over the fence, I wandered until I had some space and could curse at the bloody moon without offending anyone too much. Life was shit, and that was what I had to look forward to for the rest of my life. Lonely nights, hard-worked days, and humiliating rides where I personally insulted the sport of bull riding.

Fuck my life.

"I don't know who looked more pissed off out there. You or the bull," a familiar voice said behind me as my hat landed at my feet. "Actually, I take that back. You were definitely the most pissed one. By a long shot."

I was already smirking when I twisted around. "Why if it isn't the girl who isn't afraid to let her freak flag fly."

"Nope. I'm not afraid to be who I am. Or love who I love." She smirked right back, lifting an eyebrow.

"Rowen Sterling." I looked around. No sign of Jesse . . . or anyone else.

"Garth Black. Minus the enthusiasm," she threw back.

"What? Really? No enthusiasm? I thought that, if nothing else, one misfit could drudge up some enthusiasm for another." I grabbed my hat and beat it against my chaps to get the dirt off.

"It's hard to drudge up any enthusiasm when the best man's been missing for two months and the wedding is in two days."

Along with the life I'd left behind, I'd lost track of time as well. Could it be *June* already? "Yeah . . . about that . . ."

"Save it. I don't care what you have to say about that right now. All I care about is you getting your ass in that truck of yours and getting to the wedding on Sunday. I'm tired from tracking you down, and I'm tired from putting centerpieces together, and I'm tired from being kept up all night, so shut your mouth already."

Taking a closer look, Rowen did look beat. Her clothes were rumpled, most of her hair had fallen from her braid, and her eyes were bloodshot. I sat on the bottom of one of the empty bleacher sections. "Tell Jesse to stop keeping you up all night with his sex marathons so you can get some sleep then." I waited for Rowen to fire something back. The only time she'd let me get the last word in was never, and I was expecting more of the same.

"Unfortunately it isn't Jesse who's been keeping me up all night."

I arched an eyebrow as she plopped down on the bench beside me. "Not even married and already checking to see if that grass really is greener on the other side?"

I scooted out of reach just before her elbow came at me. "The person who's been keeping me up is the same person whose heart you broke before pulling your vanishing act."

"Josie?" It was painful thinking about her and twice as much so saying her name.

Rowen nodded. "Josie."

"How's she doing?" I asked, staring at the ground.

"I'd tell you if I thought you had a right to know. Which you don't. You giant. Ass. Hole."

"I'm not going to argue with you on that. Not even for fun." I dropped my head into my hands and squeezed my eyes shut, trying to brace myself against the pain shredding through me like tiny pieces of glass.

Rowen didn't say anything for a while. Silence, when the two of us were together, was a rare thing. "Whoa. You really are miserable, aren't you?" Rowen scooted closer and awkwardly wrapped her arm around my shoulders. "So you're miserable. And Josie's miserable. Why the hell did you up and disappear again?"

God, for so many damn reasons that didn't seem important anymore. "You, Rowen, of all people should understand why I had to leave."

"I might understand why you thought about doing it, but not why you actually did it." She gave me a few pats on the back before removing her arm. Thankfully. Rowen might be able to express her affection for Jesse like a champ, but she was an awkward mess around everyone else still. Figuring out how to give affection took a while since she'd been denied it most of her life—I understood that well. "You know I worried about the same things you're worried about: hurting the person you love, destroying their chance for a happy life. But I finally realized something,"—Rowen nudged me—"I've got some pretty great stuff to give, too. The Jesses and the Josies of the world aren't the only ones with something to give. We— the misunderstood misfits of the world—do too."

I huffed and shook my head. I might have had

something to give, but I couldn't figure out how to give it without destroying the person I wanted to give it to.

She said, "People like you and me, kids who grew up fighting for every single ounce of love that came our way . . . When we find that person we want to love, we give them a pure and boundless form of it because we know what it's like to be denied it. We know the opposite of love so well, we go a full one-eighty when we find that special someone."

I gave Rowen a half-smile. "And how does your 'special someone' feel about that pure and boundless love of yours?"

"Pretty fucking fantastic. Something your special someone never got the chance to feel because you acted like a giant. Ass. Hole."

"You know what the nice thing is about being at a zero in the self-esteem department?" I asked with some sarcasm. "Not being able to go any lower when you fire insults off at me."

"I'm not trying to insult you. I'm trying to knock, beat, shake, or bitch slap some sense into you."

"So yeah, you've got a point. I behaved like a giant asshole, but I had to. It was the only way she'd let me go. Now that she has, she can find someone else to experience that boundless love shit with. She'll find it with someone else," I said, ending in almost a whisper.

"With someone else? Who the hell do you think Josie's ever going to find that she's going to be happy with if it's not you?" Rowen looked like she was considering thumping me on the back of the head, so I scooted farther down the bench. "Colt Mason? Some other sweet country boy who bores her to tears?" I shrugged. "Puh-lease. The only boy Josie's going to be happy with is you, and if she chooses to settle down with someone else, she's just going to be pretending."

"According to you," I replied. I wondered if they'd let me ride again. That would at least get me out of having that conversation with Rowen. I'd rather eat another dozen mouthfuls of dirt than talk about Josie and what her future would be like with some other man.

"According to *her*, you giant—"

"Ass. Hole," I filled in. "Yeah, I caught that the first fifty times." And then what she'd said set in. "Josie said that? She actually told you the only person she'd be happy with is me?"

"Would it change your mind if I told you the truth?" She crossed her legs and swung her foot, waiting.

"I don't know. Maybe. Maybe not." It was an honest answer, but not the one she'd been hoping for.

"Listen, Black, I know you love her. I also know you've never told her that, and based on the coward's way out you've taken, you likely never will. That's just the saddest thing I've ever heard, especially since you've loved her for so long." Rowen wagged her finger at me, narrowing her eyes in a way that gave away she had been spending lots of time with Josie.

"It took me a little longer to figure out that Josie loves you too because she doesn't act like the total idiot you do when she's around. But I know she does, and I know she has for a while. I don't know if that love started before or after Jesse and her split up, but I know it's been there for a long time. Why the hell are you just throwing that all away without giving it a chance? If the love you two have has lasted this long while you've acted like you hate each, why wouldn't it last if you tried actually *showing* that love to each other?" She stopped just long enough to suck in a breath. "Why don't you give it a chance? A *real* one?" I exchanged a look with her. One that didn't need words to explain. "Oh yeah, that's right. Thinking about yourself again. What a surprise."

So I guess the look I'd given her did need to be explained. "I'm thinking about everyone *but* myself, for Christ's sake." I pulled off my leather gloves and tossed them so far I didn't see where they landed. "Haven't you heard? I'm a virus. The kind who can't help but infect everyone around me."

Rowen nodded, giving me almost a . . . *sympathetic* look. That was a first. "So that's what her dad told you, eh? That you're a virus? One who's going to ruin his precious daughter? Blah, blah, blah . . ." Rowen rolled her eyes and sighed.

"Yeah, that was about the gist of it. Along with lots of that blah, blah, blah stuff, too." I looked over at her from the corner of my eyes, and when I found her doing the same thing, we laughed. That was the first damn laugh I'd had in two months, and even though it was over in two seconds, it felt good. It *felt*. Which meant my numb shell was cracking. I couldn't decide if that was a good or a bad thing.

"You know what, Garth?"

"I don't know much," I mumbled.

She shook her head. "Screw what her dad thinks. This is your life to live. And that's her life to live. You only get one go around, so makes some mistakes, love who you want to love, and forget the rest." Rowen jumped up from the bleacher about halfway through her speech.

"Screw her parents? Is that something I should shout in the middle of a family dinner? *Screw you, Mr. and Mrs. Gibson. I love your daughter and she loves me and I want her to have my babies, but first I want to make wild love to her like a man on death row.*"

Rowen laughed with me again. "You might not want to say *screw you* at the dinner table because that's just rude, but I think you're good to go with the rest."

"Shit, Rowen," I said as my laughter dimmed, "what are you really doing here?" I couldn't tell if she was trying to get me to come back, or admit I was wrong, or if she wanted me to get on the phone and apologize to Josie. She could have been there for all of those reasons, plus a few dozen more.

"For a whole lot of reasons." Of course. Figures. She came toward me, stopping in front of me. "I'm here to remind you of a promise you made to your best friend to be his best man. The wedding's at seven. Be there early. In something presentable preferably. No wedding gift required. And if you don't make it, no big deal—don't even sweat it. I'll just rip your balls off later." She said that with a straight face, and I knew better than to think she was bluffing. My hands automatically covered my dick. "I'm here to remind you that you left Neil and Rose with no notice and short-handed, and they're already having to run that place without Jesse. You owe them an apology in the least, but returning for the summer and working your ass off would be better." I felt like I was being lectured, but I understood why—I *was* being lectured. "And I'm here to remind you that your other best friend—you know, the one who admitted she loved you but you were too chicken-shit to admit you loved back . . .

that person? You didn't only break her heart, you crushed her." Rowen lowered her face until she was at eye level with me. "Fix it."

I saw a pattern evolving with the couple of women I'd let past my walls. They had a way of fucking up my mind good. Josie first, and now Rowen. I needed time to digest everything she'd just said. I couldn't just respond to all that after a moment's thought. Finally, I cleared my throat and shook my head to clear it. "Anything else, Ms. Sterling-soon-to-be-Mrs. Walker?"

"Mrs. Sterling-Walker," she corrected.

"Ah, hell. You're actually doing the hyphenated name thing? Sterling-Walker?" I clapped and chuckled. "What did Jesse think of that decision?"

"Why don't you ask him?" she replied with a shrug. "It was his idea."

"Pussy-whipped, bleeding heart—"

Rowen leaned back down again and patted my cheek. "You can deny it all you want, but we all know you've been a member of that club for a while." I glowered as she headed for the parking lot. "Oh, you know, there was something else." She snapped and glanced back. "I'm here to remind you that you're an asshole and to order you to stop being such a giant one. Give it a rest, Black. It's getting old." Shooting me a smile, she continued on. "See you in two days."

I grumbled at the ground, then sighed. "Rowen?" I stood. She paused and turned to me with a smile, like she knew I'd have something else for her. Damn that women's intuition thing. "Josie and me? You really think we've got a chance at making it?

Her smile spread. "There's only one way to find out."

With a wink, Rowen continued on her way and left me to work out the biggest mindfuck I'd dealt with to date.

chapter FIFTEEN

"SOMEONE ORDER A mail-order best man?" I shouted, charging into the barn office where Mrs. Walker had directed me.

Jesse was draped over a metal chair, looking as cool and collected as any other day. The guy was about to swear a lifetime to one woman, and his forehead wasn't even beaded with sweat. "You made it." He grinned an ear-to-ear one and popped out of the chair.

"Did you have your doubts?" I shook his hand and gave him a quick, awkward manly hug. Lots of hard back patting was involved.

"Nah," he replied. "No doubts."

"That much faith in me, eh?"

"Not really, but I have plenty of faith in Rowen. Especially when she got that look on her face and headed out to hunt you down. I've learned to cease and desist whatever I'm doing if she ever turns that determined, take-no-prisoners expression on me."

I chuckled. "You always were the smart one." Jesse sat again and checked his watch. "Someone a little antsy?" If he was, he sure as hell wasn't showing it.

"Not antsy, but excited."

"Excited? For a wedding?" I wrinkled my nose. "Jess, we're cowboys. We don't get excited over weddings. Not even when they're our own."

Jesse's boot kicked mine. "Well, I'm excited about a wedding and I'm a cowboy. So consider your world officially rocked."

"Okay, I get why you'd be excited for the wedding *night* . . . but the actual wedding itself? Flowers? Long-ass ceremony? Old women in big hats? What the hell's so exciting about that?" I could see the excitement written on every plane of his face. I guess I was looking for an explanation as to why.

Jesse shrugged, checking his watch again. "In one hour, Rowen's going to be my wife. I wouldn't care if the ceremony leading up to that included electric shock therapy and bamboo shoots up my finger nails. I'd still be excited knowing that when all that was said and done, I'd get to call her my wife."

"Mrs. Sterling-Walker . . ." I gave him a sly smile, which earned me another kick.

"Yeah, yeah. I know you don't get it, but it works for us. And that's all that matters." Jesse hadn't stopped smiling since I walked in the room. Knowing him, he'd probably been smiling in his sleep since she agreed to marry him.

And then I stopped to think about what he'd just said—*It worked for them.* Jesse and Rowen were far from a cookie-cutter couple, but damn if they weren't the happiest, most in love one I'd ever had the nauseating pleasure of being around. They'd managed to figure out a way to make things work for them. The odds were stacked against them—the rebel city girl with a checkered past and the golden country boy—but they'd figured out a way to make it work. And that was all that mattered . . . I almost had to slap my cheeks to snap out of it. "So? Best man duties? Give me the basic rundown."

Jesse leaned back in the chair, and I had to suppress the urge to kick it out from under him. It was his wedding day and all—if ever a guy deserved a break, it would be that day. "I don't know. Just back me up if any of Rowen's exes show up and try to sweep her away. Oh, and try not to cuss or pull out your flask and take a swig in the middle of the ceremony." Jesse's eyes narrowed as he searched for other suggestions. "Don't piss Rowen off. Or Josie. Or anyone for that matter."

"Slow down, Sterling-Walker. Slow. Down." Jesse smirked at me. "If any of Rowen's exes show up, I've got your back—no problem. Kicking ass is one of the few things I do best." Jesse nodded. "I promise to *try* not to cuss, and you don't have to worry about any swigging in the middle of the ceremony because I'm"—I unbuttoned my jacket and held it open, patting each pocket— "flaskless." Jesse's eyes widened in surprise. "And I won't piss off your bride or hopefully anyone else, and I will certainly try not to piss Josie off."

"You know what? Just to be safe, why don't you not even make eye contact with Josie during the ceremony? Rowen promised to pat her down to make sure she wouldn't try to hide a shotgun under her dress, but it's better to be safe than sorry. So no eye contact, just in case. At that range, there'd be nothing left of you above the neck." Grabbing a piece of straw off the floor, he flicked it at me. "But with that ugly mug gone, you'd be a lot more attractive, so no worries either way I guess."

I flipped him my middle finger. "It's not like she's going to be a few feet in front of me." Jesse's eyebrows came together as I had a light bulb moment. "She *is* going to be a few feet in front of me."

"I thought Rowen told you. Josie's her maid of honor, so you two will be standing right across from each other, and you have to escort her down the aisle at the end of the ceremony."

That was why I should have been around for the rehearsal last night. I would have known Josie would be directly across from me and I could have worn a bullet-proof vest under my jacket. I had planned to talk to Josie at some point that night, but it wouldn't happen before the ceremony since it was minutes away from starting. I was practically squirming as I pictured the glare she'd have aimed at me the entire time. "Well, fuck me. And here I thought the most uncomfortable part of this thing would be the tie." I grabbed at it again, pulling it back so I could take a full breath.

"Sorry, pal."

"Sure, you're not."

A knock sounded on the other side of the door before Mrs. Walker peeked her head in. "It's time, Jess. You boys ready?"

Jesse popped out of the chair and ran his hands down his jacket. They were having a straight-up cowboy wedding—from the jeans, to the boots, to the black felt hats.

"I'm ready," I said to Mrs. Walker and hitched my thumb at Jesse. "He's *excited*."

Mrs. Walker laughed. "What can I say? I raised a deranged son." Jesse swirled his finger beside his head.

"Nah, Mrs. Walker. You raised one hell of a man." I don't know who looked at me with more surprise.

After giving Jesse a solid hug, Mrs. Walker gave me

just as solid of one. "You didn't turn out so bad yourself, Mr. Black." Patting my cheek, she slipped back out the door, leaving it cracked for us. I heard the guitars in the background playing some Johnny Cash song . . . of course.

"Okay, this is it. How do I look?" Jesse held his hands out.

"Ugly."

"Thanks for the confidence booster"—Jesse slugged my arm and headed for the door—"best man."

"Nice jeans, by the way. Good of you to get dressed up for your own wedding. Pathetic."

Jesse shrugged, my sarcasm bouncing right off of him. "What can I say? Rowen kind of has a thing for my jeans."

"No, Rowen kind of has a thing for your ass."

He paused at the door and gave an exaggerated wink. "I can't blame her. I *do* have a fantastic ass."

"Sounds like someone's boosted their own confidence," I muttered as Jesse slipped out the door. "Hey, Jess, hold up just a quick sec."

Bad timing was my M.O., but I had to get it off of my chest. I'd taken my sweet time saying it, but there I was in some big hurry to get it out right as he was about to say "I do."

"What's up?"

I sucked in a heavy breath. "I'm sorry. I'm sorry for that night with Josie. You trusted me to take care of someone you loved, and I betrayed you both. And I'm sorry." I couldn't seem to say it enough. "So fucking sorry." One more time, I guess. "I just wanted you to know. I wanted you to know I didn't plan for that to happen, or even want it to, but I didn't do anything to stop it either." I told Josie

I'd never apologized to her for that night because I wasn't sorry it happened, and that was true—it was hard to be sorry for a night I thought I'd only live in my dreams. But there was another part to it, the other side of the coin. I *was* sorry for the people I'd hurt. I was sorry for betraying one of my best friends. Well, I was sorry for betraying my two best friends. Jesse stayed quiet, the skin between his brows creasing deeper and deeper with every word. "Oh, and one more thing. I'm sorry for not saying *I'm sorry* sooner. It took me two pathetic years to apologize to my best friend for making love to his girlfriend behind his back."

"Black, what the hell are you talking about?" That wasn't what I'd been expecting him to say. "You've said sorry plenty of times before." I cocked an eyebrow. "Okay, so you haven't come right out and said those exact words, but you've shown me you were sorry. You've been showing me for a long time." Jesse clapped his hand over my shoulder. "I know you're sorry. And I forgave you a long time ago."

I let that settle in for a few moments. And a few more. "Well, shit. If I'd known that, I could have saved my breath."

Jesse's smile stretched. "It's all good. Besides, it's nice to hear the words sometimes, you know?"

"You've got that intentional look," I said, motioning at his face. "So whatever it is you're thinking, you better spit it out."

"The hard part is showing someone you're sorry—or in a totally unrelated and not-at-all applicable situation . . . showing someone you love them." Jesse's tone gave me the equivalent of a nudge. Inapplicable, my ass. "The easy part is telling them."

"Your point, Yoda?"

"You've already proven you love her. That's the hard part. All you have to do is tell her." How was he still able to talk, let alone form those kinds of thoughts, when he was supposed to be standing in front of an alter? Oh, yeah. Because he was Jesse fucking Walker.

"And that's the easy part?" I said.

"As pie."

I shoved his arm, pushing him through the office door. "Let's get you to your wedding, princess."

"I'll make sure Rowen tosses the bouquet your way, sweetie," Jesse said, adjusting his tie before buttoning his jacket.

"Bite me, Walker."

He grinned at me. "Love you too, Black."

Sliding the barn door open, I clamped my mouth closed. Dozens of faces turned their attention on the two of us. "You couldn't have given me a little warning?" I hissed at him, keeping a smile plastered on as I followed him to the altar.

"Warning," he said, waving at Clementine. She was practically bouncing in her seat.

Again, I had to fight the urge to buckle his knees out from under him. His wedding day. Dozens of people smiling at us. I should be on my best behavior. As the song the guitar player was strumming ended, he moved seamlessly into the next song. Even though I wasn't a big Cash fan, I'd been around Jesse enough to know the song—"I Walk the Line." I got the relevance, but really, the lyrics seemed more suited for a person like me than Jesse. A single guitar player was playing the song at half time, but the tune was almost haunting. I was practically wiping my eyes, and then the Walkers' front door opened and Josie stepped out. Damn. If I'd been the crying type, I would have been a sobbing mess right then.

She clutched a bouquet and wore a pretty purple dress that moved with the breeze. She was *the* most beautiful thing I'd ever seen. She always had been. And she always would be. She didn't notice me at first—not until she'd made it down the stairs to the aisle. As soon as she saw me, her smile vanished. Her skin, already darkened a couple of shades from the early summer sun, whitened. Her pace slowed so much, I worried that she would turn around and bolt. Instead, she sucked in a deep breath, shifted her gaze away from me, and continued down the aisle. When she made it to the altar, she gave Jesse her standard slug greeting, then mouthed a quick *Congratulations*.

It was another surreal moment. The three of us all together as one was about to commit his life to the woman he loved. The three of us had grown up together, lived and learned together, loved and hurt one another. Yet after all of that, we were still together, practically shoulder to shoulder, supporting one who was ready to move on to the next phase of life. Jesse, Josie, and me—an unlikely trio of friends who'd been through it all.

"Hey, Joze," I whispered to her, taking a step her direction. She greeted me back with a powerful glare. "You look beautiful."

Her glare went from powerful to lethal. Jesse subtly elbowed me in the stomach before tilting his head back. "Don't make eye contact. Keep your mouth shut. Until the end of the ceremony." One more elbow before a small smile appeared. "Please."

"Fine," I mouthed before clamping my mouth shut. The guitar player was just getting to the second chorus when Rowen stepped out from behind the front door. She looked beautiful—Jesse was one hell of a lucky man—but I only kept my eyes on her for a moment. They shifted to the woman standing off to my side.

Every eye was on the bride coming down the aisle, but mine were on the woman I could only dream would make the same journey down the aisle toward me. I could tell Josie knew I was staring at her. She was obviously ignoring me, and her middle finger was extended behind her bouquet so only my eyes would see. That was a sure sign.

The song ended. Rowen took Jesse's hands at the altar, vows and rings were exchanged, a kiss was shared that went on far too long for my liking . . . but I couldn't pay attention to any of it. The only thing I could focus on was Josie. I tried looking away from her, but it was impossible. Jesse had found the woman he wanted to spend the rest of his life with, and I had too. The only difference was that it had taken me much longer to admit that to myself. Josie and I were like oil and vinegar at times, and her temper only served to fuel mine, but we belonged together. There wasn't any more doubt in my mind. We belonged together. I'd accepted that. The trick was finding out if she still believed that.

That was how I watched one of my best friends marry the woman he loved—through the eyes of the woman I did. Once she stopped paying attention to me, her glare disappeared. Josie went from smiling, to shedding a few happy tears, to beaming, to crying, and then she repeated it as Jesse and Rowen exchanged rings. When the preacher pronounced them husband and wife, she smiled and clapped—everyone else was hooting and hollering like they were at a honky-tonk and not a wedding—but there was something sad about her expression. Her eyes couldn't mask the sadness.

As Jesse and Rowen took the trip back down the aisle together to yet another Cash song strummed on a guitar, the Walkers descended on them before they made it far. There was so much hugging and kissing and crying from all of those sisters that I squirmed where I was at the front. Once they'd made it past the Walker bottleneck, Josie moved beside me. I sucked in a breath and smiled, but she wouldn't look at me. She clearly had something to say because she just stood there, practically shoulder to shoulder with me, looking expectant.

After a few more seconds, she sighed. "You're supposed to escort me down the aisle."

"Oh." Well, that explained the look. I held out my elbow for her. "I didn't know that."

"You might have if you'd made it to the rehearsal last night." She wove her arm through my elbow, but she made sure that as little of her arm touched mine as possible. I was back to being radioactive.

"Yeah, I guess so. I had a few things to figure out." We were able to speak in normal voices because everyone was still cheering and clapping for the newly married couple who'd already made their way through the Walkers' front door.

"Well, I hope you got figured out what you needed figuring out." Josie's voice wasn't warm, and it wasn't particularly cold either. It was just . . . absent. Removed.

"I think I did." I had to tap the shoulders of a few people who were blocking our way. *It's a wedding, people, not a rock concert. Get a grip.*

"Great for you." Josie's arm weaved out of mine as we approached the porch steps. Instead of climbing them with me, she turned away and headed toward the side of the house. "Bye, Black."

I watched her until she disappeared, calculating my next move. Chase her and tell her what I needed to say before everyone sat down for the reception? Bide my time and catch her later after a few dances and a couple glasses of wine? I decided to go after her then because there was no sense in waiting. I'd waited too long already. I filed around the Walkers' house—along with everyone else who was making their way to the big white tent set up in back. I lost sight of Josie in the crowd, but I kept moving forward. We'd wind up in the same spot eventually.

Inside of the tent, everyone took their seats around white tables set with white candles and flowers. I scanned everyone, not finding her. Just when I was about to head back out to see if she'd taken a detour, Mrs. Walker slipped up beside me.

"Your seat's up here," she said, putting her arm through mine and guiding me to the other end of the tent. "Are you all ready for your speech?"

My head whipped toward Mrs. Walker. "What speech?"

"The one the best man gives during the toast," she replied, waving at someone we passed.

"No one said anything about a speech. I'm just here for the free food."

Mrs. Walker nudged me gently. "And here I was

thinking you were here for a different reason." Her gaze shifted to a person sitting at the long table in front of us. Josie. Leave it to Mrs. Walker to save the pretenses.

"Yeah . . . about that . . ." I rubbed the back of my neck as I watched Josie. "I'm not sure that reason I'm here is super thrilled with me actually being here."

"Here's a little secret I'll give away about us women." Mrs. Walker leaned in, watching Josie with me. "Sometimes we act one way but feel another."

"Are you telling me that Josie behaving like I'm the anti-Christ is all just an act?"

She smiled and patted my arm. "I'm saying why don't you find out if it's an act? There's nothing to lose in at least finding out."

"Besides my pride," I mumbled.

"Pride's overrated," she said, moving toward a table of people waving at her. "Give humiliation a try."

I didn't care if I had to humiliate myself in front of every last person on the planet, nor did I care how I had to do it—it would be worth it to get Josie to hear me out. Since Josie was on one side of the bride and groom's seats, I assumed mine was on the other side. The newlyweds weren't there yet—knowing them, they were probably getting it on right then. For Jesse's sake, I hoped people weren't right when they said the sex went downhill after the *I dos*. Maybe I could work that into the speech. Shit—a speech. I would have to thank both of the Sterling-Walkers for the heads-up on that one. As I took my seat, I glanced at Josie. She was looking every direction but mine. Was Mrs. Walker right? Could she be only acting like she hated me? I wasn't sure, but I would find out.

"Hey, Joze." I angled my chair a little toward her and

waited. "Josie?" I knew she'd heard me because her face was going a little red.

I was ready to say her name again when her head snapped my way. "You remember that little *Bye, Black* I issued back there?" Josie pointed toward the Walkers' house. I didn't have a chance to nod or reply. "That wasn't a *Bye, I'll see you in a minute.* That was a *Bye, I never want to see you again.*"

Those words, and that look on her face, gutted me. Act or no act, each of those words sliced through me. "Josie . . ." I had so much to say, so much to explain and apologize for, but that was all I could get out.

Her eyes closed and shook her head. "I warned you. I told you what would happen if you left me that night. That the . . . the . . . love I had for you then"—her voice caught, but after a moment, she lifted her shoulders and cleared her throat—"would change into something else. The opposite. It has."

I wanted to reach for the glass of water on the table in front of me, but that seemed like too much work. Every scrap of energy had just been sucked out of me. "You hate me? You don't love me anymore?"

Her eyes met mine for a moment before she twisted away from me. She was obviously done talking, but I wasn't. I would say what I needed to and apologize for fifteen years of not giving her my best every day of it.

When another round of clapping and cheering went through the crowd, I didn't need to look to know Jesse and Rowen had made their way to the tent. I stood and clapped with everyone else as my mind worked to decide what to do next. I hadn't come to the wedding with any expectations about how Josie would react to seeing me after my couple-month departure, but if I had, I wouldn't have expected her to really hate me. Maybe she'd been right, and her love had nowhere else to go but into hate. That shattered me. But maybe Mrs. Walker was right, and it was all just an act.

Jesse and Rowen hugged their way down the table. I extended my hand to Jesse while Rowen and Josie hugged. Since I pretty much hadn't taken my eyes off of her all afternoon, I saw Josie whisper something into Rowen's ear. Rowen replied with a dismissive wave. I guessed Josie was asking Rowen if she'd mind if she smashed her dinner into my face, and Rowen's wave was a *Not at all. Fire away.* That was okay. If Josie had to smash her filet into my face in order to feel a bit better so I could say what I needed to, that was a small price to pay.

"Congrats, best man. Your head is still attached to your neck." Jesse clapped the side of my arm and grinned.

"Aren't I the one who's supposed to be congratulating you?" I asked, finally diverting my attention. I might be there for Josie, but I was also there for Jesse and Rowen.

"No need to say it, pal. It's written all over that tortur-ed face of yours."

"Haha, funny man. Thank you, by the way, for letting me know about the speech I'd be making and giving me some time to prepare," I said dryly.

"You bet. Good luck." Jesse's grin jumped up a few levels when Rowen slid beside and pressed a kiss into his cheek.

"Holy shit. Rowen Sterling. Glowing. Married. I sup-pose now's the time to start packing our bags for the apocalypse."

Jesse slugged my arm. Rowen got the other. "Holy

shit. Garth Black. Present. Accounted for. Sober. Quick, no time to pack your bags for the apocalypse because it's here."

I laughed as I stepped in to hug her. "Congrats, Mrs. Sterling-Walker. You take care of my little boy and make sure he eats his peas, washes behind his ears, and that you tuck him in every night sated with a smile on his face."

Jesse rolled his eyes. Rowen lifted her eyebrows. "Planning on it."

"By the way, you look amazing," I added. I didn't know much about wedding dresses, but I'd seen enough to know that hers wasn't a typical one. In true Jesse and Rowen fashion, she'd picked out the dress that suited her, the one that worked for them, and said to hell with the rest of it.

"Nice of you to notice. Finally." Rowen inclined her head behind her—where Josie's back was as much to us as it could get.

"Yeah . . . sorry about that."

Rowen took her seat, and Jesse slid her chair forward. "Sincerity is the most important part of an apology," Rowen said. "You might want to take note in case you're planning on making any more tonight."

"I'm planning on it"—I indicated at Josie's back—"if someone decides to actually acknowledge me."

"From one stubborn person to another"—Rowen leaned across Jesse's lap toward me—"figure out a way so she *has* to hear you out. Don't let her get away from here tonight without hearing what you have to say." Rowen's eyes stayed on mine, drilling what she'd just said into me. She leaned back into her seat, but not before winding her arms around Jesse's neck and pulling him in for one long,

long kiss. Most nauseatingly in love couple alive.

Hey, maybe I could work that into the speech I had to give in—from the look of the dude carrying the mic up to the table—any minute. I wanted to ask Jesse if I could abdicate my speech-giving responsibilities, but he was still wrapped up in the kiss that was going to set some kind of record.

My gaze drifted to Josie—and the person sliding into the empty seat beside her. My fists formed at my sides automatically. "What the hell is Colt Mason doing sitting next to Josie?" I didn't care if I was breaking up their make-out session; they had a whole honeymoon to make up for it. After a few more seconds of lip locking, Jesse surfaced with a stupid grin on his face. "Well?" I nudged him to break him out of his stupor.

"Colt's Josie's date," Jesse replied matter-of-factly.

"And you didn't think to tell me this earlier?" Not that it threw a kink in my plans, but I would have liked a little more notice that Colt and Josie were there together than him slipping into the seat next to her and draping his arm around the back of her chair.

Jesse lifted a shoulder. "I'm telling you now. Besides, I'm pretty sure the only reason she invited him was to piss you off. Looks like it's working."

"Great, just fucking great," I said, scrubbing my hands over my face. Josie was with Colt, she'd all but admitted that she hated me, and the dude with the mic had just switched it on and was bringing it my direction. Could anything go worse?

When the guy handed me the mic, I accidentally tapped my water glass with it, making the glass teeter a few times before shattering when it hit the ground. Of course that made me mutter a curse which, since the mic was on and close to my mouth, sounded around the entire tent. Perfect. The first word of my speech was *that* one. Jesse and Rowen snickered, Josie was back to glaring at me, and Jesse's sisters gaped at me like I'd just set myself on fire.

Now that I had everyone's attention and the babies in the room were crying . . . speech time. "No one's ever accused me of being articulate, and after that, you can all see why—if you didn't know that already." Everyone except for the chuckling hyenas beside me stared at me with shocked expressions. "That's why I would have begged Jesse to let someone else speak, but since I had a whole five minutes of notice"—I clapped my hand on his shoulder and gave it a hard squeeze—"there wasn't a lot of time for begging. Or running away before the mic got in my hands. So even though articulate and me"— shit, was it articulate and *I*? I should have paid more attention in English class—"live on opposite sides of the state, tonight I'm going to give it my best shot. Tonight I'm going to attempt to say exactly what I need to, and I hope you all will give me a chance to do that."

My eyes shifted to Josie, who still had her back to me, but it had stiffened. "Jesse and I"—or was it Jesse and *me*? Damn it anyways—"grew up as best friends. That someone like him would even want to associate with me, let alone be friends with me, was something that took me a long time to get used to. If you've lived around these parts for very long, you know, I was a piece of—" I caught myself just in time thanks to Clementine shaking her head and wagging her finger at me from the table right in front of me. I thanked her with a wink. "I was a piece of . . . *something* . . . and Jesse was the stand-up, amazing guy he still is today. Someone like me didn't deserve a friend like him. A person like me didn't deserve his acceptance and kindness and love." Jesse and Rowen had stopped chuckling and were looking at me with something of a bewildered look, probably because I was speaking from the heart and not straight out of my ass.

"But it wasn't just Jesse and me who became inseparable. We had a third partner in crime, and the first day I saw her, I convinced myself she was an angel." Josie's head tilted, but her back was still to me. "And then when I asked her on the playground if she really was an angel and could I try her wings out, she stuck her tongue out at me and walked away . . . thus ruining my angel theory." A low laugh resonated through the room. Even I smiled at the memory. "The three of us became best friends, never doing anything without inviting the other two. Just like with Jesse, I convinced myself I didn't deserve her friendship or care . . . or love." I had to pause and clear my throat. "My whole life, I let people tell me what I did and didn't deserve, and my whole life, I believed them. But here's what I learned from Jesse." I squeezed his shoulder again before letting go.

"Who we choose to love, and who chooses to love us has nothing to do with being deserving or undeserving. It has to do with who you simply have to love and who simply has to love you. It took me years to realize that my two best friends didn't love me because I did or didn't deserve it or that I loved them because they did or didn't. We loved each other because we wanted to. We *chose* to. I know another certain someone he had to drill that into as well. A certain someone who promised a lifetime to him this afternoon." I glanced at Rowen, and she was almost teary-eyed. I'd been under the impression Rowen did teary about as often as I did.

"So that's what this guy taught me about love. It was nothing to do with deserving, and everything to do with who we want and choose to love. I learned something else about love from our other best friend." Josie was sitting forward in her seat, still not facing me, but she didn't have to—I knew she heard every word. "She taught me *how* to love. She taught me *who* I wanted to love. Even though I failed at it, stumbled over my own two feet so many times I was face-planting more than I was walking, she showed me the perseverance of love." I probably should have been looking out into the crowd or at the bride and groom, but all I could do was stare at Josie and spill my guts. I never realized how many guts I had to spill. It was a messy operation.

"I learned something else about love from Rowen. She taught me that when you do find the person you want to love for the rest of your life, it's okay to embrace change. It's okay to change yourself. Everyone likes to think that when they find that special someone, that person should accept them and their flaws, vices, and short-comings. Maybe they're an amazing enough person that they do . . . but they shouldn't have to. A person should want to change themselves for the better when they find that person. Rowen might not have come out and said it, but she showed me by example." I nodded at her as she wiped her eyes, then shot me a thumbs-up.

"So Jesse taught me something about love. Rowen taught me something about love. And the example they set for loving each other should teach us all something about love." I motioned between them. "These two are the couple to beat. The love they have for each other is the kind to aspire to. I don't know about you, but I sure wouldn't mind having someone beside me who could give these two a run for their money." A few people in the crowd clapped. I wasn't sure if it was because they were trying to give me a hint that it was time to wrap it up or if they just really liked what I was saying. Because, Jesus Christ, I was saying a lot. It was time to wrap it up before I became any more transparent. "I'm going to wrap up this hour and a half sermon with just one more thing—totally off-topic and unrelated, and I'm sorry to Jesse and Rowen and the rest of you. But I have to say this now because I have the mic, and she's close by, and this might be the only chance I get to say this." I shot Jesse and Rowen an apologetic look—they just waved me on.

"I want to say I'm sorry for hurting her when all I ever wanted to do was protect her. I'm sorry for running away and being a coward and making you cry . . . and I'm sorry for the million things I need to apologize for." Since I was staring right at her, I wasn't making my apology very anonymous. "You were right about everything. Right about how I felt for you, and why I did the things I did, and why I ran away. You were right about so much." I wanted her to look at me. I wanted to find the strength I always did in her eyes. "But you were wrong about one thing. You told me I was running away because I was afraid to admit I loved you. That wasn't it." Finally, her head turned my way and her eyes met mine. They looked as tortured as I felt. "I wasn't the guy who fell in love with you this past winter." I shook my head. Pain flashed across her face. "I was the boy who fell in love with you that day on the school bus when we were five. And I'm the man that always will."

I'd said what I needed to; I'd survived the speech. I couldn't stand to look at Josie's pained face any longer. I couldn't stand knowing I was responsible for it. So I tipped my hat at Jesse and Rowen, set down the mic, and headed out of the tent. I needed a hell of a lot more than fresh air, but it was a start. I made it all the way to the giant maple tree way back on the Walkers' property. I couldn't decide what I wanted to do more: keep walking until I'd found the end of the earth, then take a flying leap off of it, or drop to my knees and curse at the stars for shining so brightly when my own personal darkness was setting in.

I'd said what I needed to—I'd apologized—and Josie knew how I felt. She knew I loved her, just as she'd suspected. After all I'd said, she hadn't done anything about it. She'd stayed in her seat, her eyes pained, her mouth closed, and I feared, her heart closed as well. Fifteen years of build-up to when I finally confessed my love for her, and I was two months too late. As usual, my timing sucked. Knowing Josie was back in that tent, sitting beside some other guy, and that she could have been mine if I hadn't turned my back and run . . . the emotions bottled inside of me exploded. The old maple took the brunt of it.

"Now what did that tree ever do to you?" The voice came from behind me as I considered going back at it for another round.

If they weren't already, my toes were about to break if I kept kicking it. "Nothing. But in case you haven't noticed, I do a lot of fucked-up things to things and people who don't deserve it." I wiped the tree bark from my knuckles and watched Josie come toward me. In that light purple dress, with the way the moon and stars were shining, she really was an angel gliding toward me. It was such a beautiful sight—almost painfully so—the breath caught in my lungs.

"I noticed," she replied, stopping in front of me. Her face gave nothing away, but her eyes did—that fire was back.

"Are you going to slap me?" I braced myself for it.

"I'm thinking about it, but I've got a couple questions for you to answer first. Then I'll decide." I nodded. "That was some speech in there, Black. Was it real? Was it the truth?" Josie's voice was flat and emotionless. I knew mine would be neither.

"Every word." I didn't think it was possible for a voice to wobble so much over three syllables.

Her eyes closed then flashed open. "I'm here with Colt."

That was a dagger through my heart, but instead of keeping it there and letting it slow me down, I pulled it out and dropped it at my feet. "You might be here with him, but your heart isn't here with him."

That fire in her eyes spread to the rest of her face. "Who are you to tell me who I do and don't love? Who the hell do you think you are?"

I maybe should have been flinching for a forthcoming slap, but instead I stepped closer. "The person you love. The person who loves you. That's who I am." My voice didn't wobble that time. "The person who will love you every second of every day until our days run out. Until we're buried beside each other under an old tree like this. I'm not running away anymore. I'm not going anywhere, so if any of that love you used to have for me hasn't turned to hate, tell me. Please, Joze, tell me. Do you still love me? Do you still *want* to love me? Because I know I've been piss-poor at showing it, but I meant what I said in there—I've loved you since the day I met you. And I meant what I just said out here—I'm going to continue loving you until the day I die." I had so much more to say, but I'd said the important things. If she turned her back on me and I never saw her again, at least she'd know the important things. If she threw her arms around me and decided to be with me like I hoped, I had the rest of our lives to fill in the rest.

"You said I was wrong about something. Wrong about when you fell in love with me." I nodded and waited as she put her thoughts together. "Well, I was wrong about something else, too." A tear slipped out of the corner of her eye, and when I lifted my hand to wipe it away, she didn't flinch away from me.

"What else were you wrong about?"

"When you walked away from me a couple of months ago, that love I had for you did change—like I thought it would." Another tear fell, followed by another, so I just kept my hand pressed against her cheek to catch them.

"It changed to hate. I walked away, and your love changed to hate." Saying those words was a thousand times more painful than thinking them.

"No." She shook her head, her eyes dropping. "It changed when it *grew*. I realized that even though you were gone, there was no one else I wanted to love. I had no love that didn't belong to you left to give."

Oh my god. Was she saying what it sounded like she was saying? I wasn't sure, so I needed to ask. I needed to know, and hopefully my question didn't sound as lame as the one I'd asked myself. "Joze, are you saying what I think you're saying?" So much for not sounding as lame. "Are you saying you still love me?"

Her head bobbed. "So much I've been sick with it these past two months."

She still loved me. Josie Gibson still loved me, and I was finally ready to accept that love. I'd waited for that moment for so long, I didn't know what the hell to say. Or do? What did I say to that . . .? "I love you, Joze. I love you so fucking much. Yeah, I realize saying fuck while confessing one's love probably isn't romantic—"

My confession was cut short when her mouth crashed into mine. Her arms wound around my neck while I drew her close and kissed her back. That whole time I'd been anticipating a slap when I should have been expecting a kiss. The story of my life. Josie kissed me so forcefully, she managed to back me up into that old maple, and then she kissed me for so long, I'm sure the sun was thinking about rising before her lips left mine.

She was smiling with that fire still burning in her eyes. "I came here with Colt you know." Her smile went higher on one side.

"Yeah, yeah, too bad for him because you're here with me now, and I'm not letting go." Drawing her back to me, I lowered my mouth just outside of her ear. "Finders keepers."

I felt her smile on the side of my neck. She was still smiling when that sun did finally rise. It was the start of a new life for me. A new life for us. I had everything I needed right in front of me.

I didn't need eight seconds of glory when I had a lifetime of it in my arms.

epil**OGUE**

I WAS BACK on the bull again. Not in the way the saying goes, but on an actual bull that could have been Bluebell's uglier and meaner older brother. Rodeo season had been in full swing for a while, but it was my first ride since Josie and I finally figured out our shit. Well, since *I'd* finally figured out mine. The past two months had been the best months of my life. They'd been so great—I'm talking delirious, insane kind of happy—I'd come close to convincing myself I was living a different life. Josie said I'd just stopped fighting life at every turn and opened myself up to *living* it instead. She was probably right—she usually was.

Really, it didn't matter. Whether Josie's theory or mine was the right one, it didn't take away from the fact that the girl I'd spent a lifetime loving from afar, I'd get to love up close for the rest of my life. I got to touch and kiss and hold her as much as I wanted to . . . and I wanted to all the time. Luckily, she didn't mind.

So maybe I was back on the bull again in the way the saying goes, too. I don't know if I'd ever been on the bull in the first place when it came to life, but again, it didn't matter. I was there now. I was learning how to let the good things in and let the bad things pass through me, one day at a time, one lesson after another. It was a slow process and one hell of a grueling journey, but I got to experience it with Josie at my side, so fuck the rest. I was a lucky man.

Mr. and Mrs. Gibson were slowly warming up to me. Slowly being the operative word. I didn't blame them. I understood why they were practically holding their breaths for me to screw up big time. The thing they didn't know, or what they'd never be able to fully understand, was how I felt about her. I loved her, sure, but it went so far beyond that I didn't know a way to describe it. Joze was my everything. My . . . *everything*. No exaggeration. My whole day, my every thought, my every decision was somehow centered around her. She was more essential than the air I breathed because air wasn't essential to me: she was. I'd rather die from suffocation knowing my priorities were right than live a long life letting some stupid invisible compound be more essential to my life than she was. Because that was a fucking lie.

The bull shuddered, reminding me where I was and what I was about to do. The guy manning the gate was watching me, waiting. Before I gave the nod, I scanned the grandstands. I didn't need to scan them for long. A green-eyed girl wearing red boots and a killer smile stood on the other side of the arena, her chin propped on one of the rails. She was still the most beautiful thing I'd ever seen, just as she had been the first time I saw her. She winked before mouthing three words I could make out from all the way across the arena.

No, not those three words. I was on the back of a bull in front of thousands of people—not exactly the ideal time for mushiness and endearing words. Nope, she mouthed *Kick some ass*. I acknowledged her with a grin before three more words slipped out of her mouth.

Yes, those three words. The ones that had changed my life. The ones that made me want to change my life in the first place. The words I'd felt for her for so long, they'd become one of the few constants in my life. The ones I'd *felt* for her but had only recently learned how to *show* her those words. Sure, I might have been on a monster bull, about to compete in one of the biggest rodeos in Montana, but really, was there ever a bad time to hear that the person you loved loved you right back?

Nope, there never was. Never. "I LOVE YOU, JOSIE GIBSON!" I didn't mouth the words—I straight-up hollered them. I didn't care if the whole world knew it, let alone a few thousand Montanans. Flashing her a wink, I tipped my hat at Josie before giving the nod. I was ready.

I burst out of the chute on that bull with a smile on my face. I wasn't worried about staying on for a full eight. I already knew I would. When that buzzer finally sounded a handful of moments later, I smiled even wider. I'd finally figured it out.

I knew exactly what was below me—a place I didn't want to revisit. That was how I would stay on top for the rest of my life.

the**END**

about THE **AUTHOR**

Thank you for reading FINDERS KEEPERS by NEW YORK TIMES and USATODAY Bestselling Author, Nicole Williams. Nicole loves to hear from her readers.

You can connect with her on:

Facebook: Nicole Williams (Official Author Page)
Twitter: nwilliamsbooks
Blog: nicoleawilliams.blogspot.com

OTHER WORKS BY NICOLE:

CRASH, CLASH, and CRUSH (HarperCollins)
LOST & FOUND, NEAR & FAR
UP IN FLAMES (Simon & Schuster UK)
GREAT EXPLOITATIONS
THE EDEN TRILOGY
THE PATRICK CHRONICLES

CPSIA information can be obtained at www.ICGtesting.com
Printed in the USA
LVOW08s1513300616

494763LV00001B/21/P